FEATHERS

FEATHERS

THE
TALES
TRILOGY
Book 2

ROSE MANNERING

Sky Pony Press
New York

To my mother,
Karen Mannering,
I would never have written anything if it weren't for you

Sky Pony Press books may be purchased in bulk at special discounts for sales promotion, corporate gifts, fund-raising, or educational purposes. Special editions can also be created to specifications. For details, contact the Special Sales Department, Sky Pony Press, 307 West 36th Street, 11th Floor, New York, NY 10018 or info@skyhorsepublishing.com.

Sky Pony® is a registered trademark of Skyhorse Publishing, Inc.®, a Delaware corporation.

Visit our website at www.skyponypress.com.

10 9 8 7 6 5 4 3 2 1

Library of Congress Cataloging-in-Publication Data is available on file.

Cover design by Sarah Brody
Cover photo credit Ryan Jorgensen / Arcangel
Map of the Western Realm illustrated by Danielle Ceccolini

Print ISBN: 978-1-63450-165-1
Ebook ISBN: 978-1-63450-614-4

Printed in the United States of America

Contents

Part One

Feathers fell like rain from the sky. They fluttered around the couple at the center of the dancing ring, brushing their bare arms and kissing their crowns. Feathers caught the ash from the fires, creating a haze that drifted through the rose-gold twilight of midsummer and disappeared into the faraway forests and plains of the Wild Lands.

The women in the outer circles threw feathers into the sky, chanting as they grabbed fistfuls of silver, black, brown, and tawny plumes. They spun and stamped their feet, following the beat of the drums that shook the ground with a steady rhythm. They danced on, as they had been dancing all day, to mark the union of their chief and his chosen partner.

Sunset By Forest shivered as she felt the first breeze of evening. With the dancing and the chanting, she had not noticed the fading light. It had been a long day.

Feeling his new partner's tremor, Gray Morning squeezed the tips of her fingers, which were held in his large, creased hands. Then he turned to the circling tribesmen, breaking their trance.

All fell still, even the babies in the mothers' shoulder pouches. Only the feathers continued to float and whirl in gusts of air.

"Welcome, my people, new and old," called Gray Morning, his voice reaching across the flat land. "The Taone and the Walcha have been enemies forever, but now we become one. Together, we will live peacefully between the winding river and the gaping lake, and the warring will end."

He bent and took a fistful of earth churned by the heels of the dancers. As was the custom, he threw some of it into the nearest fire, muttering chants, and then he took the rest to his new partner.

Sunset By Forest stood still as he dipped his thumb in the earth and pressed it to her cheeks in arced patterns. Tomorrow, an etcher woman would carve marks into her skin over the smears in lasting ink.

As her new partner worked, Sunset By Forest took the opportunity to look at him. Though they had stood facing each other most of the day, she had kept her head bowed in respect and had only caught glimpses of his dark hair tucked behind the wolf fur that circled his brow. Now she could see that he was older than she, perhaps even as old as her father. His black eyes were lined at the corners, but his body was tall, broad, and strong. Blue patterns traced his thick biceps and trailed down his chest.

"The time for feasting is almost upon us," said Gray Morning, finishing her markings. "But as the last ray of the sun disappears, let us have our birther blessing."

Sunset By Forest frowned. She had never heard of such a thing.

The crowd parted and a dark figure approached. It was covered from head to foot in animal pelts so that Sunset By Forest could not see if it was a man or a woman. The figure walked slowly, almost regally, and stopped before the chief without hesitation or fear.

"Let us see," it said in a strange accent that was harsh and thick. From the high tone, Sunset By Forest assumed that the figure beneath the animal furs was a woman. If it was a human at all.

"Tell me about my firstborn," said Gray Morning.

The figure in furs shuffled to the nearest fire and the people melted away. It held out a hand smothered in the skin of a swift fox and caught a white feather that sailed past on a gentle breeze.

"Your firstborn?" the figure in furs muttered. "Let us see."

It bent and took a fistful of earth, throwing it into the fire. Then it took another fistful and mashed the feather into a muddy ball, rolling the mass around in its palms. It chanted, stroking the fire with its hands. The hood of its pelt coat slipped back, and Sunset By Forest saw a glimpse of a dark face with glittering eyes.

"What do you see?" asked Gray Morning, as the smoke curled and slithered into the sky.

The figure in furs turned to its chief and its eyes glowed like the moon.

"Is it a warrior?" asked Gray Morning. "A warrior son?"

"It is to be a birther, like me," the figure said, slowly.

Sunset By Forest glanced fearfully at her partner. She had whispered to the trees for a son—a son to make her new chief happy. All tribeswomen whispered for sons, but a chief's partner all the more so. Who was this birther to know what her first child would be? Who was this birther wrapped in furs to bring shame on her?

"Not a . . . boy?" said Gray Morning, his jaw clenching.

The rest of the tribe watched, the fires throwing twirling shadows across their faces. The feathers were all gone now, carried away by the evening breeze.

"An important child," said the figure in furs. "A very important child."

"A girl who will become a birther," Gray Morning corrected her.

There had been birthers in Sunset By Forest's tribe, but they had never told fortunes, and they would not have dared to speak to a chief so boldly. She was confused by this creature before her, confused and scared.

"A warrior will follow," said the figure in furs suddenly, and Gray Morning's head arose again, a smile breaking his lips.

"A warrior to follow," he repeated in a whisper, and he took Sunset By Forest's hand in his own once more. "A warrior heir."

"The first will be a birther, though," the figure in furs reminded him.

In the light of the rising moon, Sunset By Forest could see that the figure was a woman, though she looked different and strange.

"A birther to be my apprentice," the woman added.

But Gray Morning was scarcely listening, and he nodded his consent, since this first child would mean nothing to him.

CHAPTER ONE

The Boy

The first child was a boy.

Sunset By Forest lay on grass mats, her teeth clenched and her hands clasping her swollen stomach. Smoke from the fire clouded the roof of the tent, and despite the cold winter weather, her brow was slick with sweat. As another spasm of pain took her, she cried out.

"You need the birther," said West River, squatting at her side. In the time since Sunset By Forest had entered the Taone tribe, the two women had become inseparable. West River had taught the chief's partner where the Taone gathered their food and how to ride their mustang horses.

"No!" gasped Sunset By Forest. "I am fine."

"Why don't you trust the birther?"

"I do, I do," said Sunset By Forest hurriedly, knowing how the Taone felt about their birther. "But I wish to do this alone. Already I have shamed myself and brought my labor into this tent."

Sunset By Forest paused, the blue patterns of her face twisted by a contraction.

"This is not an easy birth," said West River, her voice tinged with fear. "Gray Morning won't be happy if you are harmed by this child."

Sunset By Forest nodded. "He wants his second child," she said. "His warrior son."

"I should go and get—"

"No, it is becoming easier."

West River squatted next to Sunset By Forest as the sun outside arced across the sky. She kept the fire strong to warm the chilling breezes that blew through the nooks and crannies of the tent and whispered soothing words. As evening drew in, the baby still showed no signs of coming, and Sunset By Forest's belly seemed to writhe.

Tribeswomen had tried to enter throughout the day, but West River had chased them out. She knew they would think it a great weakness that Sunset By Forest was giving birth in her tent; she should be by herself in the forest or on the flatlands. A chief's first child, even if it was a girl, should be born in the open air. The tribeswomen West River could easily get rid of, but the men were due back tonight from a hunting trip, and Gray Morning would want to see his partner. What would he think if he saw her lying on the floor of their tent, weak and incoherent?

Sunset By River lay in a trance of pain. Her amber eyes were glazed and distant, her lips whispering words that did not make sense.

"I must go and get the birther," said West River.

Sunset By River shook her head. "No," she croaked. "I am . . ."

Her words were lost in a deep groan of pain.

West River turned and ran to the door of the tent. Lifting the flap, she stopped short with a gasp for there stood the birther, her arms crossed as if she had been waiting.

"This birth is bad enough to be brought inside and yet I have not been called for?" said the birther in her harsh accent. "Did you think that you could manage it yourself?"

"No!"

"You have had three babes of your own, West River, but there are many things you do not know."

"I wished to call for you right away, Cala."

"But the chief's partner did not?"

West River bowed her head and did not reply.

"I should take this as a snub," said Cala. "I should refuse my help, but I care for this child, and Gray Morning would no doubt hold me responsible—not his stupid partner."

Cala swept into the tent, closing the flap behind her with a snap, but not before West River caught sight of the many faces crowded outside in the gloom.

The birther marched over to Sunset By Forest, who was thrashing on the grass mats.

"You should have sent for me before," she said. "And you shall pay for it now. This birth will take your strength, and you will not be able to bear another baby for many seasons."

Sunset By Forest saw a dark face swim across her vision. Since her first night in the Taone tribe, she had seen the birther many times without her fur robes; yet the birther's appearance always struck her with fear. Cala's skin was darker than anybody Sunset By Forest had ever seen. Unlike the golden brown of the Taone, it was the color of wet earth. Her eyes were large and set wide apart on her face, and she was a head taller than the tallest tribeswoman; she was taller even than some of the men.

"I don't think she can hear you," said West River.

Cala did not reply. Instead, she ordered that the fire be put out and all the smoke flaps opened. At first, West River hesitated, but the orders were barked again, and she complied. Cool air rushed through the open ceiling of the tent, and Sunset By Forest's choking breaths became smoky clouds.

"Look at the stars," said Cala. "Watch them as you have this child."

Sunset By Forest watched the glowing speckles of light and thought of soaring high to touch them. She thought of flying.

"What are you doing?" asked West River as Cala ran her hands across Sunset By Forest's stomach.

"Quiet!"

Sunset By Forest yelped in agony as Cala pressed and pushed her belly, moving the baby inside. Despite the whistling wind that chilled the air, beads of sweat gathered on Cala's brow. She gave the swollen stomach one last heave, and then rested her hands across the shivering skin, spreading her fingers wide.

Suddenly, the baby came. West River rushed up to help wash and dry the newborn, cooing with affection and relief. Sunset By Forest lay motionless on the grass mats, her breathing wheezy.

"It's a boy!" said West River with a frown.

Sunset By Forest's eyes snapped open, and she struggled to sit up.

"A boy!" she gasped. "A boy who will be a warrior!"

West River shook her head. Her friend still did not understand the traditions of the Taone tribe.

"The boy will be a birther like me. His destiny has already been spoken for," said Cala.

Sunset By River shook her head. "No!" she said. "No, you said it would be a girl, but it is a boy. A boy warrior for my chief."

"I never said it would be a girl."

Something about Cala's tone made Sunset By Forest pause.

"A boy does not become a birther," she tried to say lightly, but her voice was tinged with fear.

The thunder of hoofbeats and the babble of voices sounded outside. The men returning from their hunting trip beat their drums and yelled their greetings with high-pitched gurgles.

"Hya–Hya–Hya!" they roared.

"The chief is back," said Sunset By Forest, reaching to grab her baby. "I want to show him his warrior son." She thought that Gray Morning would put the birther in her place. She was sure that the chief would be so pleased to have a son.

The flap of the tent opened, and Gray Morning strode inside. Behind him, faces of tribesmen and tribeswomen could be seen watching curiously.

"A boy!" gasped Sunset By Forest as soon as she saw him, forgetting the proper way to greet her returning chief.

Gray Morning stopped still and stared at the baby mewing in furs.

West River knelt quickly at the chief's feet to show her respect, and then disappeared out of the tent to escape whatever would happen next.

Gray Morning's eyes found Cala in the shadows.

"A boy?" he said.

"A birther," she replied.

"No!" interrupted Sunset By Forest. "It's a boy! A boy cannot be a birther."

Gray Morning's gaze fell upon the bundle held to his partner's chest, and Cala saw the temptation flicker across his face.

"I spoke for the destiny of this child before it was even conceived," she said. "This child is not a warrior; he is a birther, and I saw it in the fire."

Gray Morning's hands clenched into fists.

"No warrior should be born inside a tent," added Cala.

Gray Morning saw the signs of birth on the grass mats beside his partner, and his lip curled.

"It was so cold outside," whispered Sunset By Forest in shame. "I had to come in."

Gray Morning turned his back on the child.

"You are right, birther," he said.

"But—"

Gray Morning pointed his finger at his partner and shook his head. "Do not shame me further!" he growled.

Sunset By Forest normally cowered in his fits of rage, but this time she wrapped her arms protectively around the baby and shook her head. "Please," she whimpered. "I want to keep my child."

"You shall raise him until your next baby," said Cala, her tone softening. "Then you shall pass him into my care."

For a moment, Sunset By Forest looked as though she might protest, but she knew that she was beaten.

"I shall call him—" she began.

"No!" roared Gray Morning. "It shall have no tribe name!"

He stormed out of the tent, forcing the eavesdroppers to scatter. In order to try to please their chief, the tribesmen and tribeswomen hurriedly lit fires and brought out some of the meat caught on the hunting trip. Sunset By Forest could hear them chanting feast songs from inside.

She cradled the child in her arms, looking at the perfect smoothness of his cheeks, and then she cried bitterly.

"My poor, nameless babe," she wailed.

"He shall be called Ode," said Cala from the shadows. "For like me, he is not of the tribe."

Sunset By Forest jumped at the sound of her voice. She had forgotten that she was not alone.

"Ode?" she echoed.

"Yes, he shall be called Ode," Cala repeated.

Sunset By Forest simply nodded.

CHAPTER TWO

The Chief's Real Son

O de's birth into the Taone tribe was not marked by a celebration. Many tribesmen and tribeswomen did not even know that their chief's first child had been born until they saw him curled up in Sunset By Forest's shoulder pouch. They tried to approach her to give respect to the new baby, but she shook her head and walked away. Those who had lurked outside the chief's tent and overheard the fuss inside soon began spreading rumors. Eventually, everyone in the tribe knew Sunset By Forest's shame.

Though Gray Morning eventually forgave his wife, when the snow had melted from the ground and springtime came to the forests, his anger at his first son still had not lessened. When he saw Sunset By Forest—now recovered from her traumatic birth and smiling as she cut grass with the other tribeswomen—he could not help but fall in love with her again. She was small and graceful. Her amber eyes were warm, and her dark hair long and thick. Her beauty and her sweet nature won her a place in the chief's heart once more, but nothing about Ode could please his father. Not his gentle mews as a newborn or his amber eyes that were so like his mother's. Not his first tentative steps on pudgy legs around the bonfire, or his broad nose that was like his father's. Gray Morning's gaze washed over his first son as if he did not exist.

When Sunset By Forest fell pregnant again, Ode was just old enough to walk and talk. Though she was pleased to finally fulfill her chief's wishes, Sunset By Forest knew this meant she would have to give up her first son. When she told Gray Morning the news he held a feast, and there was much dancing and chanting. Cala was brought forward in all her furs, and Sunset By Forest could not stop the tremor that racked her body in fear of what the birther would say this time. Ode, who was always at his mother's side, felt it, too, and took her hand.

"It shall be a warrior son. A great, strong warrior son," said Cala, looking into the heart of the fire.

Gray Morning yelled and gurgled with pleasure and the rest of the tribesmen joined him: "Ya–ya–ya!" Ode even attempted to add his own war cry to the chorus, but his mother hastily quieted him.

Ode was everything a tribe mother could wish for. His manner was gentle, and he always wished to please. It confused him that he did not ride out with the tribesmen on their hunting trips like the other little boys, and he did not understand why everyone in the tribe persistently ignored him. But as long as he could stay by his mother's side, he did not much mind. He slept curled in a ball at her feet in the tent, and he tried his hardest to stay out of his father's way. Gray Morning could go whole days never seeing his son, who crept in his mother's shadow.

Besides Sunset By Forest, Cala was the only member of the tribe to show Ode affection. If she passed him in the settlement, then she ruffled his hair, or if she happened to see him while she gathered herbs in the woods, then she would call him over and give him a sweet berry. He did not know, yet, that she would soon replace his mother.

As Sunset By Forest's belly grew rounder, Ode fetched and carried for her. Like the little girls of the tribe, he followed his mother into the forest and across the flatlands, working and foraging. West River often accompanied them on their expeditions, and though she tried to take little notice of Ode, she was not so harsh as the other tribeswomen. If she saw him trip, she would gently pick him up and dust him off. She even let her own daughter, Rippling River, play with him sometimes. Rippling River was two seasons older than Ode, and she liked to boss him around. The two would go off gathering berries or kindling by themselves when their mothers were chattering.

One afternoon while Ode and Rippling River were doing just that, Ode heard his mother scream. Dropping the sticks in his arms, he raced back through the dusty undergrowth, his bare feet pattering against the earth. It was early summer, and the sun leaked through the tall trees above, casting shifting patterns. Ode arrived in a clearing to see Sunset By Forest squatting beside a tree, her body trembling. She was trying hard to bear her pain without a sound, but groans escaped her pursed lips.

"I will leave you," said West River, calling for her daughter to follow her. "You must come back to the settlement if there is a problem," she said over her shoulder. "You must not hurt yourself for shame's sake."

"I can do it," replied Sunset By Forest between hurried breaths.

But once West River had disappeared, with Rippling River scurrying behind her, Sunset By Forest collapsed onto her back and let out a low moan. She knew that she should send Ode away, but he would be lost at the tent by himself, and if Gray Morning found him there alone, he would be angry. Instead, she threaded her fingers through her young son's and held him by her side.

"Mam hurts?" Ode asked some hours later when they were still under the tree.

Sunset By Forest nodded since she could not speak.

Ode bent forward and kissed her belly through the dyed buffalo hides she wore. He took the shawl from around his mother's shoulders and bundled it into a pillow under her head. Then he hummed quietly under his breath and stroked her damp forehead as she would have if he were sniffling with a cold in the winter.

Tears trickled down Sunset By Forest's cheeks, and for a moment she almost did not want this second son.

Mother and child remained together all afternoon. The sun beat down on the forest and the tall trees swished with the gentle wind. As the afternoon drifted into evening, Sunset By Forest began to stir. Her condition was considerably worse, yet she tried to struggle to her feet.

"Mam?" Ode mumbled as his mother thrashed around.

"Wolves!" she gasped and fell still from exhaustion.

Ode stood up and looked around. The forest was as calm and quiet as before. The evening sun cast slanting light that dazzled his eyes, and the rush of the wind was cool against his cheeks. His mother had instilled a deep fear of wolves in him from babyhood and, like all tribe children, he knew that the forest was no place to be at night.

Ode's bottom lip began to tremble. Why was his mother unable to get up? He knew they must start out for home now, and he tugged on his mother's arm, but Sunset By Forest did not move. She only groaned and clutched her stomach.

"Chief!" Ode yelled and his voice bounced off the treetops.

Ode was terrified of his father and awed by him in equal measures. He would watch from behind his mother's tunic as Gray Morning rode in proudly after every hunting trip, a carcass laid across the rump of his mustang. There was no creature so fierce that his father could not defeat with his cold eyes and strong arms. If Gray Morning were here now, they would have nothing to fear.

"Chief!" Ode tried again, but there was no reply, and he fell quiet.

Around them, the air began to cool and the sun disappeared. An owl hooted, and Ode shivered. He wondered if he should call out to his father again, but he did not want to attract unwanted attention. Beside him his mother writhed and cried with each contraction. She screamed as an agony burned through her body, and Ode hastily put his little hand over her mouth.

From far away came the long, deep howl of a wolf. After a heartbeat's pause it was answered by other howls that echoed through the forest, vibrating against the rocks and the trees. The grass opposite began to rustle, and Ode grabbed hold of a nearby stick. Clambering to his feet, his little body shook with nerves, and he raised his tiny weapon in anticipation of what might pounce at him.

A dark snout nosed through the long grass and a black-footed ferret scampered out, ignoring the little boy. The ferret sniffed the air, and then disappeared into the surrounding blackness. The stick dropped from Ode's hand and snapped in two as it hit the ground. He sank onto his knees, his chest heaving, and fear seized his insides. From all around, the wolves began to howl again—a high screech to the fat moon.

Ode squeezed his eyes shut, knowing that they were alone. The long grass rustled once more, but this time he could not bear to look. Something grabbed his arm, and he screamed.

"Hush!" said a voice.

He opened his eyes to see Cala dressed in her furs. She knelt beside Sunset By Forest and ran her hands across his mother's stomach, feeling the baby inside.

"Another breech birth," Cala said, shaking her head. "Your pride has stopped you from calling for me again, and this time you shall pay dearly for it, my chief's partner. You shall never have another child."

Sunset By Forest barely heard Cala's prophecy, so deep was her pain.

Cala turned to Ode. "Come little man, you shall begin your apprenticeship now and help me save your mother." She took Ode's small hands in her own and showed him how to push and pull his mother's body to move the baby inside.

"Your brother is upside-down, and we need to turn him around," she explained. "He needs to be born head first so that he can breathe."

Ode winced as his mother moaned in pain, but under Cala's directions, he continued. Far off in the forest the wolves howled.

"They will not get you, little man," whispered Cala when she saw him tremble. "While I am here, you are safe."

Ode gazed into her black eyes, and he believed her.

They pushed and pulled Sunset By Forest's body and she groaned as the wolves throughout the forest howled to the moon. Then, finally,

Ode's little brother came crying into the realm, and Cala heaved a sigh of relief.

"What is his name?" she asked, cleaning the child with a fur from a pouch about her shoulders.

Sunset By Forest was barely conscious, but as Ode stroked and petted her face, she slowly came around.

"A name?" Cala repeated.

Sunset By Forest looked above her.

"Blue Moon," she said at last.

Cala placed the baby in its mother's arms and pulled Sunset By Forest to her feet.

"Gray Morning will be looking for you," she said. "Your absence from the settlement was noticed, and everyone is awaiting the return of the chief's son."

Sunset By Forest glanced at Ode.

"The time has come for him to stay with me," Cala said.

Sunset By Forest looked as if she might protest, but then the baby in her arms squeaked and she understood that she was needed by another son now.

"Does Gray Morning know—" she began.

"—that I am here?" finished Cala. "No. As far as everyone is aware, you birthed the baby yourself."

Sunset By Forest nodded and began walking wearily away.

"Mam?" said Ode, toddling after her, but she pushed him firmly back, refusing to meet his eye.

Cala took his little hand and held it in her own.

"You are to come home with me," she told him.

Ode shook his head.

"Mam!" he cried as Sunset By Forest disappeared into the darkness of the forest, heading back to the settlement. "Mam!" he screamed.

But she did not look back.

CHAPTER THREE

The Storm

The night Blue Moon was born, the Taone celebrated like never before. When Gray Morning saw his partner walking through the trees at the fringes of the forest, a bundle in her arms, he let out a gurgling war cry to the moon: "Ya–ya–ya!"

He had been waiting all night, worried. He could hear the wolves howling and he had begun to wonder if he should have moved the tribe away from the forest into the flatlands where the predators would be fewer, but the dust storms that hit there this season would be equally perilous. Gray Morning had sat and pondered his decision for hours outside his tent, staring into the forest and willing his partner to appear. He did not want her shamed again for her own sake and so he stayed put, taking strength from Cala's words: *It shall be a warrior son. A great, strong warrior son.* She had never been wrong.

When he saw Sunset By Forest, he was rewarded for his patience. She walked up to him and placed the baby at his feet, while the other tribesmen and tribeswomen who were awake yelled and cried with delight.

"He is called Blue Moon," she said. She swayed slightly from exhaustion, but she smiled nonetheless.

Hasty preparations commenced for the greatest celebration the Taone tribe had ever known. Ceremonial feathers were gathered from the tribal stores, bonfires were lit, and meat was roasted. Those asleep were woken, and everyone dressed in their finest skins. Gray Morning put on his war headdress with its long tail of feathers that snaked down his back, and all the while he did not stop looking at his son.

"This warrior carries the strength of both our tribes," he roared later as his people stood before him and feathers floated through the night's air. "He will lead us forward and make us stronger. We need fear no other!"

The tribesmen shouted their assent, and then the dancing, chanting, and feasting began. Tawny feathers burst into the air, and the drums beat out the rhythm of the dance, calling in the golden dawn.

───◦◦◦───

Ode could hear the drums from the forest. "Mam left me," he said to Cala, his brow creased with worry.

"I will look after you now."

"But Mam!"

Cala knelt and smoothed down his dark hair. "You are special and that is why I must look after you," she said. "I will keep you safe like I kept you safe from the wolves."

Ode nodded. There was something about the tall, dark woman that felt very safe.

"Let me take you home to sleep," she said, lifting him into her arms.

He laid his head upon her chest and snuggled into the furs.

"I will tell you a story," she said, beginning to walk through the forest. "There was once a man who wanted power. He would do anything it took to get it—he would even sacrifice those he loved. He grew wicked. But whatever he got, it wasn't enough, and it soon became clear that he would not stop until he could achieve total ruin."

Ode clung to Cala as her swaying steps rocked him gently. He could hear the wolves howling and the gentle rustle of the forest, but he did not feel scared.

"A man like that must be stopped, and it will take someone special to do it . . . do you see?"

Cala stopped at the edge of the forest and looked down at Ode, asleep on her chest. She smiled and patted his cheek. She would tell him the story again one day and she hoped that he would understand.

⌒⊶∞⊷⌒

Ode's separation from his mother was not easy for either of them. Whenever he saw her, Ode would go running to Sunset By Forest's side, crying with relief. Sunset By Forest felt the strings of her heart pull, but she forced herself to push the child away.

"You have a new mam now," she would say, though she could not help her voice catching and trembling a little.

Despite having been usurped by Blue Moon, Ode never held it against his younger brother. Instead, the mewing bundle only attracted him. In the evenings, while Gray Morning was often preoccupied with organizing the tribe and Sunset By Forest helped the women prepare supper, Ode would creep into the tent he had once called home. Bending over his little brother, who was wrapped in furs, Ode would chatter to him and pat his head like a pet. Once Sunset By Forest caught him and her fear for what her partner would have done had he been there made her angry.

"You should not be here!" she cried. "Get out!"

Had Ode been a stubborn or bitter child he would have grown to hate his mother and father, but as it was, he loved them too much. Instead of shouting back at Sunset By Forest, he planted a quick kiss on his brother's forehead, and then scuttled out of the tent. Sunset By

Forest did not know whether to laugh or cry. She gave up trying to keep her sons apart.

One evening she even ventured to question the chief's treatment of their first boy. Gray Morning was in a particularly good mood after watching Blue Moon take his first few steps, and it was a gentle spring evening on the flatlands with the realm stretching out even and brown in every direction. The tribe had just eaten a buffalo caught on the last hunting trip and all were satisfied and smiling. Sunset By Forest and her partner were sitting before a bonfire, watching the smoke curl away into the sky.

"Blue Moon shall know Ode is his brother, won't he?" Sunset By Forest had been reciting her words so carefully in her head that they came out in a rush.

As was always the case when his first son was brought to his mind, Gray Morning's shoulders stiffened. His gaze wandered involuntarily to the far end of the settlement, past the clusters of families and friends, to the lone tent where the birther lived.

"The whole tribe knows it," he said at last. "It's hardly a secret."

Sunset By Forest smiled in relief. "Then they shall be brothers?" she said.

"Only by blood," Gray Morning spat.

His raised voice caught the attention of those nearest to them and a startled silence descended. Gray Morning sprang to his feet, his good mood gone. He kicked at his leftovers and stormed into his tent, the flap closing with a snap.

On the other side of the settlement, Ode heard the chief's shout, but he was too far away to know what was said. Like all the people of the tribe, he had a keen sense for his chief's cry that would often ring out to warn of danger. Upon hearing it, he peered out of Cala's tent, but seeing nothing amiss, he retreated back inside.

Lately, he had started to notice that he was not the only one that the people of the tribe ignored. He had seen many eyes dart away from

Cala in fear. This realization had brought him closer to his caregiver, although he still would not call her "Mam" like she asked. Instead, they settled on "Auntie."

"Auntie, how do you know what an auntie is?" he had once asked, since there was no such thing in the Taone culture.

"Because where I am from we have aunties and we have uncles."

At this, Ode's brow creased in confusion. "Where do you come from?"

Cala laughed. "A long way away," was all she said.

Ode assumed that she meant on the other side of the gaping lake, which was indeed a long way away and out of the Taone territory. The tribe traveled throughout the seasons between the gaping lake, across the plain lands and the winding river near the forest. Legend had it that the area was once shared by five tribes, but only the Taone was left, patrolling its expanse.

Currently in the mild spring season, the Taone were in the midst of the flatlands and traveling slowly toward the forest. The green thread of trees was not yet visible on the horizon and only even brown land covered in downy grass could be seen in every direction. The flatland sky was always wide and clear, and today, despite the springtime season, the sun was burning. Inside the tent, Cala fanned herself.

"Take your shawl off, Auntie," said Ode, seeing her wipe her brow.

He was squatting before the fire at the center of the tent, waiting for their ration of meat to cook. Cala ate separately from the Taone, and every time there was a killing, a tribesman would bring her a hunk of meat that Gray Morning had chosen for her.

"I am used to hotter weather," Cala insisted. "I just do not expect it in this season."

Ode was too busy staring at the dripping meat suspended over the fire to reply. He licked his lips and Cala laughed. For a moment her face was clear, but then it clouded with worry once more.

"It is *too* hot," she said.

When the meat was cooked, they ate in comfortable silence, sitting cross-legged before the fire. Ode finished his meal first and kept shooting earnest glances at the tent flap.

"All right," said Cala. "Go and sneak a visit to your brother if you wish, but you know what will happen if your father sees you."

Ode rushed to the flap.

"Do not be gone long," Cala called after him. "This warm weather worries me. I hope it will be gone tomorrow."

The next day arrived, hot and yellow. When Ode awoke on his grass mat, he discovered that he was alone. Pulling on his tunic, he wandered outside to see Cala standing in the golden dawn, looking out to the horizon.

"What's wrong, Auntie?" he asked, since he saw by the contours of her dark face that something was troubling her.

When she did not answer, he took hold of one of her long braids and tugged it. Like the other tribeswomen, Cala wore her hair in two thick plaits that reached as far as they would grow. They were wound with strips of leather and decorated with feathers, beads, and animal teeth. Unlike the tribeswomen, though, Cala's hair was fuzzy and dry. Ode liked any excuse to touch it.

As if coming back from somewhere far away, Cala shivered and looked down at Ode in surprise.

"What woke you up?" she asked.

Ode rubbed his sleepy eyes and yawned.

"I had a strange dream," he said, turning away to return to the tent.

Cala pulled him back and the tight grip of her hand made him yelp in surprise. Her black eyes bore into his, seeming to search out his very soul.

"What did you dream?" she asked.

"Don't know . . ."

"Think!"

Ode flinched at her tone. When he used to wake from a strange dream at the feet of his mother, he would wait until Gray Morning had left the tent, and then snuggle under the wolf fur by her side. Together, they would share their funny dreams until it was time to eat breakfast, and then such visions would evaporate into the morning air, never to be thought of again. He did not understand why Cala pressed him so.

"I don't remember," he said again, sorry to disappoint her.

"Next time you dream you must hold the vision, and then tell me as soon as you wake up, yes?"

"All right."

Cala gently released his arm and looked up to the sky, squinting against the sun.

Feeling as if he had done something wrong but not knowing what, Ode scuffed his bare foot across the dusty ground. A movement a few feet away caught his attention and he watched as a prairie dog scuttled through the grass and disappeared down its hole. Then he saw another prairie dog, and then another prairie dog. They were all racing across the grass and disappearing down their holes.

He grinned and wondered if he could run fast enough to catch one. He took a step forward but stopped dead. The smile dropped from his face as he stared at the horizon, and his mouth dropped open.

"Auntie!" he screamed.

Cala turned around and gasped. "Dust storm!" she yelled at the top of her voice.

A mountainous cloud of black was speeding toward the settlement. Taller than the trees, it clogged the sky and smothered the sun.

"Get in the tent!" cried Cala, before yelling, "Danger! Dust storm!"

Ode watched the wall of darkness thunder toward them, and he was unable to move. As it rolled closer, a strong wind began to pluck at his hair and he felt specks of dirt catch in his throat and nose.

"Dust storm!" the people screamed to one another.

Many ran for their tents, pulling their families with them. Others sprinted to the animals, trying to set them free of their bonds in hope that they could outrun the storm.

"My babe!" Ode heard Sunset By Forest's voice among the shouts and yells. He turned to see her herded into a tent with a group of other women, her shoulder pouch empty. He guessed she had only just woken and gone to collect water for breakfast, leaving Blue Moon in the tent alone. She screamed at the men who shoved her under cover and shouted to Gray Morning, but her voice was lost in the roar of fear.

Ode looked at the tent belonging to his parents, which was all the way on the other side of the settlement. Its flap had been left open, and Blue Moon most likely lay inside on the grass mat, unaware of what was about to hit. The way was clear now since everyone was crouched under cover, cowering in fear as the wind rushed and dragged at the ground.

Ode began to run. He sprinted across the settlement, the raging storm biting at his heels. From the corners of his eyes he saw frightened faces watch him thunder past. He heard Cala screech his name, but he did not stop. He ran on, the wind snatching at his elbows and stones pounding against his back, drawing blood.

When he reached the tent, Ode dove inside, yanking the flap closed after him with a slap. He had just enough time to crouch over his little brother, shielding him with his body, before the dust storm hit.

It clawed at his skin and lifted the buffalo hide of the tent clean off, throwing it across the flatlands. Stones carried by the strong winds smacked him on the back and dust crowded everywhere. Over the rumble of the storm, he could hear the mewing of Blue Moon, and he clung to him desperately as dust surrounded them, drowning them in thick blackness.

Despite the gale, Ode could feel his body reacting to something. His back was shaking with a new force that had nothing to do with the wind or the dust or the storm. He was suddenly filled with the desire to fly away. He wanted to soar above it all—to reach the stars. For a second he was sure that he could fly. He was about to lift off into the sky, taking his little brother with him, when a large stone thumped him over the head. Then he saw nothing but darkness.

The dust storm was over in a matter of moments, but the destruction it left behind shocked even those who had experienced such horrors before. Whole homes had vanished. Those who had weathered the storm now emerged, wading through the knee-high dust and taking in the carnage, their chests heavy with sorrow.

"My babe!" a voice screamed through the silence.

Heads turned to see Sunset By Forest running toward the place where her tent had stood, tears coursing down her cheeks. Cala hurried to join the chief's partner, wondering what had happened to her apprentice. Her eyes scanned the ground, but the dust covered everything. Then, for some reason, she looked to the sky. But the rest of the tribe were too deep in mourning to notice such strange behavior.

"My babe!" Sunset By Forest screamed, dropping to her knees, sobbing. "My children!"

Suddenly, the earth before her began to shift and she jumped aside as a hand shot up through the dust. A head smothered in dirt and blood followed, and Ode gasped the clean air. He climbed out of the debris, Blue Moon clutched to his chest, covered in dirt but otherwise unharmed.

"My boys!" Sunset By Forest yelled, and she enveloped both of her sons in a tight hug, rocking them from side to side in her arms, whispering again and again, "My boys, my boys."

CHAPTER FOUR

The Boy Birther

The Taone eventually recovered from the horrors of the dust storm and as the seasons passed, the event faded into memory. But there were two who could never forget what had happened that day. Ode remembered the moment his body had not been his own. Before the stone hit him and darkness reigned, he had felt like he could fly—he had known that he *could* fly. He kept this to himself, not even telling Cala. He felt that it was important, although he did not know why. Gray Morning, too, remembered the day his first son had proven himself to be a warrior: selfless and brave. He remembered wanting to show his gratitude, but he could not bestow such things on a male birther. He could not praise such a creature.

Luckily, over the seasons Blue Moon grew into a strong, healthy child, and his aptitude for fighting and hunting distracted his father. Gray Morning presented his second son with arrows to hold, axes to touch, and spears to feel. Before he could walk, he learned how to shoot a bow and arrow. The sight of Blue Moon wielding such weapons made Sunset By Forest bite her lip, but her partner insisted it was important.

"He is to be a great warrior. It is his destiny, so leave him be," said Gray Morning when he saw her fussing.

Blue Moon grew into the warrior son of Gray Morning's dreams. He became the youngest boy to ride out on a hunt with the tribesmen and a skilled horseman. He trained daily with his wooden practice weapons and beat the older boys in friendly matches. The Taone were in awe of their chief's warrior son, all except Ode, who would pinch his little brother's cheek and make faces at him when no one was looking. Despite Gray Morning's desire to keep them apart, the brothers were close and sought each other out as often as possible—chattering, fighting, and playing together as if there were nothing different about them at all.

Unlike the other boys of the tribe, Ode was never given practice weapons or fighting lessons. Instead, Blue Moon taught him everything he knew. Most evenings the brothers could be found brandishing blunt spears, dodging and ducking each other's swings. They snuck into the forest or went far across the plain lands, so as not to be seen, and sparred until the moon shone in the night's sky.

"Let's do that again," said Blue Moon one afternoon after a vigorous session of practice drills. "But this time, keep your knees bent."

It was winter, and snow covered the plain lands. Their boots churned the ground around them until it was creamy and their cheeks were flushed red.

"No!" panted Ode. "We need to rest."

The rough wooden handle of his hammer had rubbed his palm raw and the cold wind made his fingers stiff.

"You won't be able to say that at your initiation," Blue Moon teased. "You'll say, 'Let me take a rest,' and the coyote will go ahead and eat you anyway!"

Blue Moon grinned, but Ode glanced away. The other boys his age were training for their initiations in the wilderness and sometimes he watched them from a distance, laughing and fighting together. They were frightened and excited all at once—longing for the ultimate test in which they would become tribesmen and earn their patterns. Ode had never asked when he would begin training for his initiation. He was too afraid of the answer.

"What's going on in there?" asked Blue Moon, giving him a poke in the head with the blunt end of his spear. "There's no time to think in a fight, remember?"

"All right," said Ode, picking up his hammer and ignoring the throb of pain that slashed through his hand. "Let's practice again."

Blue Moon gave a yip of joy. "Try and beat me this time!" he cried.

Later that evening, Cala complained when Ode did not finish his dinner. The boy was listless and distracted. He moped around the tent, staring into the distance and simply grunting when she questioned him.

"It is time we began your apprenticeship, little man," Cala said suddenly and finally Ode looked up. "I have let you run around and do as you please for too long," she continued. "Your days of freedom are done, and now the work must begin."

"But I should train for my initiation like the other boys," said Ode.

Cala paused. They both knew there would be no initiation for him.

"I see no hairs on your chin," said Cala. "You are still a boy."

"But even then . . . ?"

"You will have an initiation of a different kind."

"Why?"

"Because you are special."

Ode wanted to tell her about the only time he had ever felt special: when he had been sure that he could fly. But the words teetered on his lips and something swept them away.

"Auntie, there's no place for me in this tribe," he said instead.

"That is not true. You shall make a place for yourself, for you are my apprentice and we are vital to the Taone."

"The chief wishes I did not exist."

"There will come a time when your dar will have to listen to your words."

Ode did not believe her, but he fell quiet all the same.

"Your apprenticeship starts tomorrow," said Cala. "I want you awake at dawn. I want you ready."

Ode nodded.

He had often assisted Cala in her work, but always half-heartedly. He knew that his presence made the women uncomfortable. Though he had witnessed a number of births, he always hung back in the shadows, counting the seconds until he could leave.

When Cala woke him before dawn the next day, he explained such misgivings as she rushed him along.

"Look, little man," Cala said, rebuking him. "They do not want help from either of us. You are a man, and I am not a member of the Taone. But they *need* our help, and one woman needs our help right now, so hurry up!"

Ode pulled on his snow boots and fixed his furs in place, grumbling under his breath all the while. "Where are we going?" he asked, following Cala out of the tent and into the chilled morning air.

Dawn had yet to arrive and it was dark.

"Into the forest," said Cala.

They waded through the snow in the direction of the trees. Ode was about to ask how she knew where they were going when he noticed the small prints in the snow that snaked before them. Someone had already come this way.

"It is dangerous to be in the forest alone," he said.

"Yes, the Taone are stupid," replied Cala, grinning at his affronted expression. "You said as much yourself just now. Why would someone venture into the forest to give birth where it is cold and dangerous? For pride. Stupid pride. The Taone still live by traditions that should have been changed long ago."

Ode glanced around them, hoping that there was no one to hear Cala say such things. To question the chief was to defy him.

"You need not look so worried," added Cala. "Gray Morning knows my thoughts on the matter, but he will not change his precious traditions."

They fell silent and plodded on through the darkness. Behind them, the dawn was arriving, stretching golden fingers across the lands, but it had not reached the forest yet. As they wound through ferns and bare trees, Ode swiveled his head left and right, looking for moving shadows.

"You need not fear when I am here," said Cala.

Somehow he knew she was right.

They walked a little farther, and then they heard a cry and a groan. Following the sound, they came across a woman squatting beside a tree. She was bundled in many furs and her legs trembled in an effort to keep herself upright.

"Lie down, Soft Rain, I am here now," said Cala.

Soft Rain collapsed onto her back in the snow, and Cala beckoned Ode closer. She began showing him how to feel the mother's stomach and how to maneuver the baby in her belly into the correct position. His cheeks burned as she did so, and he avoided Soft Rain's gaze.

"Ah!" screamed the tribeswoman as another contraction hit her. "Help me!" she gasped. "Please, help me!"

"You have done this once before, Soft Rain," said Cala firmly. "You can do it again. Now push."

They knelt in a huddle against the cold as the dawn rushed in all around them, warming the snow with the wintery sun. Soft Rain began to cry and whimper, clutching at anything she could reach.

"It hurts!" she yelled. "I can't do it! I can't do it!"

"Yes, you can," said Cala.

"I can't!"

Soft Rain caught Ode's gaze and held it with her light-brown eyes. "You've got to help me, I can't do it!" she sobbed.

Ode did not know what to say.

"Please!" she whined, still watching him.

"Y-you can do it," he said at last, taking hold of her hand. "We're here, and we'll keep you safe."

Soft Rain nodded before another contraction had her squirming about once more. Over the top of the woman's head Cala smiled at her apprentice.

"One more push," Cala said.

Soft Rain still had Ode's hand clutched tightly in her own, and beneath his furs, Ode felt damp with sweat.

"Come on," said Cala. "One more push."

Soft Rain screamed.

Taking a prairie dog skin from her bundle of supplies, Cala thrust it into Ode's hands, telling him to hold the baby as it came.

"But I don't know—"

"It is coming now! Get into position like I told you."

The baby was born into Ode's hands, and he stared at it, mesmerized. It opened its tiny mouth and let out a thin cry, waving its little limbs in the chilly air.

"It is a girl," said Cala, looking over his shoulder. "Do you hear that, Soft Rain? You have been granted a girl."

Soft Rain groaned faintly, lying flat out in the snow.

But Ode barely noticed. He held the baby in his hands, rubbing it with the skin to keep it warm, and watched as it wriggled and squeaked. Suddenly, two other hands began pulling the baby away from him, and he looked up to see Soft Rain tugging the bundle out of his grasp. He was forced to let go.

"What's her name?" he asked.

Soft Rain glanced up at him, and for the first time there was something close to resentment in her eyes.

"Winter's Dawn," she muttered, and then turned away.

Ode craned his neck to catch another glimpse of Winter's Dawn, but Cala took his arm.

"It is time for us to leave," she said.

She led Ode back through the snow and all the while he glanced over his shoulder, trying to watch Soft Rain and Winter's Dawn in the distance.

"Did you see how I held the baby?" he babbled. "I've never held one before, but it lay so quietly in my hands! The first person it saw was me."

Cala shook her head, but she could not help the smile that tugged at her lips.

"You barely helped me at all in that birth," she chided. "You were awkward and nervous."

"But I'd never done it before!"

"Well, you shall be doing it often from now on, so you best get better at it."

Later that day, the Taone held a celebration to welcome Winter's Dawn into the realm. Gray Morning ordered more logs be put on the fire and the drums were brought out from the store. Everyone gathered at the center of the settlement and they began to chant and sway.

"Hya–Hya–Hya!"

The women stood to dance, beating the heels of their snow boots into the ground and waving their fingers to mimic the spirits of the winds. Then the men joined them, forming an outer ring and punching and kicking the air to reenact the hunt. Like the other young boys, Ode created a smaller ring opposite the young girls and they wove between one another like the spirits of the rivers.

"Ya–Ha–Ha!" they cried.

The blue smoke from the fire whirled all around them and the beating of the drums grew faster. They danced and danced until they no longer felt the cold, and then Gray Morning held up his hands and everyone fell still.

Dressed in all her furs, Cala walked through the Taone to the fire. She had not been dancing like the others, but Ode had noticed her watching from the open mouth of her tent. When she reached the fire's edge, she bent and dug through the snow to take a fistful of frozen earth. She threw it into the flames and watched the flickering light spit.

Soft Rain stood nearby with the bundle in her arms and her partner by her side. Clinging to her knees was her son, a quiet, small boy called Silver Sky. As a family they waited to hear the fate of their new member.

"A gentle child," said Cala eventually, and both parents smiled.

Ode thought that a pretty weak destiny, but he had once asked Cala what happened when she saw bad things in the fire and she had replied that she simply tried to make the best of it. He hoped this was not the case for little Winter's Dawn. He felt a certain responsibility for her life, as if he had brought her into the realm single-handedly. He was desperate to see her once more and when the celebration drew to an end, he approached the family.

There was already a buzzing crowd around the bundle, but when Soft Rain saw him coming, she quickly turned away. Frowning, Ode tried to sidle up to her again, but still she turned away.

"How was the birth?" asked a female elder with skin in great folds around her chin.

"Quick," replied Soft Rain. "I was collecting kindling in the forest alone, and the child came while I watched the golden dawn."

The elder nodded her praise.

"A proper birth," she said.

Ode stood with his mouth hanging open long after the tribesmen and tribeswomen had moved away. For the first time in his life, he felt real anger.

"What troubles you, little man?" said Cala in her familiar, clipped accent. Ode could just see the edge of her furs from the corner of his eye since frustrated tears blurred his vision.

"She lied," he said. "She said that she gave birth alone!"

"Yes, you will have to get used to that."

CHAPTER FIVE

The Teaching of Magic

As a birther, Ode established his place in the Taone. There were no rewards and the work was often difficult, but as the seasons passed, he found peace in it. He had only to see the desperate eyes of a mother-to-be to know how much she needed a birther, regardless of what she would claim afterward. That is not to say that the desire to be like everyone else did not strike Ode so hard sometimes that it hurt. Blue Moon's tales of rough and tumble with the other boys of the tribe made Ode look down at his skinny chest and sigh.

"Hi-Hi-Hi, brother," Blue Moon said one evening, jumping out from behind a tent to surprise him.

It was late autumn and the flatlands were bare and dusty. The Taone had finished their communal meal and many were lying around the fire, dozing and warming themselves after a long day of traveling.

"Greetings, little brother," said Ode, catching Blue Moon's head under his arm and messing up his hair.

Blue Moon pushed him off with a shout.

"So, what've you been doing?" he asked when he had freed himself.

Ode shrugged. He had spent the evening whispering with Cala in a tribeswoman's tent. She had miscarried her baby that afternoon and such things would bring shame on her if the rest of the tribe were to know. Ode had held the tribeswoman's hand as she sobbed, consoling her and knowing that in the morning, if they passed each other, she would look the other way without a second thought.

"Come on, brother," said Blue Moon, pinching Ode's stomach. "Where have you been? Hanging around Rippling River? You know, I've noticed recently that wherever she is, you're not far away. . . ."

Ode's cheeks burned. "No!" he snapped.

His little brother grinned and waggled his eyebrows. Of the two of them, Blue Moon looked more like Gray Morning, with his square jaw and dark hair. He was unusually big for his age and almost as tall as Ode. Although Ode liked to point out whenever possible that there was still an inch to go yet.

"All of the boys talk about Rippling River," said Blue Moon. "They say that her eyes are like sparkling waters," he added in a silly voice.

Ode pushed him over.

"Ya-ya-ya!" yipped Blue Moon, charging back at him and almost knocking Ode flat. "Had it been this morning, I would have sent you flying," he added as Ode brushed himself off. "I beat all the boys, but it's made me tired."

"I'm sure."

"Dar thinks I might even be able to do my initiation early."

Ode tickled beneath his brother's chin. "No hair there yet," he said.

"None on yours, either!"

"There nearly is, and mine will come first."

"Maybe not."

The bellow of the chief interrupted them. Gray Morning stood on the other side of the settlement calling Blue Moon to his side. He had started giving his son evening lessons in hand-to-hand combat, as if Blue Moon needed more training. He already had bulging muscles in his arms and across his stomach.

"Boy!" Gray Morning shouted. "Boy, come here!"

"I'd better go," said Blue Moon, making a face. "See you tomorrow, brother, unless I smell you first!"

Ode laughed.

⤙⥈⤚

While his brother wielded spears and practiced hunting, Ode learned how to revive a silent baby and how to cut an umbilical cord. Cala took Ode to the forest and showed him how to pick herbs to mash into remedies. She taught him when to speak firmly to a crying mother and when to comfort her in her pain. Around the settlement these days, Cala was rarely seen without her apprentice.

"Auntie, when are you going to teach me the other stuff?" Ode asked her one night as they sat in their tent before the crackling fire.

"What do you mean?"

"I know all the birth things, but what about the rest of it?"

Cala regarded him with her black eyes.

"For a start, there is still so many things that you do not know—it takes a lifetime to learn our craft—so what are these 'other things' of which you speak?"

Ode rolled his eyes. "I mean, when will you show me how to read a child's destiny in the fire? When will you show me how to know that a mother needs our help?"

"I will not show you such things."

"But if I'm your apprentice then I need to know!"

"Those are things that cannot be taught."

Ode frowned and stared into the depths of the fire, but all he saw were flickering red and yellow flames.

"How do you do it then?" he asked at last.

Cala did not raise her eyes from the weaving in her lap. A pile of briars lay beside her, and she sat twisting them around the basket mold in her hands. She had tried to teach Ode, arguing that birthing was

37

lengthy business and idle hours were lost hours, but basketry was a step too far in the domain of the tribeswomen for him. If he was destined to be a birther, then he would face it—he was now even beginning to enjoy it—but nobody said anything about making baskets.

"How do I do it? Well, take one of these branches and I will show—"

"No!" said Ode through clenched teeth. "You know what I mean! How do you do that Magic?"

The weaving in Cala's hands stilled. "Who taught you that word?"

"I don't know."

"Where did you hear it?"

"I can't remember. Why is that important?"

"Magic is dangerous. You should not speak of it, and you cannot teach it."

"But—"

"Enough!"

Ode stomped out of the tent and into the darkening evening. The rest of the tribe were milling about the settlement; the men were reinforcing their tent pegs since Gray Morning had announced that they would stay in this spot for a few days, and the women were sorting through the stock of food. It was late summer and the Taone were at the edge of the forest, heading for the flatlands. They were stopping on their journey to harvest corn from one of their squares of cultivated land and tomorrow, while the men rode out on a long hunting trip, the women would pick and gather.

And I'll be alone with Auntie, going over everything that I already know, thought Ode. He kicked at a dusty tuft of grass and sighed. Blue Moon had asked him once if he resented Cala for singling him out from the tribe. "Mam says Cala took you away," he had whispered, almost fearful that the birther could hear them though they were not near the settlement at the time.

"She didn't take me," Ode had replied. "It was my destiny. The spirits chose this life for me."

"But don't you wish you lived with us?"

"Maybe. But then I'd have to share a tent with you, and you snore!"

At that, the conversation had dissolved into a good-natured fistfight and such talk was forgotten. However, sometimes Ode did wonder if he blamed his auntie. Perhaps it was her doing that he was cast out from his family and the tribe to be a birther. The thought made him uncomfortable, and it did not match the kind, gentle woman that Ode knew. Cala had always nursed him through his sicknesses and wiped away his blubbery tears; surely she would not do such a thing. She had her secrets, Ode knew that much, but she was not cruel.

Trying to keep such thoughts from his mind, Ode idly walked the length of the settlement. He saw a group of children playing behind the food store and among them, toddling around on shaky legs, was Winter's Dawn. Ode smiled and waved. He always liked to see how much she had grown, like a proud third parent.

Her brother, Silver Sky, saw Ode approach and gave him a wave. The boy was too young to understand the tribe's aversion to the birther and the apprentice. He thought Ode fun and interesting.

"I hope you're taking good care of her," said Ode when Silver Sky came scampering over.

"Of course! Mam told me to watch her and I am."

"Looks like you're playing games," said Ode, nodding at the cluster of children running around in the dust behind him.

"Well, I'm doing that, too."

Winter's Dawn waddled over to Ode and clapped her hands.

"Greetings, little sister," he said.

She giggled, and the two of them sat in the dust, rolling a stone between them. A moment later, Ode felt a shadow fall over him and he froze. Thinking that it was Soft Rain, he scrambled to his feet, ready to face a mother's angry glare. But it was not Soft Rain—it was much worse.

"What are you doing?" asked Rippling River.

Ode opened and closed his mouth without making a sound and a red blush crept up his neck.

Rippling River was quite clearly the most beautiful girl in the tribe. Her dark plaits were thick and silky, her brown eyes small and sparkling. She always wore a strip of leather tied tightly around her waist and a tawny feather tucked behind her ear. When she laughed it sounded like the gentle gush of a stream. Ode loved to hear her laugh.

"Were you playing with a rock?" she asked, when he did not reply.

"No."

"It looked like you were."

Rippling River giggled, and Ode thought that her giggle was even sweeter than her laugh. His blush deepened, and he shuffled his feet.

"I don't want to interrupt your game," she said, bending and scooping up Winter's Dawn, who, she held on her hip.

Ode opened his mouth to say something, but no words came out.

Rippling River giggled again, and the baby gurgled.

"She likes you," said Rippling River, and then she turned around and sauntered away. After a few steps she glanced back, saw Ode watching her, and smiled.

Ode watched her go, his chest burning. He felt giddy and light, almost as if he could fly. He sighed, and then sighed again. Supposing he ought to go back to the tent, he turned to see his brother and Gray Morning watching him. They had just finished their combat practice and both were glistening with sweat in the evening light. Blue Moon waggled his eyebrows at Ode in an annoying, knowing way. Gray Morning just frowned.

<hr />

That night, Ode dreamed he was flying. He was soaring through the air, gusts of wind kissing his cheeks. The plain stretched out before him, running on forever in every direction. He felt weightless and small. He beat his arms in a rhythmic tune that matched the steady beating of the tribe drums, but when he tried to wiggle his fingers, he could not.

Suddenly, he was no longer flying; he was still, standing in a forest that he did not know. The trees were different here, the smell was unusual, and he felt afraid. Thorns were tangled around him, and he could hear distant, peculiar sounds. Peering through the trees, he saw that he stood at the edge of a forest and he could just make out grassy land on the other side. Peering closer, he saw the grassy land dipping down and then soaring up like a huge tree. For a moment, Ode even thought that it was a huge tree since he had never known the earth to be anything but flat and even.

Studding the grassy hill were buildings that looked like tents made of wood and thatch. *How strange*, thought Ode. *That would surely take too long to pack away, and how would the mustangs carry it?*

He heard a neigh and his eyes were drawn to a horse. It was a great beast twice the size of a mustang, with thick haunches and a regal, handsome head. Ode gasped because he recognized it immediately from tales told by the tribe: a warhorse. They roamed the flatlands and forests in herds, but they were very rare. Ode had thought he'd seen one once, at a distance. This warhorse was grazing sedately, its silky tail swishing in contentment. It paused a moment and looked over at a girl who sat talking to a man.

The girl was silver. She was some distance away, but Ode was sure that he saw her correctly. The sunlight, weaker here than any he had known in his life, shone off her silvery skin and made it glitter. Her hair fell in a loose tumble of white down her back, and he could just about hear her voice, which was high and clear. Most unsettling of all, he was sure that he knew her.

Ode's heart thudded in his chest and a rush of blood surged around his body. He had to escape. He did not know this strange place or its strange people. How could he have met this girl before? He looked around him, but all he saw were thorns—a wall of them. Panic rising inside, he began beating his arms, desperate to escape.

He heard a shrill whinny and suddenly he was soaring through the air once more. He broke through the trees of the forest and shot ever higher, above the silver girl and the scene below. But as he rose, he caught a glimpse of her face and he saw that her eyes were shockingly violet, like the belly of a storm.

Ode awoke suddenly with a cry. He was shaking, and his grass mat was twisted beneath him. Through the tent's open smoke flap, he could see the distant, twinkling stars, and beside him he could hear a soothing, calm voice. He waited for his ragged breathing to slow and the images of his dream to fade. He was no longer sure of what he had seen.

The soothing, calm voice belonged to Cala, who crouched before the fire, stroking the flames with the tips of her fingers.

"Auntie, why are you awake?" he asked her.

"I heard you stirring."

"Why didn't you wake me from my nightmare?"

"It wasn't a nightmare."

Ode closed his eyes and took a deep breath. When he opened them again, Cala was kneeling at his side, pushing a mug into his hands. It was warm milk with crushed herbs—a drink she used to make him when he was little.

"What did you see, little man?" she asked.

"I don't remember."

"What did you see?" she repeated firmly.

"I . . . was flying," he said at last.

"Were you in your own body?"

"Whose body would I be in?"

"Never mind."

Ode took a sip of milk and wiped his brow with the back of his hand.

"Is this the first time you've had such a dream?" asked Cala.

He thought of the dust storm and of the way his dreams had sometimes erred on the peculiar side. Occasionally, they had felt like more than dreams. Once he had heard a voice whispering the word "Magic" in his ear.

"I don't know," he said truthfully.

They both looked into the fire and a wide grin spread across Ode's face.

"Does this mean I'm Magic?" he asked.

Cala cuffed him on the head.

CHAPTER SIX

The White Bird

From that time onward, Ode often dreamed of the silver girl. He saw her tending to horses, sweeping the doorway of her wooden tent, or riding her stallion across the grassy hills. Sometimes he saw her dressed in fine clothes that were nothing like the Taone leather tunics, walking through rooms that amazed and confused him. He did not share such things with Cala, although she would often question him about what he'd seen. These dreams felt secret.

If Ode was not envisioning the silver girl then he was dreaming of another. Rippling River frequently occupied his thoughts, and if he caught the sounds of her sweet laughter as he walked about the settlement, his face would break into a sappy smile. He would try to find ways of bumping into her if he could, and it was not long before she noticed.

"Greetings *again*, birther," she would say at first as she passed him, twirling one of her long plaits in her hand.

However, her coy smiles and teasing giggles soon turned to surly glares and flashes of panic. Some of the tribesboys had noticed the apprentice birther's attentions and they began to jeer and snicker.

Rippling River did not want her strange admirer to discourage all the others, so she tried her best to stay out of his way.

But nothing could deter Ode's infatuation. He did not wonder why it was now so difficult to bump into his loved one. Nor did he wonder why she sometimes ducked her head and scurried past him. For Rippling River, he thought he might even be able to stand up to his father and ask to be made her partner. All men of the tribe had to ask the chief's permission to acquire a partner, and Ode was not so stupid to think that Gray Morning would grant him Rippling River easily. However, he felt sure that once his father saw his deep love—for he was sure that he was in love—then he would grant them a ceremony and they would live happily ever after.

He decided that he would make the proposition to Gray Morning on the day of the Winter Feast. A love of such astonishing proportions deserved a dramatic declaration, and Ode hoped his father would be so busy organizing the celebrations that he would be easier to convince. Perhaps.

On the day of the Winter Feast, the settlement was a hive of fretting women and snappy men, all trying to prepare for the evening's entertainment. The fires were lit, the heavy snow shifted, and the piles of saved food were cooked. When the white light of day began to fade, the tribe gathered to begin the ceremony. Gray Morning, in his chiefly robes, started the chanting, and the drums were beaten in a booming rhythm. Male and female, young and old—all waved their arms and stamped their feet. Some threw off their furs, their bodies warmed by the dance, and the fires were fed until they roared.

All of a sudden, Gray Morning bellowed a cry to the setting sun. The tribe stilled and joined him in a ceremonial chant as the food was brought forward. The wailing and gurgling ended, and everyone searched for a seat, weaving through the floating ash from the fires.

While everyone settled, Ode took a deep breath and told himself that he must do it now. As the tribesmen and tribeswomen sat on the ground, Ode marched toward his chief. Gray Morning saw him coming and he paused, his huge hands folded across his great chest. Beside him, Sunset By Forest sat, her heart jumping with fear at the steely purpose in her eldest son's stride.

Ode stopped before his father, knowing that all the eyes of the tribe were boring into his back. Everyone had become quiet and still. Blue Moon shook his head at his brother, but Ode would not turn back.

"What are you doing?" growled Gray Morning.

Ode opened his mouth to speak, but no words came out.

"Get back to your seat!" hissed Gray Morning.

"No, I . . ."

Those around that heard him gasped, and Gray Morning's eyes darkened.

"No?" he repeated.

"Dar—" Blue Moon bleated, but it was too late. Everyone could see the fury in Gray Morning's face. Ode felt his legs tremble. He had not meant it to go like this; he had not meant to defy the chief, to enrage his father. Suddenly Ode wanted to be far away from here, somewhere safe. Fear surged through his body and he began shaking all over. Gray Morning stood, his hands clenched into fists as he loomed over his eldest son.

"I want to ask that Rippling River be made my partner!" Ode croaked.

There was a beat of silence, and then someone nearby began snickering. Then somebody else laughed. Another tribesman snorted, and then they were all laughing. The whole tribe, it seemed, was guffawing at the freakish birther.

Gray Morning's face twisted with anger. "Why must you always humiliate me," he spat, lunging forward.

Ode let out a shriek of fear before his body began to convulse. The Taone's laughter quickly turned into screams as they watched Ode's limbs twist, tremble, and snap in half. Before their eyes, his body contorted and became something else. Great wings spread where his hands had been and his neck grew and grew until it was long and curved. Just as suddenly as it had started, it stopped, and there was quiet.

Ode felt smaller. He could see his father staring at him in fear and horror, but he did not know what had happened. His head was dizzy, and his body seemed strange.

A scream broke the silence. It was Ode's mother, screaming and pointing and saying that the spirits had taken her son and left a beast in his place. Sunset By Forest was quickly joined by others who began screaming and crying until there was a chorus of fearful voices. A man nearby stood and drew out his dagger. He made a lunge toward Ode, the thirst for blood in his eyes.

Instinctively, Ode waddled from him and began to flap his wings. Tribesmen and tribeswomen scattered from his path, shouting curses at him as he passed. Ode beat his wings desperately, trying to fly like he had in his dreams, but he stumbled and bumped across the ground. *I must get away*, he thought. *I must get away from here.* Ode flapped his wings again, waddling as fast as he could, and this time, he launched himself into the air. The ground fell away beneath him and he was soaring through the sky. Below, he saw a tribesman throw something, but a dark figure in furs knocked him sideways and a spear whistled away in the other direction. Cala began shouting for calm and it was her voice that the wind carried to Ode as he flew away into the oncoming night.

Ode woke with a start, surrounded by blackness. For a moment, he wondered why he was not in his tent, the chilly light of morning turning the buffalo hide walls beige. Then he remembered the Winter Feast, his father's face, the screams, and the way his body had transformed into something.

He wiggled his fingers experimentally and saw in the gloom that he was himself again. A boy. He also quickly realized that he was naked. He rolled onto his back and looked up at the leafy canopy high above him, fringed with frost and speckled with stars. He must be in a forest, although he did not know where. He remembered flying away from the settlement, his body consumed with fear, and then he remembered feeling tired, his wings beating slowly until suddenly, he had been falling through the air: down, down, down. Then there was nothing but darkness.

He sat up and his arms jerked and twitched with fatigue. He leaned against a nearby tree trunk, his back slumped. He supposed that he would die now and, for the first time, the thought did not seem so terrible. Life was not worth living without Rippling River and he could see that there was no future for them now. He was surely banished from the tribe and, naked and alone in a forest at night in the depths of winter, he was unlikely to survive for long.

He shivered and hugged his knees to his chest, his teeth chattering. He was already frozen, having laid unconscious on the cold, snowy ground for some time. He was surprised that he had woken at all.

Not so far off, he heard a wolf cry to the winter moon, and he tried not to whimper. He pressed his palm to the trunk behind him and whispered to the spirits to let him die instantly and be spared the gore of a wolf attack. *They can eat my dead body instead,* he offered.

His mother whispered often to the spirits like many members of the Taone. Ode had seen her press her hands to the bare earth of the plains and the trunks of trees many a time, her lips moving soundlessly with the desires of her heart. Though she sometimes encouraged him to do so as well, it was not an act he had taken to. Cala did not do such things and when he asked her why, she had simply replied that she had her own gods, which was as elusive an answer as ever. Ode felt the spirits had done him wrong by making him a birther—and therefore a freak, so there was not a lot he had to say to them. Except now.

The wolves howled again, and this time, Ode could sense that they were not far away. He was sure that he could hear the rustle of leaves and the crunch of snow beneath their paws. They would kill him, he knew it.

He willed his body to fly away again. No matter how peculiar he had felt transforming into that winged beast, he wished he could do it now and escape to safety. He tried to harness the panic coursing through his body, but he was too exhausted. Tears of frustration and fear welled in his eyes, and he sat trembling in the snow.

He imagined that he could smell them now. The bloody tang of their panting breath and the musky scent of their thick coats. They would discover him in a moment. He closed his eyes.

A deep growl sounded, followed by a fierce chorus of barks. He could hear something thrashing in the snow and the yelp and snarl of a fight. Ode opened his eyes and found that the wolves were not upon him yet, but they were close. He held his breath and listened as they fought on, their squabble seeming to last for an eternity.

There was a high-pitched yelp, a whine, and then silence.

Ode saw a dark shadow shifting through the trees, and he held his breath. He could just make out the huge, hulking body of a male wolf, blood around its grizzly muzzle and something dead hanging limp from its mouth. It passed not far from him and disappeared into the darkness.

Ode collapsed against the tree trunk, his heart pumping in his chest. The encounter had brought life back to his body, and he stood shakily. He could not just sit and wait for death, he decided. He should at least try to live.

He began shuffling through the snow, but it was so cold against his bare feet and the wind was so icy that he fell to his knees, sobbing. For all his brave thoughts, it was no use. He raised his head to take another chilly breath and it was then that he noticed the blood. It had seeped into the snow and it was splattered against frosty leaves and icy trunks. A she-wolf lay dead before him, her wolf cub lifeless beside her. Ode thought of the lone male wolf he had seen, its mouth full of a limp bundle of fur, and he shuddered. The other cub had been taken for dinner.

Ode was wondering if he ought to lie next to the she-wolf for warmth when he heard a whine. Thinking he was in danger, he tried to stumble away, but then he saw a little snout in the bushes. He paused and looked closer. Hiding there was one little wolf cub that was still alive. Ode bent and held out his hand. The cub took some coaxing—it was so frightened—but it eventually edged out of the bushes and snuffled at his fingers. It had piercing green eyes and ashen fur that looked like the sky before a storm.

Ode lifted it up into his arms, pressing its warm, furry body against his chest. It squeaked at him and licked his neck. The experience was so surreal—to be cradling a wolf, the animal he was taught to fear most of all—that Ode almost laughed, but he did not have the energy to. Instead, he sat on the frozen ground thinking that at least now they would die together. He closed his eyes and held the cub in his arms.

He did not know how long it was before he felt a hand on his shoulder and a sudden warmth covering his body. He looked up and saw Cala, pulling a fur around him. At first, he thought he was dreaming.

"I have found you at last, little man," she said. "It is time to go home."

CHAPTER SEVEN

The Initiation

Two seasons later, in the warmth of summer, it came time for the next initiations. Blue Moon was one of the youngest applicants in the tribe's living memory and Gray Morning almost burst with pride for his second son. Despite being the smallest, Blue Moon was one of the strongest boys and he was skilled in all combat, having never tired of his constant training.

"I can't wait to get my patterns," he said to Ode the evening before the event. "Dar says I'll have them all over my body in spikes, like him, and in swirls like Mam. . . ." He trailed off, realizing that Ode would never have patterns like their parents.

"I don't think they'll improve your ugly face," said Ode.

Blue Moon rolled his eyes and gave his older brother a shove. The young wolf beside them growled and Ode quickly ruffled its furry head. "We're only playing, Arrow," he cooed.

The wolf yapped and licked Ode's fingers.

"Shall we get back to practicing?" said Blue Moon, giving Arrow a nervous glance. "This time tomorrow I'll be by myself in the wilderness."

Despite two seasons having passed since Ode stumbled through the snow into the settlement at midnight, covered with a fur and carrying a wolf pup, Blue Moon was still wary of the creature his brother had named Arrow. The Taone stayed away from Ode now more than ever. None could forget his transformation into the white, winged bird, and when he flew away that day, many had expected never to see him again. When they heard a cry that night—a child's squeal at the sight of a wolf—they had not expected to rush out of their tents in the light of the moon and see not a wolf, but a boy wrapped in fur stumbling through the snow, a pup clutched in his arms.

Had he killed the mother himself? Where had he found the fur? Whispers darted through the tribe and no one ran to help him as Ode fell to his knees before the smoking fires. Then the birther had appeared from the shadows and she had gurgled a wail of joy, insisting that everyone around her join in until the whole tribe found themselves welcoming Ode back with their chant: "Hya–Hya–Hya." Cala announced that this was a gift from the spirits, and her voice was so sure and her manner so convincing that the tribe nodded together in agreement. A few shot nervous glances at their chief, but Gray Morning stood as tall and still and silent as a stone. He had nothing to say, neither welcome nor banishment, and so the tribe had nothing to say, either. In this way, Ode was miraculously received back into the Taone, despite the unusual events of that evening. It was a miracle, and it was Magic.

However, no amount of Magic could make the tribe forget what they had seen. No one caught Ode's eye if they saw him walk by, not even the children. They were afraid of him and his wolf pup, and sometimes Cala was forced to send him away at birthings because he terrified the tribeswomen with his presence. Only Cala and Blue Moon would speak to him now; even his own mother was too scared to be in his company. She was convinced that her first son no longer existed. He had changed in the forest.

And she was right—he *had* changed in the forest. Cala said that it was his very own initiation. After all, he had been in the wilderness alone and he had made it back to the settlement alive. When Ode pointed out that he had had a certain auntie's help, she had simply waved her hand and said, "Details." However, they both knew that the Taone would not accept Ode as a tribesman and he would never receive his patterns like the other men.

If it were not for Arrow, Ode may well have banished himself. Named for the wiggly triangle of black over his left eye that resembled an arrowhead, the little pup gave Ode the love and acceptance he so craved. In the last two seasons, Arrow had grown tall and it would not be long before his puppy cuteness melted away to be replaced by the steely fierceness of a full-grown male wolf. But scampering at Ode's side, Arrow did not look so scary and Ode could not imagine being afraid of his pet.

"Come on! Make it hard for me!" jeered Blue Moon, smacking his wooden spear against the head of Ode's blunt axe.

The two brothers were fighting ankle-deep in a cool stream to "make it hard" for Blue Moon, who always wanted more challenges. The slipperiness of the riverbed certainly threw off their balance and both boys had fallen several times.

"Show me what you've got," said Blue Moon, lunging with his spear.

Ode smiled and doubled back, dancing out of the way as his brother took another swing. "You are too strong for me now," he said truthfully.

"Strong enough to do this?"

Blue Moon spun his spear in his hands and thwacked it with all his might against the handle of his brother's axe, almost sending the weapon flying out of Ode's hands. Had Ode not managed to jump back, the spear would have smacked against his knuckles and, more than likely, broken them.

Both brothers were slick and shiny with sweat, their chests heaving with the exhilaration of the fight. They had pulled off their buffalo hide tunics long ago and left them drying in dusty grass on the riverbank beside Arrow.

"All I can do is hope to tire you out," said Ode, sidestepping another of his brother's forceful attacks.

Blue Moon grinned and paused to wipe the sweat from his brow. "You think I'm ready?" he asked.

"I think you were ready a long time ago."

Blue Moon raised his spear again, but Ode quickly added, "And I think that you should make sure that you are well rested for tomorrow."

His younger brother pondered the suggestion for a moment before nodding. "Can't take any more of me?" he asked with a wink.

"Exactly."

They waded out of the stream and collected their practice weapons. The settlement stood some distance away in the rippling heat and the brothers turned toward it, hitching their tunics over their shoulders.

"Are they dropping you off in the forest?" asked Ode, Arrow lolloping at his heels, panting.

"They can drop me anywhere they want, but I'll be the last back to the settlement, just you wait and see. I'll withstand the wilderness the longest."

"I don't doubt it, but . . . be careful, little brother."

Blue Moon snorted. "Oh, you'd miss me if I was gone?"

"Only because I wouldn't have anyone to talk to."

"What about your wolf?"

"Sometimes it's nice to get a reply."

There was a pause as they picked their way over the dry, cracked ground, the bristly rushes tickling their calves.

"You don't need to worry about me," said Blue Moon. "I'll be just fine."

As they neared the settlement, the brothers returned to their quips and banter, tripping each other up and laughing if they fell. When they reached the first tent, Ode slung the practice weapons into his brother's arms and promised to see him tomorrow before he left to go out into the wild.

"Get a good night's sleep and dream of my face all night long," called Ode, as Blue Moon walked away.

The chatter of the tribeswomen cooking around the fires was too loud for Ode to hear his brother's response, so he could only make out a grumble.

Smiling, Ode pushed back the flap of his tent and ducked inside, followed by Arrow. Cala crouched before the small fire, an assortment of ingredients scattered beside her. When she saw that she was not alone, she stood and began quickly tidying up.

"I thought that you were playing with your brother," she said, gathering up feathers, thread, and what looked like dried, thinly sliced animal skins.

"We were fighting, not playing," said Ode, tugging one of her long plaits in greeting as he always did. "What are you doing?"

"Nothing. Just fiddling with a few things."

Ode collapsed onto his bed mat and began rubbing his shoulder. He had pulled a muscle in one of his fights.

"Were you looking into the fire?" Ode asked casually.

Cala knew better than to fall for her apprentice's nonchalant attitude. "No," she said firmly.

"It looked like you were."

Cala shuffled over to one of her chests and Ode could not help but notice it was the one that was normally locked. Cala's three leather chests were a rare phenomenon to the Taone, who could count the number of each's personal possessions on one hand. It took two mustangs to carry Cala's trunks whenever the tribe moved and a great deal of huffing and puffing to strap them into place, but no one questioned her right to such extravagancies. They would not have dared.

"It looked like you were trying to find out a fortune," persisted Ode.

"That is not what I was doing."

"Are you sure? What about those animal skins you had? What were—"

"Perhaps you should stop gabbling and go and get our food, little man."

Ode made a face. "I'm resting," he muttered.

"Well, hurry up. I'm hungry."

Ode longed to race over and see what she was trying to hide, but he knew she would not let him get away with it, so he stayed put. He had asked her many times what was in her locked chest and she had always given him vague answers, except for one night when, feeling particularly daring, she had whispered, "Secrets."

Ode had just finished rubbing the ache from his shoulder when the flap of the tent was pulled aside and a little face peered in.

"Birther!" it squeaked. "Birther, my mam needs you!"

Cala slammed the chest shut and grabbed her pouch of remedies from the corner. "All right, Pale Sky," she said to the child. "We'll be there in a moment."

"Not you," said Pale Sky, looking at Ode. "Mam said not you."

Ode had been sent away from many births since the incident, but it always hurt. He shrugged and looked away.

"Make sure you leave some food for me," said Cala, ruffling his hair. "Don't go eating it all again. Even growing boys don't need that much meat."

Ode did not reply. He watched as she left with Pale Sky, and then there was no sound except the distant hum of chatter outside and the crackling of the fire. He had been born a boy birther—a freak to the Taone—and now he was considered too strange even to do that. He sighed.

For a while, Ode ambled around the tent, tidying up and playing with Arrow. When the food was ready, he collected it from the tribeswomen, none of them daring to look him in the eye, and he ate his dinner alone. He left Cala's portion beside her bed mat and forbade Arrow to go near it, although that did not stop the wolf from licking his chops and sniffing the air for wafts of juicy meat.

It was only when he was laying on his bed mat, looking up at the darkening sky through the tent's open smoke flap, that Ode remembered the chest. He had seen Cala slam it shut, but he had not seen her lock it, and perhaps she had overlooked this precaution just once. He sat up and crawled over to the stack of three chests on the other side of the tent. He pushed at the chest's lid gently, expecting it to remain fastened, but it shifted under his touch and creaked open. Ode caught his breath. He had been right; in her haste to leave, Cala had left the chest unlocked.

Inside there were thin strips of animal skin folded, rolled, and bound shut with leather ties. But there was nothing else. Ode frowned and dug through the skins, but all he discovered was the wooden bottom of the chest. Feeling disappointed, he was about to shut the lid once more when one of the animal skins caught his eye. It had markings on it; shapes and symbols that meant nothing to him. He picked it up and held it toward the dying embers of the fire. The skin had flecks and dots and swirls scratched all over it, like the patterns that the tribespeople wore on their skin.

Ode ran his finger across the markings, wondering what they could possibly mean. He picked up another animal skin and unrolled it, discovering more symbols. Suddenly, a word drifted into his consciousness: *map*. He remembered the silver girl from his dreams, and he saw her bent over a similar object, tracing the markings with her finger. "The Wild Lands," she had said, stroking a shape on an animal skin. Her violet eyes widened in wonder, and she smiled.

The vision vanished, and Ode shuddered. He knew instinctively that the Wild Lands was his home. He knew that he stood in it now—a tiny part of something far bigger than he had ever imagined. His fingers shook as he contemplated that there was more to the realm than the land between the winding river and the gaping lake. All his life he had known nothing but the Taone. The possibility that there was more to life than this had never crossed his mind until now. The thought made him feel sick and small.

Ode did not know how long he sat there, hunched in a ball with the map spread open on his lap, but when a hand touched his shoulder, the embers of the fire had long burned out and the only light in the tent came from the stars.

"You've always known there was more," Ode whispered.

Cala sighed, her hand still on his shoulder. "There is always more. Does it scare you?"

"It confuses me."

Arrow was snoozing peacefully at the foot of Ode's bedroll and his paw twitched in his sleep.

"There will come a time when you accept confusion. Many strange things will happen to you, Ode."

"Why don't you just explain it to me, then?"

"Don't you think I would if I could?"

"Sometimes I'm not sure."

Cala gently removed the map from Ode's fingers and put it back in the chest. She shut the lid and locked it.

"I was making something for you when you came in," she said. "It's a gift."

From the pouch across her shoulders she took out a leather cord adorned with a single white feather. Ode flinched.

"I found this feather when I found you in the snow," said Cala, placing the cord over his head. "It's your feather, and I made it into an amulet."

"What's an amulet?"

"It's an inheritance. When you shift shape, your clothes will fall away, but this will change with you. It is part of you, and it is important."

The feather lightly tickled Ode's chest, but he could not bring himself to touch it. It was the sickening reminder that he was not like everyone else.

"So, that's it?" he snapped, his voice croaking with pain. "You're not even going to try to explain?"

Cala smiled. "Accept the confusion, little man," she said. "That is all you can do."

CHAPTER EIGHT

The Shift

Blue Moon was the last to return from the initiation, and he walked back into the settlement one late summer's morning to a chorus of excited shouts and gurgles. Gray Morning strode out of his tent grinning and embraced his son, clapping Blue Moon's bruised, scratched back over and over again until the scabs began to bleed. Blue Moon had stayed so long in the wilderness that some had wondered if he would ever return. Ode had even found himself doubting it; his chest prickling with fear since, with every initiation, there were some who were never seen again.

A feast was announced, and while the rest of the tribe scurried into action, Blue Moon tore himself away from his proud parents to greet his older brother. At the edge of the settlement, they stood before each other, both realizing that they had changed. They were not the same two brothers who had stood together at the beginning of summer.

Ode saw the wiry stealth Blue Moon had gained in the wilderness, and there was a seriousness to him now, when before he had been full of quips and laughter. His body had lost its smooth roundness and he looked jagged and fierce. His smile, however, still held a flicker of its old warmth.

"I think that we have both grown," said Blue Moon, noticing the firm set of Ode's shoulders and the shadows in his eyes that spoke of secrets.

"Spoken like a man," said Ode. "What did you do with my little brother?"

Blue Moon grinned, looking for a moment like his old self. "A coyote ate him," he replied. "And the spirits cursed him for being so cocky."

They both laughed.

"Congratulations, little brother. I can't even imagine the patterns you will get for staying out so long. Maybe you will have more even than Dar."

The wry tone of his voice must have struck Blue Moon, because he said with some wonder, "You are scared of him no longer?"

Ode realized with surprise that this was true. Gray Morning was still bigger and stronger than he, but Ode knew there were places other than the plains and the forest; places that his father had never thought of and did not rule. "No, I'm not scared of him," he finally said.

There was a pause and both brothers wished for the easy familiarity of their past.

"I feel I ought to tell you something," said Blue Moon, looking at the ground. "Dar is . . . he will announce tonight that Rippling River will be my partner."

Ode felt his fingers clench. Arrow, who was sitting nearby, looked over, his ears pricked.

"I am happy for you, brother," Ode said.

"I wanted to tell you myself. It was his choice, not mine."

"Thank you."

Blue Moon nodded, before walking away.

And that evening, after the dancing and the feathers and the chanting, Gray Morning announced the happy news. The tribeswomen cried with joy—and some with anger, since one of their daughters had not been chosen. Rippling River emerged from the crowd and she stood before her betrothed, blushing profusely and looking more beautiful than ever. The tribe began to chant again and dance for joy, the drums banging out a rhythm.

Ode watched it all from the shadows with Arrow at his side. He fought the overwhelming desire to escape it all and fly somewhere far, far away.

⚬⚬⚬

Since the tribeswomen of the Taone would not allow Ode to tend to them as a birther, he often found he had little to do. He would help Cala as much as he could, sorting through her supplies and mixing pastes and ointments, but more often than not, he was found walking alone, except for Arrow, away from the settlement to practice. What it was that he practiced, he was not sure, because he did not understand what had happened to him—how his body shifted into something else—but he knew that he needed to garner some control over it. In the same way that the tribesmen taught their bodies to hunt, he needed to teach his body to shift.

In his daily practice sessions, Arrow would sit nearby and watch as Ode changed into a white bird. Ode wondered why the wolf did not try to pounce on him, but he seemed to know that it was still his master. He observed Ode's efforts with his cool green eyes and kept watch for danger.

In the privacy of a glade or at a long distance from the settlement across the flatlands, Ode would undress and stand still, willing himself to shift. For the first few seasons, he was rarely successful. Instead, he felt frustrated and cold. Sometimes the shift would take him by surprise and before he knew it, he was changing, his arms becoming wings and his legs shortening rapidly. These moments filled him with panic and pain. The shift made his limbs burn with agony and sometimes he even hoped that his efforts to shift would fail.

"You must embrace that pain," said Cala, when he returned to their tent, moody, one afternoon.

"It would be a lot easier if you'd just *tell* me what to do."

"How should I know how it works? Have you ever seen me turn into a white bird?"

Ode grunted.

"Why couldn't it be an eagle?" he said after a pause. "Why does it have to be such a weird-looking creature?"

"I'm sure there is a reason," Cala replied, without meeting his eye.

However, as summer became winter, and then winter melted into spring, Ode found that he was achieving a shift more frequently. Sometimes the ability still escaped him, and sometimes it took him by surprise, but after a while, he no longer feared it. He had taken Cala's advice and embraced the pain until there was almost none. What he felt when he shifted now was close to exhilaration. He could fly. If he was in a good mood after a shift, Ode would let himself fly in circles, relishing the feeling of soaring above everything.

The realm looked different from the sky. The settlement seemed small and insignificant. The land looked more like the map he had found in Cala's chest. He took it out often now, with her permission, and studied the shapes and markings. He was careful not to ask questions, because he knew from experience that Cala would snatch the map from his hands and lock it back in the chest again if she felt he was growing too inquisitive, but sometimes he would burn for answers.

"What are all these other things?" he asked one evening, gesturing to the sheets of animal skins covered in markings.

Cala replied, "Scriptures," but her jaw twitched, as if she had said too much.

"What do you do with them?"

"Read them."

"What does *read* mean?"

Cala looked up sharply, and Ode quickly put the map back in the chest and shut the lid with a snap. "Never mind," he said.

His auntie hid a smile.

As Ode's shifting continued, he found himself getting used to his other form. On certain days he almost preferred it. As the white bird he was no longer the freakish birther, but rather a wild creature with no name. One day he stayed in his shift longer than normal and almost forgot himself. Flying above the forest, he had just been about to soar over the settlement—something he never did for fear of being spotted by members of the tribe—when Arrow's bark brought him abruptly back into his own body. Literally.

Ode's wings vanished, and he began to fall. With a jolt of terror, he shifted himself into the white bird once again and managed to brace himself just before he landed with a thump on the forest floor, shifting immediately back into his human form. He scrambled to his feet and brushed the dust from his hands. That he had momentarily forgotten himself terrified Ode. It had never occurred to him that it was a possibility, but he knew he must be more careful in the future.

He looked around, his legs still trembling, hoping to see some sign of Arrow or his clothes, but he'd fallen into a different part of the forest. He heard Arrow bark and followed the sound. However, when he reached his peaceful glade, he discovered that the wolf was not alone.

"Greetings brother," said Blue Moon. "Do you think that you could call your wolf off?"

Arrow was circling Blue Moon, his lips pulled back in a snarl. At Ode's whistle, he reluctantly peeled away.

"Haven't you got things to do?" asked Ode, pulling his clothes back on. It had been a long time since Ode had spoken to his little brother. Blue Moon was always busy now advising Gray Morning or looking after Rippling River.

Blue Moon grimaced. "Unfortunately yes, but I came in here to find you. I thought we could have a little sparring game, like old times. I've barely seen you recently . . . we've both been busy."

Ode noticed the wooden practice weapons in his brother's arms.

"What do you want to use those for?" he asked, unable to hide the tiny sneer that crept into his voice. "You've got real weapons now."

Blue Moon sighed. "Ode, it wasn't my fault. I didn't choose her."

"Yeah, I know."

"Then why are you punishing me? Why are you ignoring me?"

"It's not about her. It's not about you."

They paused and looked at one another.

It was about Ode. It was because he was a freak and an outsider, who wished so much that he had the life of his little brother. Blue Moon held out the wooden axe, Ode's favorite weapon of choice. "Come on, take it, I want to beat you like I used to."

Ode took the weapon.

"We haven't fought since our initiation," said Blue Moon, swinging his wooden spear in his hands.

"*Your* initiation."

"I'm not the only one who went out into the wild and came back alone. Besides, you brought a wolf with you."

Ode chuckled. "All right then, little brother, show me what you've learned."

Together they fought and joked in the glade, just like old times.

CHAPTER NINE

The Savages

That spring, Ode began to dream more frequently, and often he woke in the morning with the whispers of foreign words in his ears and the vision of other lands drifting away like smoke before his eyes. He saw the silver girl in emerald-green robes standing before a surge of people who cheered and hailed her; he saw a man who looked tired and drawn, staring at a golden disc; and he saw a little girl with yellow hair crying alone in a room, her body racked with sobs.

The visions seemed unconnected, but Ode felt that there must be something that brought them together. They were gradually becoming more vivid as the nights wore on and a sense of foreboding lingered at their edges. Ode awoke each morning and glanced at Cala, who was already awake and watching him. She did not ask what he saw, but Ode knew that she could feel it, too. They both were waiting for something unspoken.

One late spring morning, as the surface of the lake beside the settlement winked in the sunlight and the animals grazed at its banks, a scream sounded through the air. It was followed by yells and shouts, which made Arrow's fur bristle and his haunches tighten. Ode paused in his stroll beside the bank of the lake and looked across the flat land at the cloud of mustang horses charging toward them. At first, he feared that the herd was wild, but then he made out the figure of his father sitting astride his piebald stallion and galloping onward with purpose. Arrow lifted his head and smelled the breeze before opening his jaws in a soft howl. He could smell blood.

The hunters were not due back today, and the tribe instantly knew that something was wrong. More screams sounded, and women and children rushed from their tents, whispering fervently to the spirits. Ode joined their huddle, staying at the back, and waited until the hunters stormed into the settlement, halting abruptly in a surge of dust.

Gray Morning vaulted from the saddle, his brow knotted with anger. He had scratches up his arms and across his chest, but otherwise he looked unscathed. However, it was clear from the blood splattered across his cheek and the dirt smudged over his torso that he had been fighting. Beside him, Blue Moon jumped off his palomino stallion in a similar state.

As the other hunters arrived, tribeswomen began to wail and cry. Ode saw that four bodies were slumped across their mustangs, the horses' coats matted with blood. One tribesman was still alive and Cala appeared from the crowd, commanding that they take him to her tent immediately.

"What has happened?" she asked Gray Morning as the wounded tribesman was carried away.

"It was a beast," growled the chief, over the crying and wailing of the tribe. "A beast the likes of which I have never seen before."

Cala frowned and turned away to tend to the wounded. Ode knew that he should follow, but he wanted to find out more. This did not seem like a typical bear attack. The Taone hunters were experienced and skilled; it must have been an exceptional beast to defeat them.

Ode slid through the wailing crowd to Blue Moon, who was standing beside his palomino stallion, looking bewildered. Rippling River rushed from the crowd and threw her arms around his neck, showering his cheek with kisses. Ode held back and waited for his brother to send her away before he approached.

"Greetings, brother. I am more than pleased to see you still alive," Ode said.

Blue Moon jumped at the sound of Ode's voice. "I'm pleased also," he said. "I thought for a moment that the spirits would take me."

"What happened?"

Blue Moon wiped the sweat from his brow with the back of his hand. "It was a beast," he said quietly. "I have never seen anything like it before."

"But what did it look like?"

"It was . . . huge. We thought we'd take it unaware and bring it back for a feast, but it knew we were coming."

"Yes?"

"And it . . . spoke."

"What did it say?"

Blue Moon shook himself and turned away to pat his horse. "You should lay low, brother," he said. "The hunters are uneasy, and we have lost men."

"What do you mean?"

"You make them uneasy. And no one will relax with your wolf around all this blood."

Ode glanced at Arrow, who stood patiently in the shadow of a tent, away from the chaos of the settlement. His green eyes glittered in the gloom.

"Go and help the wounded," said Blue Moon. "They will thank you for that, and they will remember it."

They are my people, too, Ode wanted to shout, but he knew it was no use.

Rippling River appeared with a skin of water for her partner, and Ode hurried away. He followed the outskirts of the settlement to Cala's tent and stopped to stare at the people bunched outside. He was tempted to feel bitter. These same people had ignored him every day as they passed by the store or next to the fires. They had laughed at him and whispered about him. They had all but banished him, and yet now they looked his way with hopeful eyes.

Ode signaled for Arrow to wait and the wolf settled himself at a distance beside the lapping shore of the lake. With a sigh, Ode strode through the crowd and into the tent, determined to help.

⊶⊷

That night Ode dreamed of a battle. He saw tribesmen of the Taone charging in an unknown land against beasts that were terrifying and strange. He saw his people cut down by their enemies and left to die in the dust. He saw his father bellowing war cries that were drowned by the screams of the battle before he was pulled off his piebald stallion and beaten into the ground.

Blood splattered everywhere, pooling onto the unfamiliar landscape of rocks and rubble. Ode could smell its metallic tang and he could even taste it on his lips. He could hear the thunder of hooves, the cries of death, the beat of the tribal drums, and the almighty roars that were louder even than the screams of mountain lions or the rumbles of grizzly bears. It was in that moment that Ode knew the Taone had lost.

The vision changed, and Ode found himself in a tent that was large and rickety. He could see a woman with gray hair talking to an old man. They were not people of a tribe, for their skin was olive like the pale brown of a leaf at the end of summer and they had no patterns etched on their faces.

"No one can tell where she is," said the woman, her fingers knotted together in her lap. "My daughter has disappeared. I found her in Sago, and I tried to bring her here, but she escaped. She did not want to come."

The old man sighed. He wore stained robes and his hair and beard were pale and long. "Asha, she will come. You have read the scripture," he replied.

"Then where is she?"

There was a silence and the vision flickered before Ode's eyes. He knew that they could not see him. His spirit was in the room watching them, but his body still rested soundly elsewhere.

"We have spoken of this already," said the old man. "She will come when the time is right—when she has gathered an army among her people in the Hillands. We cannot tell when this will happen, but it will."

"But I do not have long. . . ."

The old man frowned. "But—"

"I am happy to go," Asha said, though her voice quivered. "I always thought that I might meet *him* once more, but now I find that I do not care. I only wish . . . I only wish that I could see my daughter again."

A tear snaked down her cheek, and the old man bent forward to take her hand. "You did the right thing," he began. "She can stop him. She will understand when she—"

A commotion sounded outside and a creature ran into the tent. It was built like a bear with thick muscles and a brown, shaggy coat, but it had wings curled across its back.

"There has been an attack," it said.

Asha gasped and staggered to her feet. "From the sea?" she asked. "There have been no warnings of it!"

"No, from the forest. We were hunting, and we were set upon."

"Are any hurt?"

"Just one. He is being tended to."

"Do you think they will attack again?" asked the old man.

"I believe they will, Professor."

Asha and the professor exchanged a glance.

"Will they talk to us?" Asha asked.

"I doubt it. Do you have a blanket?" the creature said.

Asha nodded and grabbed a piece of cloth. She held it out in her hand, and both she and the professor turned their heads away as the creature began to shake. It twisted and trembled as its body shrank and snapped. Its claws disappeared and its fur fell away until there was a man in its place who took the blanket and wrapped it around his naked body.

"Thank you," he said.

The man had shifted, and Ode awoke gasping with the shock of it. The amber dawn burst upon his eyes, washing the vision away. Ode saw that he was in Cala's tent, as always, and that Arrow lay at his feet. It was early and his auntie was missing. Though the walls of the tent were burning with the first light of the day, Ode could hear voices and the footfalls of a crowd outside.

He sat up and touched the white feather that hung around his neck. It felt warm.

There are others like me, he thought and it brought a smile to his lips because he knew that what he had seen was true.

"Hya–Hya–Hya!" sounded from outside, followed by a gurgle of wails.

At Ode's feet, Arrow growled softly.

Ode pulled on his tunic and walked out of the tent. In the middle of the settlement, a mass of people had gathered. Young and old, they circled Gray Morning, who stood with Blue Moon at his side in the morning light. Ode saw that the chief was wearing his ceremonial crown of feathers, which trailed down his back in a cascade of beads, threads, and russet and white plumes. It sent a chill of worry through Ode, and he hurried to join the crowd.

"It has been a long time since we have battled," Gray Morning was saying, his deep voice booming across the lake stretched out beside them, silent and still. "The spirits have granted us seasons of peace and contentment, but that time is over. Yesterday, we came across a beast that took the lives of some of our brothers."

There was a wail from the crowd and many bent to the ground and touched it, whispering words to the dead.

"We have an enemy once more, and it is time to fight," said Gray Morning, banging his fists together. "We believe the beast we found is not the only of its kind. It was trespassing on our territory, and we know there will be others. Today, we ride out and defend our tribe—we defend what is ours!"

"Hya–Hya–Hya!" the tribe chorused in agreement.

Ode saw his mother standing with Rippling River behind the chief. Both clung to one another, the blue patterns of their faces trembling with worry.

"The spirits are on our side," said Gray Morning. "Our enemy will be easily beaten. We will kneel to no other tribe!"

Many of the crowd yelped and kicked up their heels in the dewy earth to show their support.

"The Taone are stronger," added Blue Moon. "We know this land and it is ours. We will not let it be taken!"

"My son has spoken," boomed Gray Morning. "The Taone have spoken. We will fight and leave the enemy bloody!"

"Hya–Hya–Hya!" chorused the crowd. "Hya–Hya–Hya! Hya–Hya–Hya!"

Even the children joined in, crying, "Hya–Hya–Hya!" and stamping their little feet. The shouts of the crowd grew louder until they were bouncing off the lake and echoing through the settlement.

"No!" yelled Ode, and instantly, there was silence.

The crowd parted until Ode found himself standing before his father. Gray Morning's eyes darkened and his shoulders hunched with rage.

"No?" he hissed.

"No," Ode repeated, and he felt his fingers tremble like the beginning of a shift, but he used all his willpower to still himself. He would not shift, not this time.

"We can't fight these creatures," he said.

"What gives you the right to speak?" growled Gray Morning.

"I know that we can't fight them because we will lose. I have seen it."

Gray Morning roared with anger and charged toward Ode. But he stopped at the last moment. He saw that his son was not afraid and did not cower. Instead, Gray Morning stood puffing into Ode's face, his whole body clenched with rage.

"We are unbeatable," he spat. "We are great fighters!"

"We do not understand these creatures," Ode replied, his voice steady and clear while his insides quivered. "They will defeat us."

"Us? I see no patterns across your face, birther. What do you know of battles and fighting?"

"I know that we will fall. I know that if we could speak to them—"

"Speak to them? We must defeat them!"

"If you go into battle, you will die."

Gray Morning smacked his fist across Ode's face with a roar. Blood spurted from Ode's nose and he stumbled to the ground, humiliated. Arrow snarled, but Ode hastily put a hand on the wolf's bristled shoulder to calm him.

Gray Morning turned away with a grunt and stalked back to the head of the crowd. "We will fight tomorrow. Sharpen your weapons and ready the horses. Tomorrow, we will win our battle."

After a pause, Gray Morning roared, "Now!"

The people dispersed in a hurry, and Ode climbed back to his feet, blood oozing down his chin and dripping onto his chest. His face burned with pain, but he would not let it show.

"If it were not for the battle tomorrow, I would have killed you," said Gray Morning in a low voice.

The people of the Taone were rushing away and Ode could just about hear his father, though he refused to look at him.

"We need you to tend to the wounded, birther, but after we win, I can't see that you will be so necessary. We only need one birther, and I think we have one too many."

With that, Gray Morning strode away and through a blur of angry tears, Ode saw the feathers of his father's headdress ruffle in the morning breeze.

CHAPTER TEN

The Battle

That night Ode did not dream. He already knew what would happen. Instead, he woke in darkness, his mind and body empty.

"Are you ready, little man?"

The sound of Cala moving about the tent had woken him and he peered through the gloom in the direction of her voice.

"What do you mean?" he asked.

"The men are leaving for battle now, and we will follow them."

Ode slumped back on his bedroll. "Let them die," he said. "They wish *me* dead."

"You want your people to die? You want your dar and your brother to fall?"

There was a pause.

"No," he said at last.

"Then hurry."

Ode dressed quickly, but as he pulled his tunic over his head, the collar caught the side of his nose and it throbbed with pain.

"Where were you yesterday?" he asked. He had not seen Cala in the afternoon or the evening, and he had fallen asleep waiting for her to return.

"I was thinking."

"Did you see what happened in the morning?"

"I saw, but I could not help you."

"What if he had killed me?"

Cala turned to her apprentice and the whites of her eyes shone in the darkness. "He would not have killed you," she said. "He would never do that, little man. But shut your mouth now and follow quietly."

They slid into the blackness outside, Arrow a step behind them like a shadow. Ode could hear the distant hoofbeats of the horses as the warriors rode away from the settlement toward certain death. The tribesmen had spent yesterday preparing for the fight. They had gathered their weapons and painted black and red slashes across the blue patterns of their bodies to mark them for war. Gray Morning had announced they would leave before sunrise and he had forbidden the women and children to rise from their bedrolls and bid their loved ones farewell. He had insisted there was no need. The tribesmen would return before sunset the next day, triumphant.

Cala and Ode walked through a sea of tents that were carefully silent. Ode was sure that the occupants were awake, but none dared to disobey the chief's orders and come out. Ode suspected they were whispering to the spirits for safety instead and waiting for sunrise with gritted teeth.

Cala pointed at two of the packhorses used for carrying her chests and Ode climbed onto the back of the nearest. He had never been granted a horse of his own so he was not an accomplished rider, but the packhorses were stocky and easy to steer. They were none too keen on Arrow, however, who trotted at their side.

In a patter of hoofbeats, Cala and Ode cantered away from the settlement, following the trail of the tribesmen. Ode glanced over his shoulder at the sleeping tents beside the wide lake. The first rays of the sun would soon hit the water and make the light jump across its gentle waves. Before long the women would arise and light the fires for the day; the elderly would congregate by the shore, telling stories of old and watching over the children as they played. It would be almost like the thousands of days before it, but it would be the last of its kind. Their lives would never be the same again.

Ode knew it, because he had dreamed it.

———— ⊗⊗⊗ ————

Ode and Cala rode with Arrow loping along beside them for some time as the sun came up and as light splashed across the flatlands. They were heading toward the forest that stood beside the winding river and marked the end of the Taone territory. It stretched across the horizon like a fat green snake, thickening as they grew closer.

"Where will they fight?" asked Ode.

They had been riding silently since they left the settlement and his voice took his mare by surprise, causing her ears to flick back and her step to falter.

"You tell me," replied Cala. "*You* dreamed it."

"You didn't?"

"No."

Ode suspected she was not being completely truthful. He knew that she had felt uneasy these past few days, too.

"The battle was in a land I had never seen before," he said. "It was . . . rocky and dark red."

"Then it must be on the other side of the forest."

"But that isn't the Taone territory."

"Gray Morning wants a battle, and if he has to go and seek it, then he will."

Ode sighed. He knew that she was right.

As they approached the treeline, they slowed their horses to a brisk walk. The packhorses' necks were dark with sweat, and Arrow was panting heavily behind. As soon as they were beneath the canopy of leaves, Cala suggested they stop to rest.

The morning was sunny and in the shady forest, the day was pleasant and bright. Ode could scarcely believe that blood and defeat awaited them.

"Do you think we will catch up in time?" he asked.

"It depends on what you want to be in time for."

"I'm sick of riddles," he snapped and kicked at a pebble on the forest floor.

Arrow barked.

"Then I suggest you stop learning Magic." Cala wiped the sweat from her brow and swallowed. Ode realized that she looked just as nervous as he felt.

"You once told me that Magic is never certain," he said.

After a moment she nodded.

"So, even what we know could be wrong. It could all be wrong."

She smiled. "Exactly. You're learning."

Ode sighed and they lapsed into silence.

Before long, they mounted again and began trotting through the forest. The tribesmen of the Taone had left a trail of hoofprints in the dusty sand of the flatlands, but their tracks were not so clear in the forest. Ode pointed his packhorse in a forward direction and hoped for the best. After a while, they were forced to stop once more to rest before pressing on. It was afternoon by the time Ode heard the screams.

The packhorses pricked their ears and Arrow growled.

"They have not been fighting long," said Cala. "They are still banging the drums."

Suddenly, Ode remembered the blood and the violence of his dream and it became very real. He saw his people brutally killed, and he heard the echoes of their cries of pain. Sensing his distress, his horse began to shy and buck. Ode hastily dismounted and threw the reins in Cala's direction. They were at the edge of the forest now and the trees were beginning to thin.

"Ode! Wait!" she called. "We cannot walk into the battle unarmed! You have no weapons—they will kill you!"

Ode stopped and stumbled against a tree trunk, his legs shaking.

"The horses will go no farther," he said.

He was right. The packhorses could hear the sounds of the battle and they were trembling.

"We will tie them here and approach on foot," said Cala. "But we will not do anything rash."

Ode nodded, and they set off at a jog, following the cries of war. The trees disappeared and the ground became craggy. Great dusty rocks of red and russet brown rose before them in a tall wall, while the battle raged on the other side.

"No!" said Cala, as Ode started to climb the boulders. "I said we must not do anything rash. You can't run into the battle!"

"Then I will fly."

"But you—"

"I might have dreamed wrong!" Ode cried, tears of fear welling in his eyes. "It might not have to be this way."

"All right," said Cala at last. "I will wait here, but do not get yourself killed, little man. Do you promise?"

"I promise."

To shift was a release and Ode gave himself over to it wholeheartedly. He achieved his smoothest shift yet, but he scarcely noticed. Not for the first time he wished that he could be an eagle or a stronger bird that was not so ungainly or awkward. With some difficulty, he took off into the air, rising above the wall of craggy rocks. Beneath him, Cala looked on, her face taut with worry, and Arrow howled.

What he saw on the other side of the rocks almost caused Ode to shift back in shock. Just like his dream, the rough ground was covered with blood and bodies. Some were warriors from the Taone; some were horses; and others were creatures Ode did not know existed. The battle raged with the sound of grunts and the smack and slash of weapons beating and hitting. Ode saw the glint of arrows shooting through the air and the flash of spears, but it was not enough. Ode could see that some creatures were fighting with their teeth and claws, but others appeared to be using nothing. Men and women stood with their hands held out in front of them, or their fingers clenched into fists, while tribesmen fell before them, writhing. Ode did not know how they did this, but he suspected Magic and he knew for sure then that the Taone could never win this fight.

He watched two bear-like creatures take down his father's piebald stallion, and then they grabbed the chief and dragged him across the ground. Nearby, he saw Blue Moon trying to chase after them, but an unarmed man moved his hands in Blue Moon's direction and suddenly Ode's brother was twisting on the ground and yelling in pain.

Stop! Ode tried to scream, but a strange wordless sound escaped his beak.

He saw the creatures set upon the lifeless body of his father, and he saw the remaining Taone warriors lose heart as their chief was defeated. Their weapons stilled in their hands and the enemy took the advantage, seizing them and holding them captive or killing them instantly. Blue Moon still writhed on the ground, his lips foaming and his limbs shaking. It would not be long before his spirit departed, too.

Stop! Ode tried to cry again, and he began swooping to land on the battlefield. The air rushed past him, a sure sign that he was descending too fast, but Ode did not care. He fell, his wings beating and his body twisting. Down, down, down he dropped, landing with a crash on an unarmed man. The force of it caused him to shift and through his cracked, human lips he cried, "Stop!"

The man beneath Ode pushed him off and clambered to his feet.

"No!" cried Ode.

The man stared at Ode, unsure, his arms half raised.

"What is going on?" roared a creature nearby, a squirming tribesman pinned beneath its talons.

"This one just shifted," said the man. "And it's speaking in Pervoroccoian."

The other creatures were looking over with interest now and Ode attempted to hide his nakedness.

"You are beaten," said a woman. "Surrender to us, and we will spare the lives of the others."

"The battle will end?" asked Ode.

"If you surrender."

Ode turned to Blue Moon, who had stopped writhing and was trying to stagger to his feet.

"You can speak to these things?" he asked, swaying with the effort to stay on his feet. "You understand them?"

"I do. They ask that you surrender."

"The chief will—"

"The chief is dead," said Ode and his voice cracked. "You are the chief now."

Blue Moon's eyes bulged, and then his knees buckled.

"What are you saying to one another?" barked another creature. "Surrender quickly or you leave us with no choice."

"I am asking the chief," said Ode, and he turned back to his brother. "Do you trust me?" he asked. "Because if you do then you must surrender for the good of the tribe. For Rippling River and all the children that need what is left of the tribesmen to return."

Blue Moon's face crumpled and his blue patterns blurred.

"Brother . . ." Ode persisted.

"I trust you," Blue Moon whispered.

Ode turned back to the creatures. "We surrender," he said.

Part Two

Many seasons ago, two cloaked riders halted their horses on the royal road. The fading light rolled away across the flat, pale land into the distance, where the castle stood like a jagged tooth rising from the sea. Here the road was just a rough track, indented by the wheels of carts and wagons carrying goods to the royal court. Far off, merchants and servants hurried to and from the castle while the tide was out and the way cleared. It would not be long before the sea came in again and the route was cut off for the night.

Though the distant scene was busy, on this stretch of road there was no one but the riders. The slighter of the two figures lifted her hand to push back the hood of her cloak. The other rider stopped her, his fingers squeezing her wrist.

"But there is no one around," she whispered.

"Take no chances," he replied.

Their horses stretched out their necks and tried to snatch at a sprout of grass on the road.

"It is not so very grand," said the woman after a pause.

"That is a lie. Wait until we are closer before you say foolish things."

The woman sighed. "I mean . . . I am not sure it is worth all this trouble. Why were you not satisfied with Quitma? Why must—"

"We have been through this," replied the man.

The woman looked down at her gloved hands. She was barely a woman really; more like a girl, but her childhood had been ripped from her.

"How do you know it will work?" she asked.

"Because I have seen it."

"But that does not always—"

"Have you seen something different?" he interrupted.

"No," she lied.

"Then do not challenge me."

The breeze from the sea whistled through her cloak and chilled her cheeks. This land smelled sour and strange, and she missed the rich, hot perfume of her homeland. She missed the intermittent shrieks of the monkeys and the slow burn of the sun. They had left it all behind, and she did not know when they would return. He told her that they were going somewhere better. He told her that this was their prize, but it did not seem like much of a reward.

"It looks cold," she muttered.

She had seen the castle before. She had seen it every time she looked into a fire before they set out on this journey, but it still looked unfamiliar and hostile. There were no castles in Quitma, only huts made from rushes with roofs of wide, fat leaves. The grandest building she had ever seen was a palace hollowed out from a mountainside under a waterfall, which she had once called her home, but even that did not compare to the extravagant scene before her.

This was hard and precise. A thin road wound from the mainland to the castle through a flat, marshy stretch soon to be engulfed by the dark sea. Built on high rocks, the castle was encircled by a wall behind which twisted cobbled streets, snaking upward toward imposing turrets where the royal court resided in opulent chambers. The castle was huge and imposing, and no matter what she was told, the woman did not think that she would ever be able to call it home. She did not want to.

"Of course, it is cold," said the man. "This country is cold."

She knew that he was deliberately misunderstanding her and she sighed.

"Are you sure this will work?" she asked.

Sensing the man's unease, his horse tossed its head and sidestepped. The man's eyes flashed and they might have been silver or gold or violet. Or maybe it was just the light.

"Yes, of course I am," he replied.

But she knew he was lying.

CHAPTER ELEVEN

The Blood

The battlefield was awash with lifeless bodies crushed into the brown rock. Despite the dusting of carrion, Ode easily spotted the once-proud, painted feathers of his chief, snapped and beaten into the ground. He weaved his way through the wreckage to his father's body, trying not to look too closely at where his feet were treading. Gray Morning's leather armor was torn and matted with blood; the beads and the threads were smashed and snapped. As Ode approached, he saw the blue patterns of his father's face flattened in agony. The tiniest part of Gray Morning's spirit was left.

"Dar?"

Gray Morning opened his weak eyes and looked on his first son. He took a shaky breath and blood spilled from his lips.

"Where . . ." gasped Gray Morning, his body trembling with the effort of speaking. "Where is—"

"Blue Moon is alive," said Ode. "You need not fear."

"And you . . ."

"Yes, Dar?"

But Gray Morning never replied. He sighed as his spirit left him and then he became still. Ode stayed kneeling at his father's head, half expecting the chief to speak again. His whole life had been eclipsed by Gray Morning's strong, dark shadow and he could not imagine what would happen now that he was gone. Ode had always thought that one day he might gain his father's love and respect, but now it was too late.

High-pitched wails carried across the decimation as Blue Moon and the Taone warriors sobbed to the sky. They sobbed and screamed under the supervision of the creatures, mourning the loss of their kin and of their freedom. Having surrendered, they expected to be adopted into a new tribe and many feared for their future.

A black nose nudged Ode's elbow and he turned to see Arrow. The wolf had tracked him down in the destruction, but there was no sign of Cala.

"Hey! Hey, we need you!"

Ode looked over his shoulder at the man calling to him. He had been given permission to seek out his father and was given a scrap of cloth to cover his nakedness, but it was clear that he could not mourn any longer.

"Hya-Hya-Hya," he whispered to the body of his father, then he stood on shaky legs and walked away.

The Taone warriors took no notice of Ode as he stood beside them, too numb to wail or mourn the spirits of those who had passed.

"We need them to calm down," said the strange man who had called him over.

"It is their way," replied Ode with a shrug.

The man exchanged glances with a woman beside him, and one of the winged creatures with long talons growled.

"We need you to talk to our leaders," said the woman.

"Me? I am no one," said Ode. "You will need the new chief for that."

The creatures led them to the enemy's camp. Ode walked beside his brother, the new chief, as they were escorted through the rocky, unfamiliar land. He was alert should Blue Moon need him, but his brother said nothing and kept his head bowed. Behind them trudged what was left of their warriors, sobbing and distraught, and surrounding them on all sides were the creatures, ensuring that the Taone warriors did not try to fight despite their diminished numbers and lack of weapons. Occasionally, one of the creatures would say something and Ode would translate, but Blue Moon never gave a reply.

The ground became steeper and rockier until they were picking their way carefully through the russet-colored crags and boulders. A strong breeze began to whistle through the rocks, carrying an unfamiliar scent that made the tribesmen frown. Suddenly, a shimmer of cobalt appeared on the horizon and the ground leveled and the wind roared.

The party stood on a cliff face with a blue sheet rushing out before them in all directions. It was not a lake or a river or a stream, and the tribesmen gasped, some stumbling and falling to their knees in awe. The salty breeze blew and the blue sheet rustled and surged. There was power beneath its current calm and Ode found it beautiful and terrifying at once.

"What are they doing?" asked a man, pointing at the tribesmen.

"They have never seen anything like this before," Ode replied.

The man snorted. "It is just the sea," he said, adding under his breath, "Foolish savages."

Ode glanced at his brother, but Blue Moon remained impassive. Even his first glimpse of the sea could not move him.

"This way!" barked a small creature with sharp fangs.

They were led across the cliff face and down a steep pass to a camp. Tents and fires stretched out before them, and Ode knew he had been right when he warned Gray Morning that they would not win against this enemy. There were too many of them. As they entered the camp and followed the creatures, Ode felt eyes watching. They passed children and small animals, as well as other monsters and beasts. There seemed to be people and *things* everywhere. When the group stopped before a large, rickety tent, Ode knew that he had seen it before in his dreams. He was not surprised when he entered with Blue Moon and discovered an old man and a gray-haired woman waiting inside.

"Greetings, Asha and the professor," he said.

Asha paused and the professor studied Ode with interest. Some of the humans and creatures entered the tent, while the others guarded the tribesmen outside. The flaps of the door were snapped shut behind them, muffling the distant crash and rumble of the sea.

"We did not tell them your names," said a man. "And we did not teach him how to speak Pervoroccoian."

"Have you dreamed of us?" asked Asha.

Ode nodded.

"He is the shifter," said a creature who had the body of a mountain lion, yet spoke with the voice of a man. "He shifted and stopped the battle."

It was strange for Ode to hear others speaking about his Magic so openly. He was used to regarding it as a shameful secret.

"Who taught you to control your Magic?" Asha asked him.

She wore clothes that seemed strange to him. Her skirt was long and trailed on the floor, already covered in dust and grime. Unlike Ode's tribeswomen, her hair was not braided into two plaits; instead, it was piled high on top of her head and pinned in place, though much of it was tatty and fell down her neck. Ode thought that she looked old and tired.

"No one taught me," he replied.

"You had no teacher? No guardian or father from whom you inherited your Magic?"

At the mention of his father, Ode paled.

"No," he said. "No one taught me."

Asha tilted her head and studied him carefully, as if assessing whether or not she believed what he said.

"Can you only shift?" asked the professor.

"What else is there?"

A woman beside Ode snorted.

"You mean, you have never met a Magic before?" asked Asha, taking a step toward him so that he could see the fine lines around her eyes and mouth. Her olive skin was free of blue patterns and without blemish except the inevitable signs of her age. "You just . . . discovered that you had Magic?"

Ode thought of Cala, but he did not want to tell these creatures of his auntie. He knew there was a reason that she had disappeared.

"Yes."

"And that wolf is yours?"

Ode looked over his shoulder at Arrow who stood, as always, in his shadow. He nodded.

"Fascinating," muttered the professor. "I wonder how many more there are across the Wild Lands. New species: Magic Bloods and Magical Beings."

"You are a long way from your books," retorted Asha, folding her arms.

"Where did you come from?" asked Ode, thinking of the map in Cala's trunk. Though they were all speaking the same language, each human or creature had a different accent.

"We ask the questions," snarled a squat, green animal.

Ode glanced at Blue Moon, who was letting the foreign words wash over him as he stood in a solemn daze.

"We come from many places," said the professor, and the squat, green animal hissed. "We have been forced here from all over the realm."

"We have settled and grown here," added a woman.

"But this is *our* land," said Ode, the hairs rising on his neck. "This is our home—it *was* our home—and you have all but destroyed it."

"You attacked us!" sputtered a man. "You left us with no choice."

"Your mighty tribe was not enough to defeat even one of our hunting groups," added a pale-skinned boy. "Remember *that*."

"This is our land," Ode repeated. "This is our home."

The creatures began to mutter to each other.

"We were forced to leave our lands," Asha cut in, silencing everyone. She fixed Ode with a hard stare. "We had no choice, and now you will have no choice," she said. "There is a war raging in the realm, and sooner or later, it would have found you. If not us then others would have discovered this place. The realm is changing and we have been here for many seasons now, growing in number. Some have even been born here and they count it as their home, too. Tell that to your chief."

Ode wished he could argue, but something told him she was right, and surrounded by the creatures, he did not see that he had much choice.

"I must speak to my chief," he said.

He knelt before Blue Moon and the assorted audience, resting his chin on his chest in submission.

"Don't do that," muttered his brother.

"I must. You are the chief now."

"What are they saying?"

"They say that the realm is at war."

"The realm?" echoed Blue Moon.

"Yes. The lands they come from across the large lake—the sea. They want us to join them."

Blue Moon frowned; all of this was too strange for him.

"Do we have a choice?" the new chief asked.

"No."

"Then tell them that we will do what they want."

Blue Moon hung his head. If they were not surrounded by the creatures, Ode would have told his brother that they should not give up. Instead, he looked at the rickety tent they were standing in and the greasy, stained clothes of the men and women. He had an idea.

"The chief says that you need us as much as we need you," he said, turning back to Asha. "He says that he will think on your proposition."

The creatures laughed, and Asha raised her eyebrows.

"You are aware that we defeated you?" scoffed some being that was half-man and half-horse.

"And you are aware that if you do not join us then we will kill you?" added a man with fangs like a wolf.

"Your numbers are many," Ode replied. "You were always going to win, but this land is not your own." He looked pointedly at the sagging roof of the tent. "There are many of you and you have outgrown your camp, but we know where you can move to. We know how to hunt and gather and live in these Wild Lands and you do not."

There was silence.

"And so we will return to our people and think on your offer," added Ode.

Asha's mouth twitched. "So be it," she said. "I am sure you will make the right decision."

CHAPTER TWELVE

The New People

The defeat was almost too much for the rest of the Taone to bear. Many seasons of triumph had made them forget failure. Women screamed for their partners and children cried for their fathers, while the elderly wailed to the sky for their sons. Such sorrow had not hit the Taone in living memory, and Blue Moon stood at the head of it all, delivering the news with his own lip quivering. Beside him Ode watched, too fearful of what lay ahead to share the grief that gripped the tribe.

"What is to happen now?" many whispered. "Where will we go?"

Blue Moon's fingers curled into fists. "I was granted permission to come tell you the news," he said. "Tomorrow we will . . . join our new tribe."

He turned away, retreating into the chief's tent, and Ode followed as the screams of grief soared behind them.

That night, while the Taone wailed and wept to the stars, the two brothers stayed inside their father's tent. They sat, united in a silent, tense grief. Arrow lay stretched out between them, his fur rising and falling with each breath, and they stared through the smoke flap at the darkening sky. They became lost in memories of a father who had not always been gentle or kind, but who had been their father nonetheless. For a long time the only sound was Arrow's gentle, rhythmic snoring.

"What do you think Dar would have done?" asked Blue Moon suddenly.

Ode did not want to say that his father would have been too proud to bow to another, because the time for pride was gone, and Gray Morning was dead.

"He was a good chief," he replied after a pause. "But you will be a better one, brother. When the sun sets, the moon rises."

"We could disappear across the flatlands. . . ."

"We have lost more than half our men and to run would be cowardly. Besides, that would be breaching our agreement—"

"To give in would be cowardly," Blue Moon snapped.

"No, to give in would be to win. They need us. I told you before."

Blue Moon touched his father's bedroll and bit his lip. "Dar did not listen to you, and it was his downfall," he said. "I will not make the same mistake."

The brothers lapsed into silence, and they did not speak again until the early hours of the morning.

"Where is the birther?" asked Blue Moon suddenly. "I could do with someone to read the fire for me."

Ode jumped at his brother's voice. He had been thinking of Gray Morning on his piebald stallion, looking mighty and triumphant. The tent still smelled strongly of his musky scent, like the damp dust of the flatlands in the morning.

"I don't know where Cala is," Ode replied. He was beginning to worry about his auntie. He had searched the crowd for her once they returned to the settlement, but she was nowhere to be seen. He had overheard one elder of the tribe grumble that the birther should have warned them of the impending defeat.

"Can you read the flames?" asked Blue Moon.

Ode shook his head.

"Why not?"

"I don't know."

"But you can change forms and speak to enemies in their language?"

Ode frowned, and Arrow awoke with a grunt. The air in the tent was suddenly sharper and the haze of grief had lifted.

"What do you mean?"

"I may not have understood what those creatures were saying, but I could tell that they were afraid of you," said Blue Moon, the expression on his face almost suspicious.

"No, they were warriors and beasts that—"

"Yes, they were stronger, but you made them nervous."

Ode put a warning hand on Arrow's flank. The wolf's thick fur was bristling and his tail was lifted.

"Are you afraid of me?" Ode asked quietly.

"Sometimes."

"You said earlier that you would not make the same mistake as Dar. You said that you would listen to me."

Blue Moon sighed. "I do not know what I think anymore," he said.

⌘

At some point, the brothers fell asleep. They were awoken later by the dazzling glow of the morning sun, which fell through the smoke flap and filled the tent with golden warmth. The conversation of the night was forgiven, but not forgotten. Ode knew that his place among the Taone was precarious at a time of such sorrow and hostility. He desperately wished that Cala would return. He felt uneasy without her near.

The lake beside the settlement was calm and unruffled as the new Taone chief stood before his tribe and announced they were ready to join the enemy. Blue Moon declared that the union would make them stronger and he promised none would suffer. The listeners did not argue because their new chief had spoken and they were weak from mourning through the night.

"Where is the birther to celebrate the spirits of the dead?" asked Rippling River once Blue Moon had broken the news.

"Yes, where is the birther?" the crowd began asking one another.

Ode felt eyes find him in the shadows and slide across his figure with fear and resentment.

"She has run away!" spat a male elder. "She has run away in shame because she did not help us."

There were angry murmurs of agreement.

"The spirits will get their celebration when the birther returns," called Blue Moon, silencing everyone with a stern look. "For now, we must prepare to move. There are more important matters at hand."

It was with heavy hearts that the Taone packed up their tents and loaded their horses with their scant possessions. Jobs that were normally reserved for the men fell to the young boys who had not followed their fathers into battle. Ode saw them buckling under the heavy loads, their eyes brimming with tears. He offered to help, but they would not accept.

When all was packed, the tribe moved slowly toward the forest. Even the horses plodded with their heads bent low, sensing the heavy sorrow that had settled over their people. As the afternoon sun drifted across the sky, the tribe met the creatures who had been waiting for them. There were some startled gasps from the children upon seeing these beasts and beings for the first time, but many were too numb with grief to take much notice.

However, the first glimpse of the sea prompted even the most woeful heart to lift. The setting summer sun balanced on the waving waters and streaks of lavender light burst across the sky. Though others drank in the scene while pushing on, Ode stopped to stare at it, Arrow leaning against his leg.

There are other lands out there, he thought. *There is more to see and explore.* He wished that Cala were here with him now. He had so many things to ask her about her maps and the places she had been and the things she had seen. It made him excited and terrified all at once. He longed to learn from her about the rest of the realm, but more than anything, he just wanted his auntie here to tell him that everything would be all right.

Arrow's whine brought him back, and Ode followed the tribe as they wound their way down the cliff face. More creatures waited for them at the camp and a crowd had gathered to welcome the newcomers. Ode watched the faces of the Taone break into smiles as they saw men, women, and children among the monsters and beasts.

The tribe was given an area in which to set up their tents and the enemy watched in interest as the Taone settled, noticing the way they stored their food and unpacked their belongings. It was not long before the children of the Taone were playing with the enemy children, no shared language needed in their games of running and catching. Ode left his tribe mixing with their new family and followed Blue Moon to the main tent. Inside, Asha and the other leaders were waiting for them.

"I see you came to the right decision," said Asha.

"The chief would like to thank you for the hospitality you have shown his people," replied Ode. "He desires to know what you expect of him."

Asha nodded. "We need you to tell us everything about these lands," she replied. "We are forced to scavenge for food here, because this terrain is unfamiliar and it is making us weak. We have been here a long time, but not as long as you, and we desire to know your secrets. We need to be stronger."

Ode nodded and placed his hand on the crown of Arrow's head for support. He was aware that his words were deciding the fate of the Taone. Whether they chose to acknowledge it or not, he was important for once in his life and the prospect made his fingers shake.

"We can teach you," replied Ode, and he saw some of the creatures in the tent flinch.

A voice muttered, "We don't need teaching from savages," but Asha ignored it.

"Once we are stronger, we will need you to help us fashion weapons and houses. We need weapons for the soldiers and houses for the children and the elderly who cannot fight."

"Houses?" Ode echoed, and some of the audience snickered.

"They are dwelling places," said Asha, waving her hand. "They are—well—they are where people live. There is no easier way to describe it."

"They are like your tents," said the professor, who sat in a corner. "But they are made of wood and sometimes bricks."

Ode did not know what bricks were, but his brow creased. "Wood? How do you move them?" he asked.

There was silence and the creatures all exchanged glances.

"We will not be moving from this spot," said Asha. "We will stay here, expanding and growing stronger until we are ready to launch an attack."

Ode wondered how the Taone would accept this. They had been living nomadically all their lives and it would feel strange to stay in one place forever. It would feel wrong.

"What attack?" he asked.

"That is when we shall need you again," said Asha. "I told you before that we have been forced from our homes in the Western Realm by a Magical Cleansing. The people there wanted to kill us, so we ran. This has happened before, a long time ago, and we won in the end. We will win again this time."

"How can we help you in this battle?" asked Ode. "Most of our warriors are dead and many that are left are gravely wounded."

"We will have to wait before we launch our attack. It must be the right time. We will be appealing to the rest of the realm, asking anyone we can to join us. . . ." Asha bowed her head and a wistful look came into her eyes. "We are waiting for my daughter, also," she added. "She will gather an army in the Hillands and unite with us in the attack."

"She might do so," corrected the professor softly from the corner.

"She *will* do so," said Asha.

"Even so, in a few seasons our remaining warriors may be healed, but our boys will not be grown men," said Ode. "They will not be initiated, and they will not be able to fight. Not most of them."

"Some will be strong enough," said Asha. "And there are the women, also."

Ode's mouth dropped open, and Blue Moon glared at him, wanting to know what they were discussing. When Ode translated, his brother reacted with much the same astonishment.

"They cannot do that!" Blue Moon growled. "The tribeswomen will die! They have never fought, and some have never even held a weapon."

"This can all be negotiated later," Asha interrupted, guessing what they were discussing. "We have plenty of time."

Ode translated, and Blue Moon crossed his arms, shook his head.

"The chief says that we will agree to help you learn the secrets of this land," said Ode, turning back to the audience. "But we will need to negotiate the rest."

"Agreed," replied Asha. "For the time being, you must settle and become one of us. That is what you are now."

She smiled, and Ode was suddenly aware that she was right. The old life of the Taone was over and things would never be the same again.

CHAPTER THIRTEEN

The Traitor

The Taone accepted their new home far quicker than Ode could have guessed they would. Though they still mourned those they had lost and longed for their old chief, they did not dwell on the past. A battle lost was a battle lost, and they were too busy adapting to their new existence to concern themselves too much with memories.

The New People, as the Taone called the Magics, were weak and so desperate that they responded with deep gratitude if shown even the simplest tricks. When the tribeswomen taught them which weeds they could cut and stew into a broth, the New People almost cried with relief. They wanted to learn everything and they flattered their new comrades with broad, encouraging smiles. Even Blue Moon was soon won over. Ode watched his brother teaching a group of men and women how to fashion a weapon out of flint and branches. Once he had finished, the people clapped, and Blue Moon almost shone with pride.

It was only Ode, it seemed, who could not settle. Cala was still missing and he longed for her return. It made him suspect that there was trouble to come, or why else would she stay away? Sometimes he even found himself wondering if she really had simply run off to resist being shamed by the rest of the tribe for not predicting their defeat, like the tribespeople said. But Ode knew deep down that it was not true. His auntie would not do such a thing. Ode brooded over her disappearance as he wandered around camp each day, translating whenever he was needed. At first, he had enjoyed this role. He had relished his usefulness, but it was becoming apparent that the Taone were slowly learning the language of the New People. Soon, they would not need him once again.

Ode felt lonely and useless, but most of all, he felt watched. As he walked around camp from day to day, he would often feel a prickling sensation on the back of his head. When he turned, he would sometimes see the professor behind him, carefully looking the other way. All his life Ode had been different, and here, surrounded by what the New People called Magic Beasts and Magic Beings, it appeared that he was still different. What exactly the professor found so interesting about him Ode did not know and he did not want to ask.

One night, when the Taone had been with the New People for almost a whole moon cycle, Ode awoke from a disturbing dream. He sat up in the darkness and looked around the empty tent, his heart thumping in his chest. Beside him, Arrow lifted his head and licked Ode's hand, running his rough tongue across his knuckles.

Ode tried to make sense of what he had seen. The dream was vivid, but unclear, as if he had been trying to look at the sun. His eyes almost stung from the brightness of it, and he wiped away tears from his cheeks with the back of his hand. He had seen Cala, of that he was sure, and she was beside what the New People called the sea. She was waiting for him and calling to him, sitting before a small fire, the flames flickering through the night. Then the vision had changed and he had seen a mountain—towering and dark. It was silhouetted against a purple sky surrounded by clouds, and he had been reaching toward its peak, calling out someone's name, but he could not remember why or who.

Ode touched the white feather strung around his neck and despite its soft bristles and light quill, it felt heavy. He dropped it, letting it flutter back to his chest where it curved against his breastbone. As quietly as he could, he began dressing. He no longer shared a tent, but sound carried easily through the buffalo hides, and Ode knew that it was important he was not followed.

He crept out into the darkness with Arrow, a smile breaking across his lips at the thought of seeing his auntie after so long. Together, Ode and Arrow wound their way through the sleeping camp under the light of a pale, fading moon. There were creatures on watch patrolling the edges, but they were talking softly to one another in little groups and they did not see Ode and his wolf as they slid into the blackness of the trees.

Ode did not know where he was going, but he was not afraid. It was a relief to be out of camp and alone again. The constant press of bodies and chatter had been slowly turning him crazy. Too many times these past few days, he had wanted to shift but always he made himself squash the urge. The New People were open about their Magic, but Ode felt eyes upon him at every move, and he did not wish to draw more attention to his gift. He did not feel comfortable around these people and he did not want to make himself vulnerable. Now, finally alone, Ode felt the tension in his body leak out into the night.

Arrow felt it, too, and he went bounding ahead, dancing across the craggy land and chasing any birds or squirrels he could find.

Before long, Ode could hear the low crash of the sea and he could feel the fresh wind breathing against his cheeks. He followed a narrow, coastal path that was rocky and steep, the sea appearing on his right over the edge of a cliff face. Ode stepped carefully in the darkness and ignored the bursts of wind that would sometimes gust from nowhere and threaten to push him off the path.

Ahead, Arrow paused and raised his head. He was almost invisible in the darkness except for the white fur speckled across his chest and Ode nearly walked into the back of him. The wolf sniffed the air, his hackles rising, and then he bounded into the undergrowth with a yelp. Ode followed, ducking under branches and climbing through bushes until he emerged in a clearing. Arrow was sniffing the ground, his tail wagging, and Ode could make out the remnants of a fire nearby. This must have been the place from his dream.

"Auntie?" he hissed. "Auntie? It's me."

He waited for several long moments, but there was no answer.

Ode wondered if Cala was sleeping nearby, but Arrow could not seem to pick up a trail and he kept sniffing in circles.

The desire to shift had been plaguing Ode since he left camp and he decided to give in to it. He told himself that he might be able to see more from the sky and perhaps spot where Cala could be hiding.

As Ode's bones cracked and his muscles tore, he was filled with a surge of release. He had not shifted in so long that he felt shoots of pain, but the relief was overwhelming and the pain short-lived. As the white bird, Ode spread his wings and shook, stretching his feathers in a pale fan. He launched himself into the sky with some difficulty, but just as he finally began to ascend, he saw something move in the trees. The shock made him shift back, stumbling onto the ground. He grabbed his clothes to cover his nakedness while a figure stepped out from the shadows. The professor took an object from his pocket and began scribbling on it.

"What are you doing?" asked Ode, pulling his clothes back on.

He began frantically trying to think of plausible excuses to explain his midnight wandering.

"I'm making a note," replied the professor. "It's a book full of my observations. Do not tell Asha. She would take it away because we have no paper, but I need it, you see, to make notes."

"No, I don't see."

Ode glanced at Arrow who was licking his paws calmly, appearing not to notice the professor.

"What have you done to him?" Ode asked.

"Do not fret, he is fine. It is just that he cannot smell me. Or see me. I have not spent a lifetime studying Magic without picking up some tips on how to use my own gifts."

Ode wanted to run. He wondered if the professor had heard him calling for Cala. He had been so sure he was alone; it had not occurred to him that the professor might have Magic of his own.

"Why are you here?" Ode asked.

"I am studying you for my book. Before the Magical Cleansing I was a great professor at a university dedicated to the understanding of Magic, and before that I traveled across the realm, finding creatures and building archives. I made it to the Wild Lands a few times before, but never found much except the odd moorey."

Ode could not understand much of what the professor was saying, but one thing had piqued his interest.

"You traveled across the realm?" he asked.

"Yes, I suppose you do not know about the other countries—"

"I know of them. I have seen maps."

"How?"

Ode knotted his fingers together. "Where did you go in your travels?" he asked instead.

"Everywhere. I have been as far across the realm as I can manage, but there are still areas that are a mystery to me. There are still species I have yet to record."

Ode thought of Cala's map with all its different lands. He wished that he knew more.

"Have you ever left the Wild Lands?" asked the professor.

"No."

"That is . . . peculiar. Your shift reminds me of a creature that is not native to these parts, as far as I know. How many other Wild Landers have Magic?"

"Just me."

"Impossible," replied the professor, his voice becoming steely. "You are lying."

The professor was old, but Ode did not know the power of his Magic. He did not know what he was capable of.

"It is imperative that you tell me the truth," added the professor in a low voice. "I must know who taught you your Magic."

He came closer and Ode felt a coldness creeping over him. He wanted to run, but he found that he could not. He wanted to tell the professor to release him, but he could not utter a word.

"I taught him Magic!" said a voice.

Cala emerged from the darkness, her face set in hard lines.

"Leave him be," she said. "And come out of your hiding, woman, I know that you are there," she added, raising her voice to the trees around them.

After a moment, another figure glided into the clearing, and Asha approached the bewildered huddle. As if broken from a spell, Arrow jumped up, a snarl rumbling from his jaws.

"I knew something was strange here," said Asha, throwing back the hood of her cloak. "I knew that you people were hiding something!"

"Only I have been hiding," said Ode quickly. "The rest of the Taone know nothing of this or Magic. They have come to you peacefully, I swear it."

"If only what you said were true," hissed Asha. "Who is this woman who hides from us, and why do you meet at night in secret?"

Ode glanced at Cala, unsure of what to say, but his auntie was barely listening. Instead, she was staring at Asha with her top lip pulled back in a grimace.

"Asha, can you not see?" whispered the professor. He had been quiet until now, staring at Cala as if mesmerized.

"Yes, she is not from the Wild Lands, I see that plainly enough. Woman, do you come from Fasheba or Dagero? How did you get here? Speak."

"I come from someplace far away," spat back Cala.

"No, Asha!" cried the professor. "Can you not *see*? Can you not *see* the resemblance?"

Asha froze and a little gasp escaped her lips. In the darkness her face became paler, and for a moment, Ode thought she might faint.

"You know him," Asha whispered. "You have the look of his people, the—"

"Yes," snapped Cala. "I have the high forehead and the wide mouth. Yes, I know him, and yes, he knew you. For a while."

"He loved me!"

"I doubt it."

"Who are you?" cried Asha, her eyes large and wild now. "How do you know him? What are you doing here? Where is he? Speak!"

"No," said Cala with a smile.

"And you?" said Asha, turning to Ode. "You know him? How? You must speak to me!"

Ode shook his head. "I do not know what you are talking about," he said, edging away.

"The boy knows nothing," confirmed Cala. "Leave him alone."

"The others are coming as we speak," said Asha. "I raised the alarm, and if you do not speak now then they will *make* you speak! Tell me, how do you know him?" Asha's words bounced from the trees and screamed across the land, silencing even the distant rumble of the sea.

Cala's smile widened. "You said he loved you?" she said. "Well, he loved me most of all."

Asha shook her head. "No," she whispered. Then she cried louder: "No!"

The crashing sound of footsteps and the heavy plod of many feet could be heard.

"We are here!" Asha shouted out. "Hurry!"

Arrow started to bark and snap his jaws at the air. Ode stared at his auntie, realizing that he barely knew her. In that moment she became like a different person.

"Run," she said to him.

The crash of feet and the roar of voices drew closer.

"We are here!" cried Asha. "Hurry!"

The professor continued to stare at Cala, his mouth open like a gaping hole.

"You must run," said Cala. "Run, little man!"

Ode turned and disappeared into the trees. He transformed into the white bird and flew away, Arrow following from the ground. As he sailed through the dark sky, Ode heard shouts and cries, but he did not turn back.

CHAPTER FOURTEEN

The Betrayal

Ode leaned against the trunk of a tree, his stomach growling for food. He had landed here in the early hours of the morning. After his night flight, he had crashed through the leaves of the trees around them and tumbled to the ground, his head ringing with Asha's shouts and screams. Shivering, he curled up on his side until Arrow appeared, Ode's clothes hanging from his mouth. As the morning light started to break through the darkness of the forest, Ode pulled on his leather tunic and tried to understand what he had witnessed.

He replayed the events of the previous night over and over until his head spun. He did not know his auntie—that much was clear. Who was the man she and Asha spoke of? What was the importance of it all? Cala had kept too many secrets. He could not remember her having mentioned anything like this before; not in all the many seasons they had lived together. Ode felt a bitterness begin to lodge itself in his chest. She had been keeping things from him—she had lied to him. His auntie was not his auntie at all.

Ode could guess what Cala's fate at the camp would be now. The New People would present the Taone with Cala and his tribe would condemn her to death. They would call her a traitor—they had always had their suspicions and they did not like what they did not understand. As leader, Blue Moon would have to agree with his people, and Ode knew that his brother felt no kinship with the birther. He would not find it difficult to have her killed.

Ode was angry with Cala. He was furious and for a moment, he thought that perhaps she deserved what was coming to her. But then he remembered that she had tried to be a mother to him when the rest of the Taone cast him out. They had always been outcasts together. Ode knew that he could not let her die. Much as he hated her in that moment for her secrets, he could not let her suffer.

As evening descended, Ode climbed to his feet on stiff, aching legs, knowing what he must do. With Arrow trotting beside him, he strode through the forest, guessing which way to turn. Now that he had made his decision, he was eager to get on with it and he did not have trouble finding the rocky coastal path that led to the camp. He followed it cautiously, in case there were any Magic Beasts or Magic Beings around, and it was not long before he grew so close that he could hear the faint shouts of children playing and the distant clang of pots and pans as they were washed after dinner. Ode edged as near as he dared and then stopped. He worried that if he went closer, the Magics would sense him with their special gifts. For a while he waited in the shade of the trees, unsure of what to do. He heard the chatter of some tribeswomen as they spoke to each other in a mixture of their own language and the words of the New People and he wondered when they would forget that they were once Taone.

Ode did not know how long he had been waiting when he heard a sound behind him. He jumped and turned to see the professor, who held out a wrinkled hand in greeting.

"Do not fear, I am here to help you," he said.

Ode looked at Arrow, but the wolf appeared to see nothing. He wondered if he should run, but something in the professor's manner made him pause.

"Why would you help me?" Ode whispered.

"You need to get to your teacher and I can take you to her. With me, no one will see you pass—that is my gift. I have been waiting for you all day."

"Why would you help me?" repeated Ode.

The professor sighed. "Sometimes I do not trust Asha," he said. "She is blinded by . . . incidents from the past. I do not know what will happen to us, but I feel that I must do this. I know that you are important."

Ode swallowed a mixture of suspicion and excited fear that burned down his throat.

"How do you know this?" he asked.

"I feel it."

"There must be a reason."

The professor smiled wryly. "You have become distrustful and that is good. You must be questioning those around you always. But your answer is that I have seen the white bird you turn into before. Do you know what it is?"

Ode shook his head.

"It is a swan, and it is not indigenous to these parts. I have traveled across the realm studying creatures and I have only seen a swan in one place: the Scarlet Isles."

"Where is that?"

"In the Western Realm. It is where the Magic Cleansing is spreading and this is not a coincidence. Nothing ever is."

Ode was silent.

"Come now, we must go," said the professor. "I am old and often I grow too tired to use my gift."

Ode hesitated, unsure if this was a trap.

"How will it work?" he asked.

"Walk behind me and stay close," said the professor. "Try not to look directly at anyone."

Ode stared at the professor's lined, pale face and decided that he was telling the truth.

"All right," Ode said at last and then he pressed his palm to Arrow's head to guide the wolf beside him, who still seemed to see nothing.

With his eyes fixed on the ground, Ode followed the scuffed edges of the professor's robe in front of him. The air had grown quiet and still, but as much as Ode wished to look up, he did not. He felt bodies swish near him and he sensed the warmth of the fires as they passed. He kept his hand on Arrow's head, willing the wolf to stay calm.

"You can look up now," said the professor.

Ode raised his head to see darkness and pools of shadow. They were at a corner of the camp he had never visited before, far away from the tents and chatter. He glanced over his shoulder and saw two guards standing nearby, one male and one female. He gasped in surprise but both were oblivious to his presence. Turning back, he saw that the ground before them was churned to mud and there was a sharp, sickening smell in the air. Arrow began wagging his tail and, as one of the shadows moved, Ode realized it was Cala.

"I prayed that you would come, little man."

Ode did not know whether to comfort her or shout at her, so he said nothing, his shoulders twitching.

"What is wrong, little man?" asked Cala. "Speak to me."

Ode pressed his lips together.

"You do not have long," warned the professor. "I am growing tired."

Cala's eyes shone in the gloom and sought Ode's. Much as he tried to resist her, he knew that he could not. She was crouching on the ground, her hands and feet tied to a post. Ode could see that the knots had been pulled too tight and her skin was chafing.

"Have they sentenced you to death?" he finally asked.

"Yes. At first light," she replied in rasps. "I brought some of them into this realm but . . . no matter. Things are changing, and they are afraid. They want to get along with the New People and much as some would try to argue for me . . ." She glanced at the professor. "That woman would have me dead."

"Asha?"

Cala nodded.

"She is lost in her own pain and jealousy," interrupted the professor. "Her decision cannot be excused, but it can be understood. You have not seen the devastation of the Magical Cleansing. You do not know what we are facing."

"That may be," replied Cala through clenched teeth, "but nothing will be helped if I am dead."

Ode saw her wince as she tried to move her hands. He took a piece of flint from his boot, which was fashioned into an eating knife, and began to saw through the rope. He could feel her eyes on him as he worked and he could smell her familiar, comforting scent mixed with the rancid odor of their surroundings.

"We must hurry," hissed the professor. "I am becoming weak."

Ode freed Cala's hands and began to work at the bonds on her feet, sawing with the knife as best he could.

"When I am free, I must go from here," Cala said.

Ode did not look up, but his hands faltered. "Without me?" he asked.

"You cannot come with me. It would be too dangerous. I am going to . . . I am going to search for someone I knew long ago."

"The man you spoke of with Asha?"

The professor looked over with wide eyes. "You must get him to help us," he said. "You must bring him—"

"I must do nothing!" snapped Cala. "You do not understand what you are dealing with. You do not understand what he has done and what he will do to get what he wants."

"Who is he?" asked Ode.

The last of Cala's bonds fell away and she touched the raw skin gingerly. With great effort, she climbed to her feet.

"He is powerful . . ." she began.

"A sorcerer," interrupted the professor, "such as the Western Realm has not seen in many a lifetime."

Cala grabbed Ode's arm and pulled him close to her. "He is just a man," she whispered in his ear. "You must remember that, beneath his power, he is still only a man. His name is Abioy, but keep that to yourself until the right time."

"What are you saying?" asked the professor. "What is this whispering? Do not forget that in a few moments I could have you captured again!"

Cala narrowed her eyes. "I am captured only if I want to be," she hissed.

The professor frowned and Ode looked behind him at the backs of the guards who were oblivious to their escaping prisoner.

"I am helping you because I believe that it is in the best interest of the Western Realm," said the professor. "But perhaps I am mistaken."

Cala smiled. "It is too late for mistakes now," she said.

Arrow emitted a deep growl and Ode felt the hairs on his arms rise. The professor's fingers twitched and he shook his head.

"Guards!" he yelled. "Guards!"

The guards turned and their faces quickly flooded with shock and rage.

"Run!" cried Cala.

At first, Ode felt like he could not move. He stared at the guards stumbling toward him, his body in a numb panic.

"Run!" cried Cala again, shoving him.

Ode's legs jumped to life and he turned and raced into the trees, Arrow close behind. He saw Cala disappear in the opposite direction and then he heard distant shouts and angry screams. He hoped that she had not been captured again. He ran and ran, his legs unable to stop.

Branches clawed and bit at Ode's arms and face, and he fought the urge to shift. He did not want to lose his clothes again. He did not think that anyone was following him and he slowed his pace, his chest pounding with hurried, painful breaths. Even Arrow did not sense any danger and slowed to a trot at his side.

So it was a shock to both of them when someone grabbed Ode from behind and pinned him to the ground.

CHAPTER FIFTEEN

The Banishment

Ode felt the breath knocked from his body and his head pounded with the beat of his heart. Arrow was snarling. Someone was talking to Ode and shaking his shoulders. As his surroundings slowly came into focus, he saw the familiar patterns of Blue Moon's face floating above his own. His brother had one hand clamped upon his shoulder, while the other was fending Arrow off with a spear.

"Call back your wolf!" he said.

Ode lifted his free arm and waved it in the direction of Arrow's growling. He felt a rough tongue lick his fingers and Arrow's snarls subsided to a grumble.

Blue Moon lowered his spear, but he did not let go of his brother.

"You've caught me," Ode wheezed.

"By chance you ran past me back there."

"So, you tackled me to the ground? You could have just called a greeting."

Ode tried to smile and sit up, but Blue Moon pressed him back down.

"I was hunting when I heard the commotion," he said. "I know you've released the birther—you have, haven't you?"

"I thought you just said that you knew."

Blue Moon's fingers bit into his skin and Ode saw that his little brother was in no mood for teasing.

"The New People have told us tales of the birther," said Blue Moon. "They have said that she is evil."

"Did you ever see her do evil?"

Blue Moon frowned. "She didn't do much good," he said. "She didn't save Dar."

"The New People killed him."

Pain flashed across Blue Moon's face and he pressed down upon his older brother, forcing the air from Ode's chest so that he gasped.

"What's going on?" Blue Moon asked.

"I don't know," Ode wheezed sincerely.

Blue Moon glanced around before releasing Ode, who spluttered and coughed, climbing unsteadily to his feet.

"You know that I should kill you, brother?" said Blue Moon. "You have released a captive and there are creatures crashing through the forest right now looking for you."

Ode nodded. "I was raised in the Taone and I know the penalty for betraying others," he said. "But we are not the Taone anymore. Things are different."

"Yes, they certainly are."

The point of Blue Moon's spear sunk to the ground and he stared off into the trees, his eyes filled with memories of the past. He did not look so much like a chief then, but only a young, lost boy.

"I don't know what to do," said Ode.

"You can't stay, or you will be their next prisoner."

"But I don't know where to go."

"Fly off somewhere?"

Ode shook his head.

"Summer will end soon," said Blue Moon. "The cold winds will come. What will you do then?"

"I don't know."

"There seems to be a lot of things you don't know."

"There always has been, and there always will be," said Ode, and the two brothers surprised themselves by smiling.

"You will have to go from here," said Blue Moon, his smile fading away.

"I know."

"You will need warmer clothes and weapons to defend yourself."

Ode looked down at his worn buffalo hide tunic and soft, summer boots. He would be easy prey when the winds came and he only had his piece of flint to protect him.

"I have nothing," Ode said.

"If you meet me here at sundown, I will bring you what I can."

"Brother, thank—"

"No, don't thank me. There is something I must tell you," said Blue Moon. "I should have told you before, but these days have been too much."

Ode saw the knot of pain in his brother's brow and the rigid lines of his face. For a moment, he looked so much like Gray Morning.

"When we charged into battle, Dar knew that we would lose," said Blue Moon, his voice faltering. "He told me that he would die. He–he said that I must live, and he died protecting me."

"He would have wanted it that way," said Ode. "He was saving the new chief of the Taone. Without you, the rest of the tribe would have been lost."

"No, that is not what I need to say. You see, he wanted me to live to . . . to return to the tribe and tell them that you were to be the new chief."

Ode felt the ground beneath him wobble.

"I don't—" he began.

"Dar knew that you were right, and he knew that he should have listened to you. It was just too late."

"He didn't know what he was saying!" Ode babbled, his words coming out in sharp bursts. "In the excitement of the battle he became confused."

"Maybe. But that is what he said. Only, I didn't do that. The Taone seemed to assume that I was the new chief. So did you."

Ode nodded, staring off into the trees. He could not imagine the mighty Gray Morning admitting he had been wrong. Besides, his father hated him, didn't he? Ode remembered the painted feathers beaten into the battleground and he winced. It was too late to wonder now.

"I thought you should know," said Blue Moon. "I know you think he hated you . . . but I am not so sure."

"Thank you."

Blue Moon nodded and turned to walk away. "I will see you later," he said over his shoulder, then added with his old smile, "Chief."

⸺⚬⚬⚬⸺

It did not cross Ode's mind that his brother might be laying a trap. Ode knew that they had grown apart, but they were brothers and he was sure that Blue Moon did not want to hurt him. He went to their meeting that evening without fear of ambush, so he was surprised when Arrow halted suddenly in the forest, his hackles rising.

Ode knew to trust his wolf's instincts and he crouched down and edged into the shade of a tree. He waited, and then he heard the voices, too—a low murmur nearby. He had spent the day wandering through the forest and waiting until sundown, deliberating what he would do and where he would go. He had been careful to stay far away from the camp and he had not seen or heard anyone.

"Where is he?" asked a strange voice.

Ode flattened himself against the ground and Arrow hid beneath the branches of a bush.

"He will be somewhere here," replied Blue Moon in the language of the New People, stumbling over their words.

"Why not call out to him?" suggested another voice.

"If I do that then he will know something is wrong."

It was just as Blue Moon uttered these last words that Ode understood. His brother was speaking loudly and this was peculiar. To the ears of the New People he was whispering, but the Taone did not speak at all when they were hunting, if they could help it. When they did, it was in the softest tones, so the sound could easily be mistaken for the hush of the wind through the leaves or the tread of a pronghorn's hoof. Blue Moon was warning Ode to stay away.

"Are you sure he will come to this place?" asked another voice.

"Yes," said Blue Moon. "But we are making too much noise. Let me leave these supplies here; we will make less sound without them."

As if to prove his point, he rustled some branches.

"But he will expect you to bring them, will he not?"

"It won't matter," replied Blue Moon. "You will attack before he has time to worry."

There were murmurs of agreement.

"It is lucky that we came across you back there," said a voice. "You would have found it difficult to carry out this plan by yourself."

"Yes," replied Blue Moon. "It is very lucky."

Through the trees, Ode saw a group of figures pass by. They were all Magic Beasts by the shapes of their shadows, which Ode knew was a strike of good fortune. Had a group of Magic Beings come across Blue Moon, they may not have been so easy to convince; many of them had the gift of foresight and some could even sense when others were lying.

Ode waited with his breath held until they had passed and he could no longer hear the crash of their steps through the forest. When he was sure that they had moved on, he darted as quickly and quietly as he could through the trees. He could see tracks that his brother had left behind to guide him—deep prints in the mud that were as unusual as Blue Moon's loud whispers, for the Taone hunters were taught to leave no signs of their passage.

Beside a tree he found a leather bag containing food, a fur cape, boots, and some extra necessities including a small dagger. He grabbed the bag and, hoisting it onto his shoulder, began to jog through the trees. He allowed himself one last look at their planned meeting place and he mouthed silent thanks to his brother for his kindness. He knew that without the help of Blue Moon and these supplies, he was unlikely to get far in his journey.

As Ode turned away to sprint off into the forest, a flash of white caught his eye. He did not stop to look for fear of the Magic Beasts returning, but pressed on. It was only later, when his sprint had slowed to a jog, that Ode was sure he had glimpsed the professor in the trees, watching him.

<hr />

That night it grew dark quickly. The forest had grown thicker as the day passed and Ode's pace had slowed to a brisk walk. Arrow trotted at his side, panting, his gray form slithering through the tree trunks. The beams of greenery above shrouded the light of the moon, and when Ode walked into a branch for the fourth time, he knew that he should stop for the night.

Ode had slept alone in a forest before, but tonight was different. He did not know this place. There could be wolves, mountain lions, bears, or worse. Trying to ignore the rapid beating of his heart, Ode crawled under the branches of a sprawling bush, dragging his bag after him. Arrow followed, and together they lay in the undergrowth, trying to ignore the unfamiliar sounds around them.

Ode buried one of his hands in Arrow's heavy, soft coat, thankful that he had his companion with him. He thought of the tent that he had slept in for as long as he could remember, with its comforting scent of smoke and earth. He thought of Cala, who had been torn from his life, and Gray Morning, who was lost forever. He thought of the rest of the Taone, realizing that he might never see them again.

It struck him like a chill. He had been so preoccupied with the events of the last day that he had not considered that he was actually leaving. He was departing, never to return. The beat of the drums and the plumes of ceremonial feathers were now only memories from his past. There would be no more Winter Feast and there would be no more birthing celebrations. He was no longer a member of the Taone.

Ode's eyes stung with tears of grief and fear. Somewhere in the forest, an animal howled to the moon, and he buried his face in Arrow's fur to muffle a sob. With his free hand he grabbed hold of his amulet and held it tightly, squeezing its bristly impression into his palm.

I am alone, he told himself. *I am banished.*

Part Three

In a castle surrounded by a forest, a young, silver-skinned woman walked through hallways alone. She was dressed in silks and jewels that glittered in the light of her candle, and the heavy hem of her emerald robe dragged across the carpet, whispering behind her. She could hear the distant sound of voices and merriment from one of the ballrooms, but as she traveled farther, the sounds grew faint, until they were only a hushed murmur.

She stopped before a large oak door and slid inside, shutting it carefully behind her. In the dark room she breathed a sigh of relief, smelling the comforting aroma of crackled pages and old scrolls. She felt her way through the dark to a table, upon which she knew there were oil lamps. As she lit them, she smiled to herself, remembering the days when she did not have to do such things.

The lamps threw a warm, yellow glow across the room, illuminating the rows of shelves that towered everywhere, stuffed with books and scrolls. The library, like the castle, had once cared for itself, but when the enchantment ended, it had left a mess. There were odd papers strewn on the floor and teetering stacks of tomes in corners.

The silver-skinned woman unclasped the emerald robe from around her neck and heaved it onto a nearby chair where it fell with a thump and a puff of dust. She stretched her aching shoulders and stroked the amulet around her neck, tracing her thumb across the rose etched into the center of the golden disk.

Taking one of the oil lamps, she began walking slowly through the shelves, reading the titles imprinted on the books' spines. She was looking for something she had seen in a dream, but she was not entirely sure what it was. Occasionally, she pulled out a book that seemed promising and began leafing through the pages, but soon she would sigh and discard it before continuing her search. The oil lamp in her hand burned brightly, guiding her way through the maze of shelves as the night wore on, and the only sound was the soft tread of her jeweled slippers on the floorboards.

"Beauty?"

She jumped at his voice, almost dropping the lamp in her hand. She had been so absorbed in her reading that she had not heard him enter the room.

"What are you doing?" he asked.

"Looking for something," she replied without turning.

"You disappeared after the coronation. No one knew where you had gone."

Beauty sighed. "I stayed for a while," she replied, turning to face him. "But everyone seemed happy enough to talk and eat among themselves. I did not think that they would notice I had gone."

"I noticed."

Beauty saw his hunched shoulders beneath the green velvet of his jacket. He looked just as uncomfortable as she felt in these regal clothes. She had asked him that morning if they must go through with it and he had replied that they must, for the Hillanders needed a queen to follow.

She put the oil lamp down on a nearby shelf and shuffled to his side. Sometimes she still felt shy with him and taking his hand, she could not help the blush that crept onto her cheeks.

"I am sorry, Beast," she said.

The Hillanders called him General and some even referred to him as the king, but to Beauty he would always be Beast.

"I came here to find something," she added. "But I wanted to be alone, too. All those people and the way they looked at me . . . I do not know if we will win. I do not know what will happen to them. I cannot keep them safe."

"We have an army and we have loyal followers—" he began.

"We have farmers and bakers! The Hillanders are good people, but most of them have never held a sword." Beauty turned away, letting her white hair fall into her eyes so he could not see her fear.

"That is true," said Beast. "I cannot deny it. But we have my army, too, and yes, I suppose they have not fought since their enchantment—and some barely know their own names—but they were once good soldiers."

They looked at each other and then smiled.

"And we have you," he added, taking hold of her hand once more.

"All right, you have charmed me," she said. "For now."

"Come back to the ballroom and bid your guests good-bye. Farmers and bakers they may be, but they live by custom, and they would like to see their host before they leave. Their host and their queen."

Beauty twitched at the word.

"Do you ever wish that we were spending our days in here again?" she asked. "All we did was read and talk."

"Perhaps. But you are forgetting that I was also covered in fur then, with fangs down to my knees."

"Yes." Beauty giggled. "Perhaps I had forgotten that."

"Come on," he said, gently tugging on her arm and leading her to the door.

As she scooped up her emerald robe to leave, a book across the room caught Beauty's attention. She knew immediately it was what she had been looking for and she ran to grab it.

"What is wrong?" asked Beast.

Flipping the cover open, her fingers trembling, Beauty poured over the pages. She was vaguely aware that her silvery skin was beginning to glitter in the lamplight, as it did when her Magic overtook her.

"It is a swan," she whispered.

Beast looked at the page she was studying, which was filled with sketches of a large, white bird. He frowned.

"They are native to the Scarlet Isles," he said. "I have seen them before."

"It is what I have been dreaming of," said Beauty, her eyes large and luminous in the shadows. "But I do not know what it means."

CHAPTER SIXTEEN

The Wandering

Ode did not know where he was going, but he walked endlessly through the wilderness. He tried to keep the sea to his left, but often he wandered off course and found himself doubling back and following his own tracks. His days became nothing but the steady rhythm of his feet beating the ground and his arms swinging with his pace. He tried to put faith in his own Magic, convinced that he would have a dream or a vision soon, telling him what lay ahead. But the days trickled by and no answers came.

Each morning Ode awoke with fresh aches and pains that he tried to stretch out in the rising sunlight. He slept fitfully, worried always of danger, and his tiredness swelled until it was like a cloak draped across his shoulders, dragging him back. Arrow, too, was suffering; his usual gliding gate slowed to a stiff plod and he stopped to sniff their new surroundings less and less. One day, both awoke and found that they simply could not continue. Tears of frustration rolled down Ode's grimy cheeks, and he lay still, giving in to his sore body. He rested for the whole day, ate and slept a little, and then finally pushed onward the next morning, hopeful that wherever he was heading, he would reach it soon.

But the forest around Ode seemed to go on forever. Every so often the trees would begin to thin out and he would find himself wondering if this was the end. But then they would reach the crest of a hill and another expanse of green would unfold before them in steady, leafy hills that disappeared into the horizon. The ground was as uneven as it had been at camp and was still the russet brown color of autumn. Ode often thought wistfully of the dark damp earth in the forests of the Taone territory or of the dusty grasses of the flatlands. He longed for familiar and comforting surroundings.

The food and water Blue Moon had given Ode quickly ran out, so each day was a battle against twinges of hunger and stabs of thirst. Ode was not a hunter, but like all Taone members, he could forage for food and find water. On good days, Arrow would catch a rabbit or a squirrel and Ode would roast it, barely able to wait until it had cooled before stuffing it in his mouth. On bad days, there was nothing but berries, and on a few occasions, there was nothing at all.

Ode knew that he was growing thinner. He could see that Arrow was also becoming weaker and his coat had lost its glossy shine. Every night Ode went to sleep with one hand clutching his feather amulet, desperate for a dream to foresee what would happen next, desperate to know when their suffering would end. Red and orange leaves were beginning to flutter from the trees like fiery rain, and one morning, Ode awoke with frost in his hair. He began wearing the fur cloak Blue Moon had given him and he tied on his winter boots, but he knew that he would not be able to survive the snow when it came. He told himself several times a day that his Magic would intervene and he would not be wandering in this wilderness forever, but still the dreamless nights came and went.

As the leaves continued to fall around them and the days trudged onward, Ode began to lose faith. He had no energy to shift and often he worried that his Magic had disappeared completely. It seemed that he could do nothing but put one foot in front of the other, walking for hours. Often he was so wrapped up in the monotonous rhythm of his strides that he would forget how vulnerable he and Arrow were until it was almost too late. Several times they had come across wolves, bears, and mountain lions. The first time they encountered a bear, Arrow fought it off, but as he grew thinner and weaker, the pair found themselves hiding from predators instead. If winter came and they were still wandering, Ode did not know what would kill them first: a pack of wolves or the freezing cold.

One evening they were plodding through endless miles of trees when Ode heard a twig snap. At first, he thought nothing of it since the sounds of the forest had become as natural to him as his own breathing. Even when Arrow paused and raised his head, Ode did not sense the hint of danger. Instead, he hoped that a squirrel was nearby as they hadn't eaten since morning.

Arrow barked and Ode looked over his shoulder with a frown just in time to see a glint of flint as something slashed at his arm. He ducked, but it was too late and the thrown spear tore at his skin, slicing a hole in his fur cloak. He shouted in pain and clutched the stinging wound. Then he began to run.

As he sprinted through the trees, Ode saw shadows following. He heard the chatter of an unknown language and he felt the press of bodies chasing him. Fallen leaves crunched underfoot and the air whistled with more spears.

Arrow galloped at his side and Ode leaped over bushes and darted through trees, trying to lose his attackers. His breath heaved in his chest and his body tingled with fear, but he was weak and he knew he could not keep running. When he had thought of his demise in the never-ending forest, Ode had never supposed that other tribesmen would kill him. He had imagined wolves or starvation, and it had not occurred to him that, of course, there must be other tribes than just the Taone residing in the Wild Lands. For a moment, he was jealous of this tribe and their ignorant existence. If only the New People had landed here and invaded their territory instead, then everything would surely be as it was before. But Ode did not have time to feel too bitter. His attackers were shouting to each other and when he stole a glance over his shoulder, he saw three men charging after him. The sight of them almost made Ode stumble, for they were so different from the Taone that it was hard to believe they called the same land home. These men were short and squat with thick, dark hair. Their skin was pale, unlike the chestnut brown of the Taone, and they were covered in tawny fuzz from foot to crown. They were also gaining on him.

Ode willed his body to shift, but he knew it would not; he had no energy to spare. His legs were beginning to slow and each hurried breath was scorching his chest. He did not see a fallen branch until it was too late. He caught his foot on it, and with a cry he tumbled to his knees. Arrow faltered and Ode's body smacked against the ground with a thump that made his teeth ache. He lay on the cold forest floor, waiting for hands to grab him from behind or for a spear to slice through his skull—whatever came first.

After a moment of nothing, he lifted his head and saw the three men standing a little distance away, watching. They had their spears raised, but they did not look like they were going to attack. They were standing beside a tall, fat trunk with markings etched into its bark. Ode could not make out exactly what the markings were, but he instantly understood. He had trespassed onto their land, and they were protecting it.

He climbed shakily to his feet, his legs wobbling from the run, and faced them. They were peering at him curiously, and he wondered if he was as strange to them as they were to him. He lifted his hand in greeting as the Taone did, but they did not respond. They stayed standing by their boundary with their spears raised, warning him that he was not to turn back.

"Don't worry, I'm leaving," he called out to them.

They flinched at the sound of his voice, but otherwise, they did not reply.

With Arrow panting after him, Ode limped away through the trees. He did not make it far before he collapsed, knowing that he could go no farther that night.

He dropped his leather pack onto the ground near a bush and pulled out his supply of water, taking eager gulps and then pouring the rest out for Arrow. While Ode tried to clean the wound on his arm, the wolf slunk off into the darkening forest, hunting for dinner. Ode's cut was not deep, but it still throbbed and bled. He knew he was lucky that the spear had not buried itself in his arm and he was *very* lucky that the arrowhead had not been poisoned.

Tearing a length of leather from his tunic, Ode wrapped it around his bicep and tied it in place to stop the flow of blood. He hoped it would not get infected; there was no Cala now to make a potion to take away his fever. There was no one.

Ode was building a small fire when Arrow emerged from the darkness, a rabbit dangling from his mouth. Ode praised him and began stripping and cooking the meat, his mouth watering and his hands trembling. Once eaten, the food improved his mood a little, warming his belly in the chilly darkness, but as more and more light disappeared, the temperature dropped and he edged closer to the fire, Arrow cuddled up at his side.

When the darkness was complete, Ode extinguished the fire and the two of them crawled beneath a nearby bush. Shivering, they lay on the cold ground side by side, with the fur cloak flung over them. After a moment, Ode realized that he could see whiteness raining down through the branches. He lifted his head and peered at the spiraling, white flakes falling all around them, his jaw clenching in fear. The snow had come.

CHAPTER SEVENTEEN

The Red Cloak

While the last of the leaves still clung to the trees in the forest, there were only light dustings of snow. Ode sometimes woke in the morning with whiteness frosted all over him, and often as he walked, tiny flakes would cascade from the sky in ominous whirls. He watched the remaining leaves obsessively, longing for them to stay—longing for autumn to stretch on and never change into winter.

But there was no escaping the chill that laced the air. It gnawed through Ode's flesh and made his bones ache from the moment he woke until the moment he slept. As the cold increased, his daily pace slowed, until sometimes he wondered if he was barely moving at all. The forest continued on forever and gradually became whiter and whiter as the days passed.

One morning the snow began at sunrise, pattering against Ode's head and clinging to his cloak and Arrow's gray fur. When the pair came to a stream, it was frozen over and Ode had to break the ice with his dagger before they could get a sip of the chilled water that made their stomachs sore with its bite.

The snow persisted as they walked on until it outlined the bare branches they passed and collected in a layer beneath their feet. The light flurry grew thicker and faster until snow was covering everything and Ode found himself ankle-deep in pure coldness that drenched his boots. Gust after gust of snow became a blizzard that whirled and twirled through the air, rushing against Ode's cheeks and burying itself deep in Arrow's fur. Soon neither could see where they were going.

Ode huddled farther down into his cloak, desperate sobs beginning to rack his throat. He grasped the feather around his neck, stiff with cold, and he longed to feel his Magic again. He had never wished to be the strange birther as much as he did now. All those seasons he had spent despising his gift, and now he wanted it desperately.

I cannot have walked through this snow for nothing, he thought. *This must all mean something. Whatever it is, do it now. Now!*

Ode fell to his knees in the snow and prayed that he would be saved from this hellish whiteness. He was so deeply entrenched in his misery that the sudden vision took him by surprise. He saw red. It flowed around him and through him. He heard women singing in a strange language, their voices soft and gentle like a summer moon. When he opened his eyes, the vision was over, but the red did not fade.

Ode blinked several times yet a spot of red remained, surrounded by the white snowstorm raging above. As he tried to understand what the vision meant, he realized that the red was a figure. A cloaked figure in the distance. Before he knew what he was doing, Ode was stumbling toward it, shouting.

"Help me!" he yelled. "Wait!"

The figure turned. It was a man heavily laden with leathers and furs, a red cloak slung over his back. He stared at Ode sliding toward him in the snow with astonishment.

"Help me!" cried Ode, sprawling at the man's feet.

Arrow galloped up behind him, whining.

Ode took hold of the edge of the man's red cloak and gripped it tightly in his hands.

"You must help me," he gasped.

The man bent to help him stand, but Ode was already unconscious.

───⊗───

When Ode awoke, he was deliciously warm. He had forgotten how it felt to breathe without coughing and to lie down without shivering. For a while he remained still, wallowing in the heat. Then, gradually, his body came alive and before long he realized that his back ached and his feet were sore. His chest was raw and his stomach throbbed. He finally opened his eyes.

He was inside a wooden tent, like the kind he had seen in his dreams. Furs and other materials covered him as he lay on a strange, raised bed mat, and a fire flickered in the corner. The tent was large and square, and Ode supposed it must be one of those "houses" that the New People had spoken of. He tried to sit up, but gasped with pain and collapsed onto the bedding, clutching his sides.

From over the edge of his raised bed mat, he heard a squeak of excitement and a black nose thrust itself into his face, sniffing and snorting with delight.

"Arrow . . ." Ode tried to say, but his dry throat only croaked.

The wolf began licking his cheek and Ode could hear the swishing pump of his companion's wagging tail. He reached out a hand to pet Arrow's head, and the wolf licked and slobbered at it. As he did so, Ode noticed the bruises and cuts on his arm and he frowned. His wrist was bandaged and there was another bandage at his elbow, too. He suddenly wondered how long he had been in this house and who had brought him here. In his foggy mind he could just about remember the snowstorm and a figure in red, but it did not feel real.

He relaxed back on the pillows, trying not to worry his tired mind with such thoughts. For now, he was simply happy to be warm and sheltered. He was about to drift back into sleep when someone entered the house.

Again, Ode tried to sit up, but buckled with a yelp of pain.

"You woken!" said a man, closing the wooden door and stamping his boots to shake off clumps of snow.

Ode stared at him.

"It be good you woken. I be scared you too far gone. I be scared you die."

Ode knew that the man was speaking another language even though he could understand him. Much like the New People, the inflection and tone of the man's voice sounded odd to him, but he could grasp the meaning of the words.

"Who . . ." he tried to say, but his croak dissolved into coughing.

"Do nay overdo it now, do nay overdo it," said the man.

He was tall and broad with light-brown skin like the pebbles at the bottom of a stream. He had a thick, dark beard and warm, brown eyes. Over his many leathers and furs, he wore a red cloak tied with cord at his neck.

Once Ode had stopped coughing he curled into himself, exhausted. He did not care who this man was or why he was here—he just wanted to be lost in sleep again.

"You understand me? You hear me right?" the man said.

This time Ode did not try to reply, he simply nodded.

"I thought it be so," said the man. "I been wondering if I imagined you running toward me in the snow, speaking in mountain language."

The man was carrying an armful of chopped wood and he hastily pushed it into a corner. Then he stood watching Ode with a wide smile.

"You probably wondering how long you been here," he continued. "Well, it be a long time. Like I said before, I be worrying for a while whether you make it through, but I guess you did. You had fevers and sicknesses and when I found you, you was almost dead anyway. That wolf not left your side the whole time you be here. He give me a hard time when I first tried to nurse you."

Ode glanced at Arrow, who was looking back with faithful green eyes.

"Me and the others be keen to ask you where you come from and why you come here," added the man. "We all so sure you sent from the gods to us."

Ode closed his eyes. He did not have the energy to form any answers.

"Yes, you better sleep now," said the man. "You got plenty of resting that needs doing. We be speaking when you're ready."

But Ode found that he could not return to the delightful nothingness of before. For the next few days he floated in a semiconscious state, overwhelmed with memories of the past. In his wanderings through the Wild Lands, he had been so focused on staying alive that there had been no time to dwell on what he had left behind. Now warm and fed, he found his mind drifting toward the Taone and his dead father.

Blue Moon said that Gray Morning had wanted Ode to be the new chief. Was that merely the fear of defeat talking, or had his father really meant it? Ode would never know. Gray Morning had always made it clear that he hated his first son, but perhaps it was not so simple. Sometimes such thoughts would bring frustrated tears to Ode's eyes as he lay in bed, staring at the wooden roof. He was angry at what could have been and he was distraught there was no way to change it. Gray Morning was dead and gone.

When he was not thinking of his father, Ode wondered how the Taone felt now that he had disappeared. He suspected they were relieved, perhaps even happy. He doubted even his own mother was sad. Sunset By Forest had treated him differently ever since he shifted at the Winter Feast. She was suspicious and scared of him now, like everyone else. Blue Moon at least, Ode hoped, would miss him. He could not be sure of this, but he clung to the thought, wishing it to be true.

And Cala? Ode did not know what to feel about his auntie. She had become powerful and intimidating to him, when she had once been soothing and kind. It was her fault that he had been exiled to the wilderness. She had sent him off, and then abandoned him. Ode remembered their parting with bitterness curling the edges of his memory. He did not know if she had ever really cared about him. Looking back, it seemed as though he were merely a tool in whatever she was planning. A tool that did not work out. He was glad, at least, to be away from her and the New People's war; it seemed like a dangerous problem that did not concern him now.

If it were not for the frequent interruptions of the man in the red cloak, Ode would be lost in such thoughts. The man appeared at intervals throughout the day, speckled with snow and eager to check on his invalid. His name was Erek, and Ode quickly discovered that he was the leader of whatever tribe this was. Erek liked to talk. He would start chattering as soon as he entered the house and he would not stop until he left again. For a while, Ode was happy simply to lay still and listen, but soon it became clear that Erek wanted answers.

"You be awake four days in a row now," he said, entering the house covered in flecks of white that clung to his closely cropped hair and long beard. "Perhaps you be trying to sit up?"

Ode had known that he would not be able to get away with laying silently in bed forever, and as his body grew stronger, he was beginning to feel stale and trapped. He needed to escape his thoughts, but summoning the energy to move was proving difficult.

"That throat be good enough to talk yet?" asked Erek.

Ode nodded and shifted himself into a sitting position. His body still ached from some bruises that had yet to heal, but he could withstand the pain now.

"So, let be starting with how you got here," said Erek.

He took a stool from beside the fire and placed it next to Ode's bed.

"I walked here," said Ode.

"But why? Where you be coming from?"

Ode shrugged. "I don't know," he said. The foreign language sounded strange in his mouth, but he spoke it without thinking.

"You nay be knowing how you got here?" echoed Erek with a frown. "No."

"You nay be knowing where you born or nothing?"

"No."

"You nay be knowing how you can speak mountain language?"

"No."

"Seems you be lying," said Erek.

He did not say it unkindly, but Ode felt nervous all the same. He swallowed and looked around the room. In the days he had been bedridden, its contents had become familiar to him. He had discovered that it was not a house but a "hut." Erek spoke of the room as if it were small and bare, but to Ode it was large and cluttered. He could not work out why one individual needed so many buckets, furs, and knives. Erek had five times more items than Ode had ever owned in his lifetime.

"Strange to nay know where you come from," persisted Erek.

"Where do you come from then?"

"I come from Shadeet originally. Most people be telling that from looking at me, but nay you, I guess. I'm a Kin though, you understand?"

"A Kin?"

"Means I be a Kin of the Scarlet Isles," said Erek, motioning to his red cloak. "I went there when I be a boy and became a Kin of the Castle Temple in the mountainous islands," Erek paused. "I be seeing this nay mean much to you."

Ode rubbed his head.

"If I be looking at you and guessing your origins, I be thinking maybe a boy from a tribe," said Erek. "You nay look like much tribes I be seeing around here, though. Skin the wrong color."

Ode looked down at his bare hands. "I don't remember anything," he said. "I woke up in the forest in the winter and that's it."

"What about that wolf?" asked Erek.

"I don't know where he came from."

"What about the feather around your neck?"

"I don't know," said Ode, fighting to keep his voice steady.

"I nay believe you."

The fire crackled. Erek was about to say more when a knock sounded at the door, which meant that someone was delivering the stew. It seemed that a man called "a cook" made the food for this tribe and they ate separately in their different huts. Ode had yet to meet the other members of the tribe properly, though some had come to the door once or twice to speak to Erek and he had caught glimpses of red cloaks and long beards.

"Best be eating this up for strength," said Erek, handing him a bowl.

They finished their dinner in silence, both staring into the fire, deep in their own thoughts.

"You be knowing why we here?" asked Erek suddenly.

"No," replied Ode. "Why?"

"To tell the tribes about the gods. We be here five seasons now, but still they reject us. They run from us, and they attack us, and they nay want us here. You be the first we got to speak to."

"Maybe they don't want to hear it."

Erek snorted with laughter. "Well, no," he said, before his face became tense and distant once more. "But we be here for no reason then. This nay a kind land to us—this winter is . . . a test. This place be flat, and there is nay beauty."

"Are the Scarlet Isles hot?"

"They be the same as here, but it be mountain country and it be beautiful. The air be different, and well, I suppose it be home. You be knowing what it like to have a home?"

Ode shook his head, trying not to think of the flatlands and the forest.

"I be thinking me and the Kins will be leaving this place once it confirmed from the Castle Temple. There be no point staying longer. We wasted enough time. What you be doing then?"

Ode blinked; he had not thought that far ahead. His days had been spent in an aching, sick haze, and he had planned nothing. He had been too busy thinking about the past.

"I think I must follow you," Ode said, because he did not know what else he would do.

Erek gave him a searching look. "You be sure you don't remember where you come from?" he asked.

"No."

"So be it."

CHAPTER EIGHTEEN

The Great Great Lake

A letter from the Castle Temple sanctioning the return of their
missionaries arrived two days later, carried by an eagle. Erek
rushed to tell Ode the good news and it was clear from his wide smile
how eager he was to go home. Ode wished he could share in the
excitement, but it all meant very little to him. He was following the
Kins because he did not know what else to do. Anything was preferable
to wandering in the wilderness again. He knew what it was like to try
to fend for himself and he would go anywhere before he was forced to
face the cruel loneliness of the Wild Lands.

"My prayers be answered!" Erek cried, bursting into the hut with
a scrap of parchment gripped in his hand. "We be leaving right away!"

He was so thrilled that he did not elaborate. Turning around, he
ran back outside to share the news with the other Kins, leaving Ode
to accept that his period of healing was over. It was time to move on.

While the arrangements were made to decamp from the settlement,
Ode attempted to regain his strength before he was faced with another
journey. He did not know how far away the Scarlet Isles were, but his
struggle through the thick snow of the Wild Lands was all too vivid

a memory. He knew he needed to build up both his health and his confidence before setting out.

At first, Ode slid out of bed and wobbled around the room, leaning against Arrow's head for support. After a few days, once he could manage several laps around the hut without tripping or losing his breath, he piled on some of Erek's furs and stumbled outside.

The cold bit into him the moment he opened the door. With his chest rasping, he shuffled through the snow and studied his surroundings. For almost a whole moon cycle, he had seen nothing but the inside of the hut and at first, the whiteness of the snow was startling. There were eleven huts bundled around him and that was all. Everything else was snow, and folds of it stretched away on every side until they disappeared into a forest at the horizon. Out of that forest, Ode could see three red dots bobbing toward him. He waited, huddled against the chilly air, until they were closer, and when he recognized Erek leading the group, he waved.

Erek smiled and called out a greeting.

"You be out of there, I see," he said, when they were closer. "That be good. You be needing to be strong enough to travel."

Even the thought of traveling made Ode feel sick. "How far is it to go?" he asked, his voice making clouds.

"There be a sea to cross, so it be far."

Ode thought of the sea he had seen at the settlement of the New People and he wondered if it was the same one.

"This be a good time for you to meet two special Kins," said Erek, gesturing to the men beside him.

One was short and squat with fair skin and blue eyes, while the other was tall like Erek, but thin and with a mop of red hair. They greeted Ode with kind curiosity.

"All the Kins be dying to meet you," said Erek. "I be fending them off 'til you strong enough. Many be wanting to talk to you."

Ode tried not to seem nervous and smiled.

"We be in the forest there trying to meet Wildlanders, but they nay seem to want to see us," said Erek, shaking his head.

"Many moon cycles and still we nay be gaining their trust," added the Kin with red hair, who then introduced himself as Molash. "We be meaning them no harm," he added.

Ode almost felt responsible, though he did not know this tribe. He hung his head, not knowing what to say, and shivered.

"You be looking worn," said Erek. "Perhaps you be going and laying down now. You be joining us tonight for planning instead?"

Ode nodded and retreated to the hut gratefully. His excursion outside had made him tired, and he climbed back into the bed, his eyelids already heavy. Next to him, Arrow settled himself on the wooden floor with a sigh.

As Ode drifted into sleep, he heard the Kins outside discussing him. His knowledge of their language baffled them, and they could not agree on how it could have come about. It baffled Ode, too, and he could not explain it either except that Magic must be involved. But he sensed that this would be dangerous to admit. As far as he could tell, no one spoke of such things here.

⁀⧫⁀

As his strength returned, Ode began to practice the fighting drills he and Blue Moon used to perform together. He no longer spent days tucked up in blankets inside the hut, and he started to feel like himself again. When he could be of help to the Kins, he offered his services, often chopping wood for the huts or slicing vegetables for the cook's stews. The Kins treated him with respect and gentle interest, welcoming him into their clan instantly. They were not like people Ode had ever known before; they were not suspicious or demanding or cruel. They were quiet and dignified. It was only Erek who chattered so much.

"But I suppose they do not know about me," Ode whispered once to Arrow on one of their solitary walks through the snow, collecting firewood. "If they knew what I could do then they'd think differently."

Ode was surprised that he did not feel the urge to shift. Since his Magic had all but deserted him in the wilderness, he had not felt its force again. He thought back to his time with the Taone, when he had crept away daily to transform. Now, he did not feel the need. It was like his Magic had almost disappeared.

Ode was just beginning to understand the daily running of the Kins' settlement when another eagle arrived, announcing that the clan were to leave right away. Belongings were strapped onto horses that were slighter and, in Ode's opinion, not as strong as the mustangs from his homeland, and everything was made ready for departure. The huts were cleaned and shut up for their next residents, the messenger eagles were set free to travel back to the mountains, and the area around the settlement was cleared.

On the last night, the Kins gathered and drank a strange liquid they had been saving for a special occasion. Ode was allowed a sip and he had to stop himself from spitting it right out. The bitter taste made his eyes water.

"There be plenty of this wine waiting for us at home," announced Erek, and the rest of the Kins smiled and nodded with pleasure.

Ode was surprised by their quietness. He compared it to the Taone, with their drums and their dancing and their feasting, and he wondered how these men could show their happiness simply by smiling and nodding.

"Let us sing a song," said Erek, breaking the silence.

He began to clap his hands in a simple, steady rhythm and to chant warbled noises. His voice was soft but clear, and one by one, the rest of the Kins joined in until they were all singing. They crooned mournfully and their eyes stared off into the darkness around them, seeing a land that was far away.

Ode listened and tapped his foot to the beat, thinking of the flatlands and the forest that he would never see again—with a mixture of relief and regret. He did not know what mountains were, but they sounded different and exciting. Squashing any longing for his lost childhood home, Ode stared into the nearby fire and told himself that there was no point looking back. The Taone as he had known them did not exist anymore. They were the New People now.

The next day, the Kins rode out into the snowy whiteness. Erek led the party and when Ode asked how he knew where he was going, the Kin replied, "I *feel* those mountains pulling me." Then he took out a piece of parchment from his cloak and added, "The map be helping me, too."

Ode looked at the parchment longingly, urging on his dun packhorse so that the two men were abreast of one another.

"You be seeing a map before?" asked Erek.

"A few times."

"If you be knowing there's a realm out there, you nay be like other tribe boys."

Ode shrugged, but did not take his eyes off the map.

"All right then," said Erek, handing it to him with a chuckle.

Ode examined it closely, scanning the shapes and sketches for something he recognized, but it was not like Cala's scrolls.

"I be thinking we be about here," said Erek, leaning over his saddle and pointing at a spot.

Ode realized he must be looking at a small section of the Western Realm's map in detail. He traced the shapes for meaning, but gathered little.

"You read?" asked Erek.

"What does *read* mean?"

"These be words," said Erek, pointing at the tiny markings dotted over the map. "They be names of things, like this one say the *Scarlet Isles*."

Ode stared, fascinated. "How can you tell?" he asked.

"Because I read."

"How can I read?"

Erek smiled. "I be teaching you," he said.

But that night a heavy snowstorm came and there was no time for reading lessons. Huddled in one of the shelters, Ode's mind was drawn back to his days spent lost in the wilderness. He buried himself in his furs, longing to forget the fear and the loneliness of that cold, starving time, but it throbbed through him anyway. Arrow curled into his side, and together they lay shivering until morning.

In the light of day, the storm did not seem as bad and Ode chided himself for being silly. Some of the Kins also looked a little shaken as they emerged from their shelters, but everyone smiled when they saw the morning sunlight. After breakfast, they all packed up and pressed on, forming a wiggling snake that slithered across the white land and went on seemingly indefinitely.

The journey to the sea was hard on all of the Kins, and Ode wondered how some of them could stand it since they were far older than he. They had insisted that he use a saddle because their horses were not used to being ridden bareback, but Ode found it stiff and awkward. The saddle gave him sores and the relentless cold was unbearable at times. But Ode never heard the Kins grumble. He saw them wince in pain and he heard them gasp in agony, but they did not utter a word of complaint. Even when the eldest developed a hacking cough and had to be ministered ointments by the others, he never moaned. Their endurance rubbed off on Ode and he found himself also shrugging away aches and pains.

One evening around the fire, Molash asked Ode if he regretted accompanying them on their journey, and Ode answered truthfully that he did not. He felt there was a lot he could learn from these people.

A few of the Kins even won Arrow's grudging affection. The wolf sometimes nuzzled up to those he liked, offering his head to be petted or his back to be rubbed. The Kins were not scared of him and they fed him tidbits of meat and tickled his chin. On one occasion, Arrow managed to warn the group of a nearby mountain lion and thus received a sort of honor status among them.

As the days stormed by, the clan edged closer to the coast until one morning, Erek announced they would reach it by sundown. He explained to Ode that they were heading toward a small harbor town with merchant ships that could take them to their island, Holli—one of the islands of the Scarlet Isles. When Ode finally saw the harbor town with his own eyes in the fading light, he could barely comprehend it. The huts there were large and tall. They were so close to each other, packed into tiny spaces, and built so high they soared like trees. There were many people walking about, and Ode saw cobbled paths that wound around and in between it all like threads sewn into a tunic. There were dogs, cats, and horses everywhere. Children scurried about and a salty breeze blew in off the sea. Ode could hear the crash of the waves and the constant murmur of many voices. He was terrified and thrilled all at once.

Erek led the Kins through the cobbled streets and Ode noticed that people paused when they passed and ducked their head in a respectful greeting. The party finally stopped before a huge house that the Kins later explained was an inn. Erek disappeared inside and arranged for rooms for the night and a place on a merchant ship leaving tomorrow, while Ode waited outside with the others, trying not to show how uncomfortable he felt. Finally, Erek reappeared and the party unloaded their horses, stabling them in a nearby barn.

Inside the inn, Ode looked at everything with round, amazed eyes. The rooms were too large, and there were so many of them. The amount of furniture bemused him, as did the people who sat inside drinking foul-smelling liquid. The owner tried to make him leave his wolf in the stable, but Erek gently insisted that Arrow must stay with them.

"I never seen a tame wolf," said the owner in a different language, backing away. "Not a big one like that. If he do damage, you have to pay."

"It'll nay come to that," replied Erek with a firm smile.

By the next morning, news of the tame wolf had spread. There was a crowd gathered outside the inn as the Kins departed in the direction of the harbor, and Arrow shied away from the people, unused to such attention. Ode, too, felt himself trying to duck out of view. This town was strange and scary to him. He had not slept well in the uncomfortable, lumpy bed at the inn and he was starting to worry. It was becoming clear to him that life in the rest of the realm was nothing like his past with the Taone.

The ship was an even bigger shock. Ode had sat in canoes before and what lay on the sea now seemed to him like a giant canoe with add-ons. He turned pale when Erek explained that they were supposed to live on the ship. Anxiety choked his throat, and it was with stiff, unwilling legs that Ode forced himself onto the deck. Arrow was also unsure and kept whining softly and butting Ode's hand with his furry head.

On deck, the floor shifted and swelled under Ode's feet as the ship rocked. The shouts and bustle of the sailors made him jump and fidget, but most disconcerting of all was the great stretch of green-blue that seemed to go on forever. It was like a lake without an opposite shore. Ode had admired the sea back with the New People, but he had been standing on dry land at the time. It had never crossed his mind that he would be expected to travel on it.

"How you be faring?" asked Erek, patting him on the back.

"I am . . . I am unsure about this journey."

"We all be feeling that way!" said Erek with a laugh, but when he saw Ode's petrified look, he paused. "I know this be difficult for you, but it be the only way back. That be the misfortune of living on an island. All the Scarlet Isles be like that. Once you become a Scarletion, it be part of life."

Ode did not reply, for it had not occurred to him before that he was leaving the Wild Lands and, with it, his old self. He was soon to become a Scarletion.

"Let us be getting you settled with a bunk," said Erek.

Ode stepped gingerly on deck, as if at any moment the boards beneath him would disappear and he would fall through into the sea. He followed Erek down a ladder into the bowels of the ship and the rancid, salty smell made him gag.

"Be nay worried, you get used to it," said Erek cheerfully.

Clutching his stomach, Ode twisted with Erek through low-roofed passages, past barrels, sacks, and dead rats.

Arrow, who had leaped into the dark after him, sniffed the dead rats and growled at those still scurrying in the corners.

"The sailors be loving him if he catches them rats," said Erek. "They be not so sure about a wolf when we walk on, but I be telling them he be good. He be good, yes?"

Ode nodded, too afraid to speak in case he vomited.

Erek stopped at a squat, damp room with white sheets hanging from the ceiling and dim light emitting from a tiny, round window.

"Perhaps you be laying a bit, yes? Get you some sea legs before you come back on deck?"

Ode glanced at the filthy, stained floor and Erek chuckled.

"Nay, in the hammocks," he added, and when Ode did not move he demonstrated, climbing into one of the white sheets that swung from the ceiling.

Ode blinked at him, wondering if this could be happening.

"Scarletions sleep this way?" he asked, at last.

"Nay! This be just sailors. Don't be looking too fussed now, you be getting used to it. Give it a try."

Ode carefully climbed into one of the sheets and lay swinging from side to side like a stiff corpse.

"There now," said Erek. "Just be laying there a moment."

Ode closed his eyes, and Erek left the room. Beneath him, Ode heard Arrow prowl around the room, sniffing the rotten floor and snapping at the rats. Ode tried to think calming thoughts, but the terror of life on this ship for days on end brought a sweat to his brow. Above him, he could hear heavy footsteps running back and forth and shouting as the sailors prepared to set sail.

Suddenly, Ode's stomach clenched and his eyes snapped open. He barely had time to sit up before he vomited over the side of the hammock, his bile pooling on the floor. He groaned and collapsed back against the foul sheet. It seemed that he was destined for another bout of sickness, but Ode did not realize that this one would last for days and days. It would go on and on until he finally set foot on firm land again.

CHAPTER NINETEEN

The Journey

The passage across the Route Sea almost killed Ode. He barely left his hammock, and when he did, it was only to snatch a few breaths of fresh air on the top deck before he hurried back to the dim cabin below. The Kins were kind and they sat with him often, nursing him with ointments and prayers. Ode liked it best when they sang to him; their voices drowned out the constant crash of the waves and for a moment, Ode could pretend he was not on the ship.

Erek tried to cheer him up with tales of the land they were traveling to. It was Erek who explained that they were crossing what the Western Realm called the Route Sea, though other nationalities had different names for it. He attempted to fill Ode's mind with mauve-crested mountains and temples strung with prayer flags that fluttered in the wind, but the images seemed too vague and surreal to Ode. They were lost in the slap of the waves against the walls and the shrill cries of the seagulls the sailors kept on board to carry messages between ships and the land.

Several times the ship was hit by terrible storms and Ode feared they would all perish. On these nights he would tumble out of his hammock and crouch on the filthy floor, his arms wrapped around Arrow's furry shoulders, who would lick his cheek and whine. There he stayed in the darkness for hours on end, as the ship flopped and rose against the waves, sure that the waters would engulf them at any moment.

At night, the hammocks were full and the cabin stank of stale, unwashed bodies. The sailors grew irritated with Ode, and they teased and taunted him for his seasickness. Ode's misery onboard the ship was so deep that when Erek told him they would soon be reaching land, he scarcely believed it. He could not remember anything but the sickly sway of the waves under his feet and the salty stench in the air.

One day, Erek came to fetch him, and despite Ode's slurring protests, the Kin ushered him up on deck. Ode stumbled and tripped under Erek's guidance to the edge of the ship to peer out at the endless blue. Except, this time, at the end of the blue there was a distant shadow of land. It was brown and smudged against the darkening pewter winter sky, but it was there. A cry of relief escaped Ode's lips and the Kins around him smiled.

"We be home!" cried Erek. "We be almost home."

That evening they reached the shore and Ode was first off the ship. Seeing him move so fast made the sailors laugh. They bid farewell to the Kins before beginning to unload their produce ferried over from the Wild Lands. Wood, coal, and caged animals were pulled out of the ship's undercarriage and carried into the harbor. Ode walked past a boxed cougar, half-dead from the passage, and he had to force himself to turn his sad eyes away.

Keen to secure lodgings for the night, the Kins took their belongings and entered the city. If Ode had thought that the harbor town in the Wild Lands was big, this city was like nothing he could have imagined. At the end of each street, another four emerged, forking in different directions. There were people everywhere, laughing and drinking on corners, and gambling and stealing in the squares. Ode walked through it all with his hand buried deep in Arrow's coarse coat, clinging on to something familiar. He still felt dizzy from his time at sea and it was almost easier for him to imagine that this new place was a strange dream.

"You have nay chosen an easy life with us," said Molash, falling into step beside him. "This can nay be like anything you know."

Ode nodded his agreement.

"The mountains be quieter, and you will like it better."

Ode hoped he was right.

The Kins spent the night at an inn, and the next day they awoke early since Erek said it was important to leave before the city "came alive." Ode did not know what this meant, but if what he had seen the night before—all of the bustling and shouting people—had been the city asleep, then he agreed they should leave as quickly as possible.

The Kins strode through the cobbled streets in the early morning light, heading for the road south that went out of the city. Even though the sun had not yet risen, Ode saw people scurrying across their path and some even lay asleep in the middle of the street. He was surrounded on all sides by high, towering houses and there was not a tree in sight, let alone a forest. The flatlands of the Wild Lands seemed like a distant place now.

"As we be traveling down this road, the land be even and long," explained Erek, while the party trudged out of the city and into farmland. "Right now, they be covered in snow, but in the summer they be lush and green. The brightest green you can be imagining—emerald colored. It be beautiful."

Ode nodded and tried to envision the flat snow-covered land around them in the summertime.

"Is it like that in the mountains?" he asked.

Erek shook his head. "Nay, it be hot, dry, and brown in the mountains at summertime. The valleys is where there be water and food grown for us. But the mountains be a beauty of their own."

Ode tried to imagine those soaring bumps as they traveled on many flat snowy roads. He waited for the mountains to appear, but the land remained even and there was nothing but blanketed whiteness, occasionally punctuated by rickety dwellings. It was not until he finally saw them one afternoon, looming out of the horizon like distant bruises in the sky, that he truly appreciated what Erek had meant when he called the mountains *magnificent*. To Ode, they seemed ethereal—as if they possessed a Magic of their own. But he decided to keep this observation to himself.

"You live there?" he asked, and the Kins chuckled.

"All of the temples be in the mountains," said Erek. "This be just the beginning. The mountains go on, one after the other, all the way to the opposite side of the island."

"That's a long way," said Ode, trying to imagine it.

"All them that be committing their lives to the gods live here," explained Molash. "It be the place closest to the gods that us can get in the realm."

As the mountains inched closer day after day, the ground under Ode's feet began to rise. Around him, the season was nearing its end and the thick snow started to soften and melt. One day there was even a burst of sunshine that made everyone in the party smile.

Ode paused to relish its warmth on his cheeks, and it was then that he noticed the group was gaining altitude. If he looked behind him, he could see the flat lands they had walked across sinking below. Forever climbing upward, he had not realized they had come so far. When he looked ahead, the land kept inclining. He wondered if it would rise so high they could touch the clouds.

Each night, when the Kins made camp to eat and sleep, Erek would regale Ode with tales of their mountain existence, and the higher they rose, the more excited Erek's storytelling became. He told Ode about their lives devoted to the gods and how the temple ran with each Kin and Kiness—a female member of the temple—taking on their fair share of work.

"Why do you devote your life to the gods?" Ode asked him one evening.

They sat inside their shared tent, wrapped in furs.

"At first, it be nay my choice to go to the mountains," said Erek. "I nay pretend otherwise. Shadeet be not a wealthy place and my parents had ideas for me. They sent me here for a better life, but I nay regretted their decision."

"Why?"

"You be ever told of the gods?"

"No," Ode lied, thinking about Cala. "I only know what I have gathered from traveling with you these past moon cycles."

"I be wanting to tell you more, but I be hoping you would ask yourself."

"I'm asking now."

"Our scriptures be saying that when the realm begun, Magic reigned free across the land and it be difficult and dangerous."

At the mention of Magic, Ode stilled, and beside him, Arrow lifted his head.

"The gods be the ones that created it, placing Magic Beast and Magic Being and all other beings besides in the realm," Erek continued. "They be the ones that control it all; they be the ones that made it all; they be like our parents, you see? That be why I give my life to them, for when I die, I be reunited with them."

Ode nodded, but he barely heard Erek's words. He was too shocked by the mention of Magic. He had never heard the Kins speak of it before.

"Perhaps that be all I should say now," added Erek. "But I be telling you more over time."

And from then on, every night Erek told Ode a little more about the gods. He explained that some of the Kins and Kinesses believed that the gods had spoken to them directly. He told Ode about the multitude of scriptures that had been passed down through generations, foretelling great events and setting rules for all beings. Ode listened to Erek attentively, yet he could not help but feel excluded. He was used to feeling freakish and unwelcome and he believed that a life of such blessings could not be possible for the likes of him. If the Kins knew of his Magic, he felt sure they would cast him out.

By day the Kins continued their journey. The winter finally melted into spring and buds began forming on the trees and bushes they passed. Ode saw that beneath the snow, the thawing ground was dusty and scattered with shingle. The farther they traveled upward, the more the trees and grass began to disappear until there were only low, scrubby bushes. The earth became browner and rocky, while the air thinned. Ode's head started to ache and his chest choked on every breath.

"That be altitude sickness," said one of the Kins, when he saw Ode slumped against a rock with his head between his knees. "You be getting that for a while 'til you get used to it."

As the party climbed higher, Ode's sickness grew worse. He stumbled through the journey, vomiting often, and at night he clenched his teeth until his jaw ached. Every day became an unforgiving upward struggle, and Ode could not enjoy the incredible view of rolling, craggy mountains that surrounded them. He had no relief until they finally reached the first mountain pass—a small dip between two craggy peaks.

"It be down into the valley after this," said Erek, offering Ode a swig from his canteen.

"And then are we close?" gasped Ode.

"Nay! Then it be up another mountain. There be many more mountains to go yet." Erek saw Ode's expression and quickly added, "But it be getting easier for you. I be making you something to help when we get in the valley, yes?"

Ode nodded glumly and stared at the brown and black humps that lay before them. Some were so tall that their peaks were still iced with snow. Others looked so steep and stony that Ode thought it impossible to climb them at all. The road from the city had disappeared long ago, and now they were only following tracks worn by many seasons of past travelers.

On the road out of the city, the party had frequently passed families moving from village to village and farmers herding animals between fields. Such company had gradually decreased as the ground steepened, but now in the mountains, every so often they would climb a rock and come across a stranger, taking Ode by surprise. The mountain people were small, dark-haired, and shy. On one day they saw an old man herding goats across a slope and on another day, they passed children picking berries from bushes.

"Nam-yeh!" the Kins would call, waving.

The mountain people would nod and some would whisper, "Nam-yeh," back at them with their heads bowed.

Erek explained that the mountain people lived in small villages nestled in the rocks. He said they frequently exchanged and shared food with the temples, but as a rule, they liked to keep to themselves.

"Were they here first?" asked Ode, thinking of the Wild Lands and the New People.

"We nay know," said Erek. "Some think they descend from those that left the temples and the gods to live life alone. We be happy and peaceful with one another, that be all that matters."

The valleys between the mountains were luscious and cool. On the brown slopes, the spring sunshine could be fierce, reminding Ode of his summer days in the plain lands, so it was often with relief that they descended into a shadowed valley where rivers bubbled and trees grew. As the days passed, Ode's sickness lessened as he became accustomed to the thin air, until he felt almost normal again. Then he woke each day with a smile as the sun spilled onto the mountains and the sky warmed to a bright blue.

The days wore on, and they climbed through several more mountain passes until they came across their first temple. The Kins were excited to see it, perched on the crags opposite and carved out of the rock. It had red-painted walls and, from what Ode could see at a distance, carved pillars with fluttering strings of multicolored flags.

"Is that the temple?" he asked.

"Nay, but that be another temple we know," replied Erek.

"Who lives there?"

"Kins and Kinesses from a different order," he said. "We be from the Castle Temple—a temple aligned with the royal family of the Scarlet Isles. Our temple be farther on. It be the highest temple around."

As the party entered another moon cycle, they began to come across more temples. All of them were painted red, but Ode could tell, even from a distance, that they differed in size and condition.

Life had become a cycle of walking then sleeping, walking then sleeping, and Ode began to wonder how he would cope with living at a temple like the many he had seen. He could not imagine himself eating and sleeping in such a place.

It was mid-spring when they finally reached the Castle Temple. They came to a mountain pass and all of a sudden, it appeared there on the rocks across a valley. It was the largest and highest temple Ode had seen. Its sprawling red walls bled into the rocks and its carved details shimmered in gold. There were strings of triangular prayer flags strung around it and across it, arcing and weaving like colored fringing. Ode felt a knot of apprehension form in his chest. They had been traveling for many moons and they had finally arrived, but he did not feel the same glee as the Kins around him. This place was still so unfamiliar.

"Thanks be to the gods!" cried the Kins.

The party began to descend into the valley and Ode noticed that this land was cultivated. There were crops growing and goats and sheep grazing in herds alongside thick, fat animals the Kins called yaks. In the distance, Ode could make out tiny red dots that looked like people watching over the animals.

"Nam-yeh!" Erek shouted, cupping his hands so his words echoed across the mountainside.

At his voice, the red dots jumped up and down and waved back.

"Nam-yeh!" they shouted.

The party strode on, forgetting their sore legs and sunburned necks. At Ode's side, Arrow began to trot, his pink tongue lolling from side to side as he panted in the heat.

The next mountain had stone steps cut into it, which twisted up the slope. Running from the top to the bottom were what looked like little barrels set on poles. Ode wanted to ask what they meant, but the Kins were too busy storming up the steps to focus on anything but the temple. Ode followed them, sweat trickling down his back and darkening his tunic. His stomach was strange and tight, and he was not altogether sure how he felt about finally reaching their destination.

The party stopped at the top, gasping for breath. In front of them stood the temple in all its imposing glory, and out of its doors poured a gaggle of Kins and Kinesses in bright red cloaks with big grins.

Beside him, Erek turned and patted his shoulder. "This be your new home," he said.

CHAPTER TWENTY

The Temple on the Mountain

O n closer inspection, the Castle Temple was colorful and worn. To his surprise, Ode discovered that he liked it almost instantly. The red painted walls were cracked and peeling, while the carved wooden pillars were chipped and scuffed. Mismatched, faded rugs spread across the floors of the galleried hallways running between dusty flagstone courtyards, and cobwebs clung to every corner. The rooms smelled of incense and cooking and echoed with prayers and laughter. It was welcoming, friendly, and not what Ode had expected.

He felt his unease slip away as the Kins and Kinesses fussed and cooed over him, taking his heavy pack off his shoulders and pointing and exclaiming at the gray wolf that stood at his side. He could tell that they assumed he could not understand their language since they discussed him loudly with one another.

"It be a Wildlander, finally! Our prayers be answered, and we be blessed."

"He be frightened, poor boy!"

"Will he be making himself one of us?"

This last question was directed at Erek, who smiled and put a reassuring hand on Ode's shoulder.

"Quiet now, my brothers and sisters. Our guest be knowing everything you say, so watch your tongues."

There were some gasps of shock and a few reddened faces. Ode was stunned to hear a collection of murmured apologies.

"It's . . . no matter," he stuttered in reply. "It is nice . . . to meet you."

The crowd stared at him with open fascination.

"We be weary from our travels," said Erek. "And I think it best we speak to the High-Kin now so that rest be soon after."

Nods of agreement followed and they were led down hallways and across a courtyard to a tall, separate building with a heavy red curtain in place of a door. This was held aside and Ode entered a dim, colorful room strung with prayer flags that wound across the beams and around the pillars. Erek told him to kick off his shoes at the entrance before they padded over the worn, stained carpets. They passed benches set out in rows and fading murals painted on the walls. In front of them stood a huge golden statue of a cloaked figure, and beside it knelt an old man with a long black beard.

"High-Kin!" bellowed Erek.

The old man smiled and struggled to his feet with a wooden cane. "My returning brothers," he said. "The gods be blessing me with your homecoming. You be the last missionaries to return, but nay the least."

"How fared my other brothers and sisters in their trips?" asked Erek.

"Good, good. Spreading the message of the gods in new lands is nay easy." The High-Kin's brown eyes fell on Ode and Arrow.

"High-Kin, this be a Wildlander that returned with us," said Erek, standing aside. "He be speaking our language, and he be here to join us."

The High-Kin nodded and turned to Ode.

"Where did you learn to speak like us?" he asked.

Ode fidgeted under his gaze. "I don't know," he answered at last.

There was a pause.

"Do you wish to be a Kin?" asked the High-Kin.

Ode glanced at Erek, then at the other Kins behind him.

"I don't know," he said again.

Erek looked disappointed.

"To be a Kin is nay a simple choice," said the High-Kin. "But the gods be bringing you here for a reason, boy. It be right that you unsure—Kinhood be a big decision. Until you decide, you will live and work with us. You will spend time with the gods and they be telling you what to do. That be acceptable to you?"

Ode nodded.

"About my wolf . . ." he began.

"Do it bite?" asked the High-Kin.

"Not unless he's made to," replied Ode, resting a hand on Arrow's head.

"Hmm. It be staying as long as nay harm come. It may even be of use." The High-Kin smiled and tugged on his long beard. "Erek, you done a great thing bringing this boy to us. He be a gift from the gods, and I be expecting we learn plenty from him."

Erek bowed his head in thanks.

"And now it be time for your resting," said the High-Kin. "Let me greet all of you, and then we shall prepare you a supper."

One by one the Kins approached the High-Kin and he hugged them, whispering a welcome in their ear. While he waited, Ode could not help but notice that the High-Kin's eyes strayed to him often between greetings and their edges were tinged with curiosity and something a little like fear.

Later that evening, the whole temple met in the eating hall: a vast, bare room with a tall ceiling. The High-Kin called Ode to the front and introduced him to the High-Kiness—a smart, older woman with a tightly wound headdress, who greeted him with a nod. The High-

Kin explained to everyone that Ode was to join the Castle Temple and work with the yak herders in the valley. Ode looked out at the sea of red cloaks and felt his cheeks flush. Kins and Kinesses of all ages sat in rows on cushions placed on the floor, balancing their bowls in their laps. They stared at him with polite curiosity, but when the High-Kin had finished the introduction, they began chattering and laughing with one another.

Ode listened quietly to their conversations, sipping his rice and broth, from his seat in the corner of the hall next to Erek and Molash. He noticed other men and women who did not wear red cloaks and he assumed they must be like him—undecided about the gods. Erek explained that many were failed Kins and Kinesses who had not passed their exams and who had lost their faith. They lived in the temple community until they decided their future with the gods.

After supper, Ode met the other yak herders he would be working with. The group of boys looked him over with undisguised resentment, since he was the first Wildlander the temple had seen and everyone was making a great fuss. They greeted him sullenly and led him back to the tall building with the cloaked gold statue that was called the Room of the Gods. Inside, all the members of the temple were gathering, cramming themselves onto the benches and crouching against the walls. Ode took a place at the back and watched the ceremony with interest.

The younger Kins and Kinesses pinched and teased one another, while the older members prayed and sang together. A golden gong sounded each time a new part of the ceremony began, and Ode noticed a group of girls giggling, their covered heads bobbing as they whispered to one another, while an old man sat in the middle of it all picking his nose. It seemed that ceremony participation was not mandatory.

That night, Ode followed the other yak herders down the steps of the mountain to the valley. The boys held out their right hands as they descended, turning the barrels Ode had noticed earlier that ran in a row from the top to the bottom. As the barrels rotated, a little bell inside chimed, so their descent was accompanied by a chorus of silvery tinkling that rang across the valley. When Ode asked what they were doing, the boys mumbled that the barrels were prayer wheels and if you passed down, you were to turn them in the direction of the moon and think of the gods.

"But we don't think of them," sneered the oldest boy, and the others snickered.

After passing herds of goats and sheep in the darkening valley, the boys led Ode to a small hut nestled between the rocks. They begrudgingly explained that they took turns watching over the yaks to keep them safe from wolves and beasts, their eyes flicking to Arrow without comment. Inside, the hut was sparse but clean, and Ode took a free bed in the corner. The light was fading quickly outside and he was weary. One of the boys disappeared to relieve another from his night shift on the mountainside, while the rest climbed into the beds. As Ode drifted off to sleep with Arrow on the floor beside him, he heard the boys whispering cruel jibes and insults at his expense. He shut his eyes and told himself he did not care.

CHAPTER TWENTY-ONE

The Killings

Despite his unfriendly peers, Ode found that he settled into the daily patterns of the Castle Temple. The day began when sunlight reached the valley, and if he was in the hut, it streamed in through the shuttered windows, rousing him from sleep. If he was on the mountainside tending to the yaks, then he watched it spill over the rocks, bathing them in buttery gold—one of the most glorious sights he had ever seen.

Yak tending was not difficult, and he soon felt comfortable perched on the rocks watching over the stocky, horned creatures. Before entering the mountains, Ode had never seen a yak before. He thought them similar to buffalo, but with a thicker, shaggier coat. They were peaceful enough and did not make much fuss as long as Arrow stayed at a distance. In the mornings, women would come from a hut farther down the valley to milk them, and if Ode was on duty he would help them carry their pails up the mountainside, trying not to spill any on the steps.

Breakfast was always at the temple and a golden gong announced its arrival. Then Ode and the other yak tenders, along with the sheep and goat herders in the valley, would hurry to the eating hall. At mealtimes, Ode always sat next to Erek or the other Kins who had accompanied him on the journey from the Wild Lands. They welcomed him with smiles and chatter while they ate, before disappearing into the temple hallways after their meal to pray and complete their chores. Ode would watch them leave with a heavy heart, wishing he could follow.

Instead, his day would be spent either with the yaks or working on the crops in the valley. He was glad it was springtime since the bright weather made the work almost pleasant. His life at the temple was not too different from his days with the Taone, though Ode looked back on those seasons as if they were distant dreams. Sometimes he would be reminded of it—he would remember Blue Moon's playful taunts or would think of Cala's comforting, peppery scent. Sometimes he would wake in the night and lie in terror of what he had left behind. If he was not a member of the Taone, what was he? If he was not the freakish birther, then he was just a boy.

Often the yak tenders would ask him questions about his past. Ode was so afraid of revealing something that he would always reply, "I don't remember," until they began taunting him with the phrase. They hissed it in his ear at night and shouted it across the mountainside during the day, throwing pebbles at him as they passed. Their taunts would make Arrow snarl, but Ode held him back.

After Ode had been at the temple for one moon cycle, the High-Kin asked to see him. Ode went to the meeting with mounting trepidation, worried that one of the yak herders had reported him for some imagined crime. Unlike the rest of the Kins, who slept in dormitories, the High Kin and High-Kiness had their own rooms away from the distracting noises of the temple, and it took Ode some time to find the right place in the maze of hallways.

Inside, the High-Kin's room was much like every other room in the Castle Temple: red and dusty. There were chests bursting with scrolls, and scripture copied from the originals in his own neat handwriting lined against the walls. The High-Kin sat cross-legged on his red cloak, which was spread across the layered rugs, with his head bowed.

Ode had come to covet those red cloaks. Sometimes a number of them would hang in one of the hallways, waiting to be washed, and if Ode happened to pass, he would hold out his hand and let the rough cotton whisper through his fingers as if he were descending the steps of the mountainside and turning the prayer wheels. The cloaks represented true acceptance into life at the temple. The Kins were kind and loving toward him, but he knew that without the red cloak, he would always be separate. He wished he could announce that the gods had chosen him that very moment, but he did not want to deceive those who had been so generous to him.

Trails of smoke from burning incense curled around the edges of the room and made the air hazy. Its rich, spicy scent reminded Ode of the fires the Taone would dance around in the summer while singing to the sky.

"You be waiting long?" asked the High-Kin, catching sight of him. "I never be hearing you enter the room."

"I would not be a Wildlander if you had."

The High-Kin smiled.

Ode sat on a cushion opposite the old man with Arrow at his side and watched as the High-Kin climbed shakily to his feet, leaning on his staff. Slowly, the High-Kin picked his cloak off the floor, shook it out, and shrugged it onto his shoulders, tying the cords in place as he settled himself back on the floor.

"I called you here to ask how you be faring in your new life," he said.

"It's hard sometimes, but—"

"Hard?"

"Different. There are so many things to learn."

The High-Kin tugged on his long dark beard, which fell in curly waves and pooled in his lap. The midday spring sunshine from the open windows made his bald head shine.

"What be making it hard?" he asked.

"Just the new ways things are done," Ode replied, but he could feel the High-Kin's brown eyes searching his own.

"If there be a particular something or someone making it harder, you be telling me, yes?"

Ode nodded, but he did not want to talk about the yak herders. He felt almost sure that the High-Kin knew and Ode was ashamed. He wanted to be gentle and humble like the other Kins and Kinesses; he had seen how they loved one another and he had rarely heard an angry word shared between them. Besides, the yak herders had warned him that there would be repercussions if he attempted to snitch.

"There be nay more to say on that subject then?" the High-Kin persisted.

"No," said Ode.

"If you be saying so. But how are you faring overall?"

"I like it here," Ode replied truthfully.

"So much that you be thinking of saying the vows?"

Ode looked down at his hands, brown from a morning of work on the mountainside. His nails were lined with dirt and no amount of washing before meals seemed to change that.

"I want to take the vow," he answered truthfully, "but no gods have spoken to me."

There was a pause.

"At least you be speaking the truth. How you be finding the ceremonies?"

"They are nice but . . . I don't feel anything."

The High-Kin nodded. "There can be nay forcing it," he said. "Keep your heart open, and if the gods be wanting to take you, they will soon."

"I hope so," Ode muttered, and the High-Kin hid a smile.

"Anyway, I be calling you here with a task in mind," he said. "I be hearing how well you be working in the valley. Many be impressed with your willingness and your skill."

Ode could not help the flush in his cheeks that overtook him.

"They are?" he said before he could stop himself, and then quickly added, "I've been trying hard. I'm very grateful for all that you have done for me."

The High-Kin nodded and studied him for a moment.

"You be an interesting boy," he said. "You be almost nay a boy now."

Ode felt himself blush further. It had not escaped his own notice that he had grown recently. Throughout his wanderings in the wilderness of the Wild Lands he had become thin, and there had been no opportunity for him to fully regain his strength during his journey to the mountains. Now, with three meals a day at the temple and the bright sunlight warming his back as he worked in the valley, he knew that he had surpassed his original weight. He was the tallest of the yak herders by far, and the broadest, also. His legs were knots of muscle and his shoulders were wide and strong. He had recently caught sight of himself in a drinking trough and not recognized his own reflection.

"You say we been good to you," said the High-Kin. "But you been good to us, too. You been working your hardest and the yaks been the safest they been in many moons. There be nay killings from the mountain wolves or the lions when you been around."

The High-Kin glanced at Arrow, who was stretched on the floor, watching the conversation with his calm, green gaze.

"But there be problems with the sheep," he added.

Ode nodded. He had heard of such things at mealtimes. He knew the temple expected to lose some livestock to the beasts in the mountains, but the harsh winter had made many predators hungry and bold.

"We be losing a high number of sheep and many be saying there be a pack of wolves that be taking them. Since you proved yourself with the yaks, you be willing to tend to the sheep for a time?"

The High-Kin had barely finished speaking before Ode heartily agreed to do everything he could. He was flattered and knew this would mean some time away from the yak herders. He tried not to wonder whether that was the very reason the High-Kin was suggesting it.

Following their meeting, Ode hurried down the mountainside, the tinkle of the prayer wheels pealing after him as he went. He strode across the valley, past those working in the fields, some with red cloaks slung over their shoulders out of the mud, and past the women milking the goats, who called a cheery greeting to him as he went.

"Nam-yeh!" he shouted back over his shoulder.

On the other side of the valley, Ode picked his way up the mountain slope, following a well-used track to the shepherds' hut. He knew some of the shepherds, but when he entered, they were not pleased by his announcement that the High-Kin had sent him. Ode sighed quietly to himself and wondered if it would be like the yak herders all over again.

But the shepherds, if they resented Ode, did not resort to calling him names. Most were older men and women who were naturally quiet and withdrawn, and they kept their comments to themselves. Ode swapped places with one of their members and, after a few trial shifts over a period of days, he was finally permitted to watch the sheep at night. There had been more killings recently and the team were disheartened. The lead shepherd, a woman with white hair and brown eyes named Leai, sent Ode to his shift that evening with a warning that should a pack of wolves attack, Ode must be on his guard. It would not do to play the hero and lose his life.

Ode took his time finding a suitable perch for the evening. He had become accustomed to the mountainside across the valley where the yaks grazed, developing his own particular seats that he enjoyed, seats settled into the crevices of rocks or cocooned by scrubby bushes. He was unfamiliar with the curving of the land here and it took a while to become comfortable in the fading light. Arrow was forced to stay back and slither through the undergrowth since the sheep would scatter in a panic if they so much as sensed him near.

The cupped valley began to darken, as if the light were being poured out of it, and the coolness of nighttime arrived. The mountains were notoriously cold after sundown—even in the early summer—and Ode wrapped his fur coat tightly around himself. He was seated on an overhanging rock with the sheep grazing below and he could see the peaceful quietness of the valley stretching out before them. There were pinpricks of light from the huts of workers across the mountainside and in the valley, like yellow stitches in black velvet. He imagined the groups of men and women he knew from his days working in the fields, sharing stories after dinner at the temple, gathered around the fire with mending in their laps or a bucket of peas to shell. He had often seen them collected like that in groups, and he had always wondered why it could not be like that with the herders. Those who watched the livestock all seemed distant and separate.

Ode looked across the valley to the Castle Temple, with its glowing blaze of lights, cut into the rock. He would swap even the groups of men and women gathered around the fires in the valley to be in the temple surrounded by the Kins and Kinesses. Inside those red walls, life seemed so pure. Ode had often been sent to the temple in the evenings to complete odd jobs, and he had noted the pleasant evening hush that descended as the sun faded from the sky. The younger Kins and Kinesses would retreat to their dormitories to practice their prayers, watched over by the older members. Candles would alight as many wandered off in groups to read scripture together while the moon steadily soared into the sky. And Ode wanted to be among them. He wanted it desperately—he wanted it too much.

Ode pulled himself off his perch and trudged down the mountainside to collect some sheep that had drifted away. He gathered the herd back together, then returned to his post. His mind often wandered while he watched over the animals and he speculated, not for the first time, whether that was the very reason the High-Kin had placed him there. It would be too easy to muddle along in the valley with the friendly groups of workers and to never have the time or the space to contemplate the gods.

Ode rarely thought of the Taone or his past life if he could help it. The memories were too painful and too distant. Sometimes during ceremonies, when the Kins and Kinesses prayed, he would mutter about Cala and Blue Moon, asking for their safety and protection, but he would not let himself think too long on such things. These days, he made a conscious effort to push them from his mind. He did not often think of his Magic, either, and he suspected that it had all but disappeared. Sometimes he caught himself wondering if he really ever did transform into a bird. He certainly felt no desire to do so anymore.

Hunched on the rock, Ode looked up to the vast sky. It was black and flat now, scattered with stars like freckles. Ode wondered if there were eyes watching him; he wondered if he was not alone.

If you are the gods then tell me to join the temple, he pleaded.

Around him the lights of the huts were gradually extinguished as the workers fell asleep. Opposite, the temple was fading to a pale glow as many went to their beds and only those intending to pray or read into the night kept their candles flickering.

Send me a sign, please, Ode prayed. *Show me what I must do.*

Arrow growled and Ode's eyes snapped open.

Ode could just barely see his wolf's crouched, gray form in the moonlight, hackles high and mouth pulled back in a snarl. The sheep had heard the sound and were beginning to run away—round shadows disappearing down the mountainside. Ode clenched his jaw and felt for the dagger tucked into his boot. He wondered if it was the pack of mountain wolves everyone had been chattering about at mealtimes. His heart began to hammer at the thought.

Arrow's growl grew louder and deeper as Ode edged off his rock and stood behind his companion. His fingers folded around the handle of his dagger. Though he sometimes practiced the fighting he and Blue Moon had once trained for together, he knew that the reality of a battle was different and he was afraid.

Ode crept a little closer and held the dagger high, poised ready for a fight, but it was not a pack of wolves he saw. His held breath whooshed out in a gasp, and he almost stumbled. Before him in the moonlight was a snow leopard. He knew that it must be the infamous mountain beast, for there was a painting of one in the temple. He also knew that they were rare. Erek had told him that he would most likely live his whole life in the mountains and never set eyes on such a creature. But before him now was an animal with a long, squat body and silvery fur marked with black rings. Its head was small and its tail long. It had piercing blue eyes, and it stood frozen, one of its large front paws lifted.

Arrow's growl exploded into a bark and he leaped off his haunches at the snow leopard. The two collided with screams of rage and snapped and scratched at each other. Their roars tore through the quiet of the night and Ode felt sure the whole mountainside must be awoken. The two animals fought fiercely on their hind legs before the leopard swiped Arrow away with its great claws. The wolf was knocked back with a whine and a line of blood stained his fur. Ode saw the leopard get ready to pounce and he instinctively ran forward, his knife in his hands.

"No!"

Ode stepped but one pace before a flash of red leaped from the shadows and jumped onto him.

He felt the knife in his hand tear at something. There was the sound of ripping before Ode fell against the rocks with a groan of pain, the knife knocked from his grasp. He looked up to see a small figure with a red cloak scrambling through the darkness. He knew instantly that it must be a Kiness, for the knife had cut her headscarf in two and it was falling away.

"Jet!" she cried, and the leopard responded with a purr.

But Ode scarcely noticed, for he was looking at her hair. As the headscarf dropped away, a tumble of thick, golden waves like the dazzling blaze of the sun escaped down her back. He heard her cry in alarm, and he saw her snatching for the scraps of material to cover herself. He wanted to call out to her, but he was mesmerized by the luminous shine she emitted.

In an instant, she had disappeared, fading into the night. The leopard followed, and Arrow growled after it. Ode, meanwhile, was left with sunbeams in his eyes and his heart stolen like some kind of Magic.

CHAPTER TWENTY-TWO

The Kiness

There were no sheep killings that night. Once Ode had recovered from his moonlit encounter, he stumbled down the mountainside to collect the panicked sheep, relieved that none were missing. Arrow's cut was not deep and only his dignity suffered a lasting wound. Once he had allowed Ode to fuss over him and clean his injury, he retreated to the undergrowth, growling quietly to himself.

For the rest of the night, Ode sat in a daze. He watched the sun slowly stretch over the peaks of the distant purple mountains and he saw bright yellow light fall into the valley, but he barely noticed. He could think of nothing but the Kiness he had seen and the beautiful radiance of her golden hair.

When Leai came to relieve him that morning, she saw that none of the sheep had been taken and could not contain her amazement. She patted Ode on the back and congratulated his skill, but Ode said nothing.

"I be hearing an almighty uproar in the night," she said. "That be you fighting off the wolves?"

Ode nodded dumbly, for he did not know what else to say.

"You be a blessing for us," she said.

Ode felt like a fraud, so he bowed his head.

But even once he had retreated to the wooden hut to rest for the morning, he could not forget the Kiness. He tried to eat, but he was not hungry, and he tried to sleep, but he could not, due to the spangles of golden light that danced across his vision when he closed his eyes.

That evening, he followed the other workers from the valley up the steps to the temple for supper, but his thoughts were elsewhere. When the yak herders hissed jibes at his back, he did not notice, and when one of the milkmaids tried to share a joke with him, he looked back at her blankly. Inside the eating hall, he scanned the crowd for the golden-haired Kiness, but if she was there, he could not see her.

Ode was sulky and preoccupied throughout dinner. He let Erek chatter away beside him and grunted occasionally to pretend he was listening, but he did not register what the Kin said. Spooning hot broth into his mouth, Ode looked up often, studying all of the Kinesses in his line of sight and prompting some of them to frown back at him. He felt sure that if she were there, he would just *know*; her unrivalled beauty would radiate from her. Once the meal finished, a crowd gathered around him to offer congratulations for his successful night fighting away the wolves.

"You be a hero!"

"If you be watching our herds then they be safe!"

Ode stared at his hands and tried to ignore the glares from the yak herders, who were making faces at him from the other side of the room.

"I barely did anything," he answered truthfully, but the crowd all shook their heads and chided him for being so modest.

At the first opportunity, Ode slipped away, leaving the crowd still huddled and babbling in the eating hall. He hurried across one of the courtyards, his sandals scuffing the flagstones, and disappeared down a quiet, dim hallway with a sigh of relief.

"Psst!"

Ode jumped and peered into a shadowed room beside him. He could just about see the outline of a person crouched against the wall.

"Come in, and pull the curtain across!"

It was her. Ode's heart pumped in his chest. He darted into the room and pulled the velvet curtain across the doorway so fast that Arrow was left stranded on the other side, growling.

"You be telling your wolf to be quiet?" she said, her voice like the soft gush of a stream. "We be found if he nay quiet."

Ode's throat was suddenly dry and he just nodded dumbly.

"Well, be getting on with it then!"

"Hush," Ode croaked at the curtain, and Arrow quieted on the other side with a disgruntled snort.

"That be better," said the Kiness.

As Ode's eyes adjusted to the darkened room, he saw that it was indeed the girl he had met last night—the one who had been bathed in moonlight. She wore a red cloak neatly tied over a shapeless brown dress, but even that could not detract from her astonishing beauty. She was small, fair, and graceful, with delicate features and large blue eyes. A line of neat, careful stitches curved across the pale fabric of her headdress where it had been sewn back together.

"I be having to say I tore it myself," she said, noticing him looking at it. "The High-Kiness nay believe me truly, but she be too busy to bother much."

Ode simply nodded.

"I be seeing you run out of the eating hall and I rushed down the other hallway to catch you. I be hearing them all around you in the hall talking about last night. . . ."

The girl bit down on her full, red lip and her blue eyes grew worried as she paused, waiting for him to answer.

"I . . . I didn't tell anyone," Ode sputtered eventually.

"Praise be to the gods!"

The girl raised her hands toward the ceiling and collapsed against one of the many desks in the room, clearly in relief. They were in a temple classroom, normally full of young Kins and Kinesses learning their scripture during the day.

"You know that Jet was nay ever going to hurt the sheep, yes?" she quickly added. "You know that we was trying to protect them?"

Ode nodded vaguely, staring at her headdress again. He longed to see the golden shine of her hair folded beneath the pale tucks. He could still remember it, flashing like a glittering ray of sunshine.

"You will nay tell the High-Kin or High-Kiness any of this . . . will you?"

Ode paused. He desperately wanted to please her, but he did not like the idea of keeping secrets from the High-Kin or High-Kiness. He did not want to deceive those who had given him so much.

"Why were you there?" he asked finally.

"To protect the sheep, like I be saying."

"But, why did you have a snow leopard with you? And aren't all Kins and Kinesses supposed to stay in the temple after dark?"

The Kiness kneaded her long, elegant fingers together. The more Ode looked at her, the more he became convinced that she was the most beautiful girl he had ever seen. He had to stop himself from reaching out to touch her cheek; he longed to know if its shining, pearly luster was real.

"Jet is my . . . friend. I found her many seasons ago, and I be only able to see her at night when it's dark and the others asleep."

"The snow leopard is your companion?"

"Yes."

"Kins and Kinesses don't have companions!"

"You have a wolf, do you not?" the Kiness faltered and quickly corrected herself. "I mean, you be having a wolf, yes?"

"Why did you just—" began Ode, frowning.

"I be leaving now," she interrupted, still twisting her fingers. "I be having to go or else they be wondering where I am. Just be promising me that you nay be telling anyone. I nay know what would happen if it was all found out. I be only trying to help."

The girl gave him a beseeching look as she gathered herself together, and Ode felt panic bloom in his chest. He did not want her to go. He wanted them to talk in this classroom all night.

"I won't tell," he said recklessly.

"Thank you," she whispered, then overwhelmed him with a sweet smile that made his cheeks flame red.

"But what is your name?" he cried as she pulled back the curtain from the doorway to leave. "Please," he added, when he saw her deliberating.

"My name is Briar," she answered softly, at last.

"Briar," he repeated.

And then, with another shimmering smile, she was gone.

All night, Ode felt as if he were floating among the purple mountaintops. He could not sleep, all he could do was dream of Briar. He was sure that he must never have set eyes on her before, for he surely would have been struck instantly by her beauty. There were many Kinesses at the temple and they were always coming and going, so it was possible that their paths had never crossed. But if he had never seen her, then he hoped desperately that none of the other boys or men working in the valley had either. Sometimes he heard the yak herders laughing and joking about the milkmaids or the Kinesses. He did not like the way they talked and the thought of them snickering over Briar made him furious. At one point in the night, he sat bolt upright and punched his pillow, so overcome by the very thought of it.

In the early hours of the next morning, he finally drifted into a light, fitful sleep, plagued by thoughts of golden hair that burned like the summer sun and blue eyes as calm and deep as a lake. He awoke to fervent voices barking orders and a fluttering sensation in his chest. His first thoughts were of Briar and he gazed around the room with a dopey grin.

"Glad someone be looking so happy," said the shepherd in the bed next to him. "You not be hearing the news yet, then."

Ode quickly wiped the smile off his face and listened as the others told him about the massacre during the night. The wolves had come again and destroyed almost a quarter of the flock. The shepherd on duty had tried to stop them and had been injured in his efforts. He had only managed to save his own life by leaping down the mountainside and hiding in a crevice.

"I know it be not your turn to look after the sheep again, Ode," said Leai, her face appearing worn with worry. "But will you take the night shift this evening?"

Ode nodded.

That morning in the eating hall, the night's killings were all anyone could talk about. The room vibrated with gory details and scandal. Ode, however, had other thoughts on his mind and he looked for Briar everywhere. He loitered around the crowds of young Kinesses, and he scrutinized every headdress that passed, but he did not see her. He was on his second lap of the eating hall when Erek called him over.

"There always be a seat next to me for you, you knows that. Why you be walking around the hall looking for spaces?" Erek asked.

Ode mumbled something about not noticing him and finally sat down, feeling gloomy. If he could not see Briar at mealtimes, when could he see her? He did not know what he would do if he never set eyes on her again; he could not even bear the thought.

"Those wolf killings on your mind?" asked Erek quietly.

Ode nodded, because that seemed as good a reason as any for his remoteness.

"Thought that be it," said the Kin, slurping his water. "Your wolf be acting strange, too."

Ode looked at Arrow, who was staring intently back at him. All night the wolf had nudged him and growled as Ode tossed and turned in his bed.

"I reckon they put out a few shepherds tonight to watch over the flock so you nay need to worry, yes?"

"Yes. Thank you, Erek."

"Welcome, boy. Welcome. These wolves be running away with their tails between their legs with you and your animal on watch tonight."

Ode hoped he was right and he prayed for it that evening at the ceremony in the Room of the Gods. Again, he searched the packed temple for a pair of large blue eyes in the smoky incense haze. But he saw none. The room overflowed with bodies and it was difficult to decipher the person beside you, let alone anyone else. Ode let the chants and whispers wash over him as he stood in his usual spot at the back and he added his own words to their prayers. He asked that the flock be kept safe tonight, and he asked that he might be given the chance to see Briar again soon. He felt bad for lingering longest on the latter request.

That evening, as night poured into the valley like black water cascading into a well, Ode trudged across the mountainside to the remaining flock. He was joined by three shepherds who were to stand watch with him and all were quiet and solemn. They felt the weight of their responsibility keenly and each was a little afraid of the gory stories they had heard repeated in the eating hall that evening.

After agreeing on a warning signal, the shepherds went their separate ways across the mountainside, carrying weapons they did not know how to use. Ode had offered to watch from the highest point in front of the mountain pass that led into a neighboring valley. He wanted to be far away from the others so he could daydream of Briar in peace. He found a comfortable vantage point from which he could see some of the flock and settled down on a rock, wrapping his furs around him.

He started by imagining bumping into Briar in one of the long hallways of the temple. He invented a gentle summer afternoon after he had spent the morning working in the fields. His shirt would be damp and sticking to his body and she would be impressed by his size and strength. He imagined catching her by surprise when no one else was around and when they collided, her headdress would topple off to reveal her long, glowing curls. He was about to envision stroking the soft curve of her cheek when he heard a growl.

The summer afternoon of his dreams disappeared and Ode found himself surrounded by darkness. Arrow was growling a warning nearby and Ode shrugged off his furs, scanning the shadows for danger. The flock was some distance off and he could not hear anything amiss except for his wolf's growl. He grabbed the dagger from his boot and climbed off the rock onto the dusty ground. He tried not to think of the bloody carcasses he had seen that morning littering the mountainside.

Ode flexed his shoulders, his heart beating against his chest, and it was then that he saw a pair of glittering eyes watching him.

Before he could cry out a warning, the mountain wolf had burst from the shadows and it was all Ode could do to tumble out of its path. Arrow rushed from the bushes, charging to Ode's defense, and the two wolves snapped and circled one another, spittle oozing from their sharp teeth.

A distant howl echoed from farther down the mountain, and Ode heard one of the shepherds whistle a warning call. He stumbled to his feet and grabbed for the axe resting beside his things. He had been given it before his shift, but he had never wielded such a weapon in real combat and he had hoped he would never have to. The axe felt awkward and heavy in his hands. He tried to swing it menacingly at the attacking brown wolf, but he narrowly missed clobbering Arrow over the head, so he retreated.

As Ode backed away, movement from above caught his eye and he jumped aside just before another large, white wolf pounced from the overhanging rocks of the mountain pass. Sweat gathering on his brow, Ode whistled the warning call as loudly as he could and prayed there would be a shepherd free to come to his aid. His signal bounced between the rocks, but no one appeared, and in the distance, he could hear snarls and shouts as another attack commenced elsewhere.

The white wolf and the brown wolf backed Arrow and Ode into a corner and began moving in, their bodies crouched low to the ground and their lips pulled back to reveal sharp, glinting teeth. Ode swung his axe and clipped the white wolf's muzzle, drawing a spurt of blood that made him gasp. The white wolf howled in fury and launched himself at Arrow, knocking both of them to the ground in a writhing, snapping tussle.

Ode watched them frantically, his axe raised, but he did not want to swing it again for fear of hitting Arrow. The brown wolf joined the fight, grabbing hold of Arrow's neck in his jaws and Ode heard his companion whimper. He dropped his axe and grabbed hold of his dagger again instead, ready to jump into the skirmish, but a cry stopped him.

"Wait!"

Ode turned to see a silver shadow soaring from the rocks above. It landed gracefully with an almighty roar that made the wolves pause. Jet, the snow leopard, launched herself into the fray, scratching and biting at the white wolf until his hold on Arrow's neck slackened.

Ode watched as a red-cloaked figure came running across the rocks toward them. In the darkness her fair skin shone like moonlight and her red cloak swirled about her ankles like a rosy mist. Ode's eyes were so transfixed by Briar that he did not see a dark shape leaping at him.

"Watch out!" Briar screamed.

Ode barely had time to turn before the brown wolf attacked him.

Part Four

A silver figure stood on the shore of the Wild Lands. Her white hair rippled in the salty breeze like streams of moonlight and her emerald robe pooled at her feet, damp with sand. She was so young. The cluster of Magic Beasts and Magical Beings that had formed to greet her were unsure if she was a girl or a woman or something else entirely. Ethereal though she was, she did not look like the warrior queen they had been hoping for. She did not look like the commander of a rebel army.

"I suppose I ought not to ask how you knew I was coming," she said.

The small ship on which she had sailed across the Route Sea bobbed on the distant waves behind her. A rowboat traveled back and forth ferrying her guards and council, but these men and women looked suspiciously like farmers and fishermen. Only the tall, broad man with a scar across his eye who stood at her side seemed as if he might understand battle tactics and warring.

"We foresaw it," said one of the Magic Beasts, a creature with tusks and horns. "We only just barely saw that you would come . . . you are difficult for even our best seers to work out sometimes. You are too powerful."

The silver-skinned woman pursed her lips. She wished that she were astride her warhorse since she felt small and awkward on her feet. She missed the reassuring presence of Champ, her companion, but he would not have liked the journey.

"But there is one who has been anticipating your arrival far longer than all of us," added a black-haired woman from the group of Magical Beings. "Your mother has been calling for you often, Beauty."

"*Queen*," corrected the man with a scar across his eye.

Beauty flinched and tried not to appear as nervous as she felt. "This is my general," she said, gesturing to the scarred man. "He will accompany me to your leaders. The rest of my party you will feed and make welcome. This has been a difficult passage for us."

She spoke clearly, with all of the dignity and strength she could muster, and she hoped it was enough.

The Magic Beasts and Magical Beings exchanged glances.

"As you wish, Queen," one creature replied at last.

They led the newcomers to their camp in silence. The men, women, and children of all nationalities that they passed paused to watch the procession and stared with undisguised curiosity as a silver-skinned queen wound through their makeshift huts and tents. Finally, the group stopped before a large barn that was so new, its wooden walls still smelled freshly chopped.

"Our leaders are expecting you inside," said a Magic Beast with fangs. "We will feed your people while you speak."

Beauty nodded in what she hoped was a queenly manner. Then, with her breath held, she waited as the doors of the barn were pulled open. Without giving herself a moment to turn back, she strode into a room filled with Magic creatures of various shapes and sizes. Her general followed, never more than a pace behind her, and his fingers twitched as if he longed to take her hand.

"Greetings, Queen," said a collection of voices.

The barn doors closed and a nearby fire crackled. Beauty frowned and took a step closer to her general, wishing she did not have to wear the encumbering robe that twisted around her ankles.

"Why is—" she began, but the words fell from her lips when she saw an old woman wrapped in blankets beside the fire, shivering despite the warm spring weather.

"Asha . . ." Beauty whispered.

"We keep it burning for her," explained a bare-chested man in halting Pervoroccoian. "She says that she is always cold."

He had blue patterns tattooed across his dark skin and there was something familiar about his face that Beauty could not quite make out.

"Beauty, my child, is that you?" asked the old woman in a trembling voice.

Beauty swallowed, unable to reply.

"My queen would like some privacy with her mother," said the general. "Alliances and such can be discussed in a few moments, yes?"

The Magic creatures reluctantly nodded their consent and began filing out of the barn, mumbling as they went. The last to leave was an old man who walked with a stick. He smiled at the silvery woman and chuckled to himself.

"We have met once before," he said. "Do you remember?"

Beauty shook her head.

"It was at the docks of Sago when I was trying to transport Magics out of the country and bring them to safety. You were just a little girl . . ."

"Lyan!" said Beauty suddenly, remembering the kind lion-like creature with a bushy tail. "Is he here?" she asked.

"I am afraid I do not know. There were many that did not survive the Magical Cleansing or the passage to the Wild Lands."

"Oh."

The old man tapped his stick upon the floor and made to leave.

"Your mother has spoken of nothing but you for as long as I have known her," he said over his shoulder as he shuffled out. "Be kind, for she has tried to do what is right even if she has not always succeeded."

Once they were alone, Beauty's shoulders sagged and her royal mask fell away. She felt a hand reach out and touch her elbow.

"I am still here," said Beast. "But I will go if you would prefer?"

"No, please stay."

Beauty knelt before her mother—this woman who was like a stranger. She wanted to accuse Asha of abandonment and cruelty, but the time for such things had passed.

"I thought you were dead when I left you in Sago," Beauty said, finally. "I almost did not believe it when I dreamed that you were still alive."

Asha was shriveled and gray. She looked seasons and seasons older than the woman Beauty had met in Sago.

"I feared you would not come," Asha croaked. "I feared you hated me . . ."

"No," said Beauty, but she did not sound convincing.

"It is fine. I know I have not been a mother to you, but I have loved you from afar—please know that. I am so blessed to see you one last time, and I am thankful that there is someone who will look after you . . ." Asha's eyes wandered to Beast standing nearby.

Beauty blushed. "I can look after myself!" she snapped.

"I know, I know." Asha sighed. "But you have found love and that is a powerful kind of Magic that I never had."

"My father must be a cruel man."

"I would once have defended him, but I think he deceived me. I was a girl when we met, and I was impressed by his Magic and his skills. I followed him across the realm, and then one day, in the mountains, he disappeared. I have been trying to do what he wished of me since—building an army to fight against the Magical Cleansing just as he did during The Red Wars—but I have not heard from him since. I think he never loved me at all."

Asha began to cough and her whole body shook with the effort. Tears trickled down her withered cheeks, and Beauty took hold of her hand.

"Mother, you once told me that I must lead an army of Magics and . . . you are right. I have been gathering rebels in the Hillands and we come here now to join with your people."

"That is good, my daughter."

"Together, we will march on Pervorocco, and we will end this Magical Cleansing."

"Be careful of your father."

"No matter about my father."

"Yes, Beauty! Do not think that he is not in this somewhere. He is controlling all of us in some way. Do not let him use you like he used me."

Beauty glanced over her shoulder at Beast, who was staring at his hands.

"We know he is capable of great evil," Beauty said. "I will heed your warning."

"When he created you, you took some of his Magic," Asha wheezed. "He thinks that he is powerful, and he is right, but he gave away part of himself to you. You must remember that."

Beauty nodded. "I will not forget," she said.

"For now, it is just good to see you once more, my child."

Beauty squeezed her mother's thin, frail fingers.

"It is good to see you also," she said. "Truly."

Asha smiled and took her last breath.

CHAPTER TWENTY-THREE

The Night Shift

Ode felt sure he was dreaming. A pair of large blue eyes looked down at him from a fair, beautiful face. Briar gently touched his cheek, her fingers like the stroke of a feather against his skin.

"Can you hear me?" she asked again.

He did not want to answer; he just wanted to keep feeling her touch.

"If you can hear me, I need you to speak."

Ode blinked and gulped away some of the grit at the back of his throat.

"Why aren't you speaking like the other Kins and Kinesses?" he asked in a croaky voice.

Briar blushed. "At least you are alive," she said, and Ode dared to believe that she sounded pleased.

He did not want to take his eyes away, but behind her head he could see the night's sky studded with stars, and all at once he remembered the wolf attack.

"Where's Arrow?" he asked.

At the sound of his name, Arrow appeared, pushing his snout into Ode's face and snuffling at his ears.

"It is all right. Your wolf is here, and he is safe," said Briar. She giggled when Arrow began washing Ode's forehead with his rough tongue.

"That's enough," Ode groaned, pushing him off.

"Can you sit up?" asked Briar.

Ode did not want to sit up; he wanted Briar to stay knelt over him forever.

"That wolf jumped on you and I think you will have some scratches and bruising," she added. "But there should be no lasting damage."

Ode imagined her examining him, and he blushed in the darkness. Wishing he did not have to move, he struggled onto his elbows and winced. She was right about his aches and pains.

"How did you find us?" he asked.

"I heard about the killings last night and came out to keep watch, too. It was Jet who heard the wolves attacking you."

Ode looked over at the snow leopard who sat some distance off, licking her paws, her long tail flicking from side to side. There were two dark, motionless bodies next to her—fur matted with blood.

"We would have been killed without you," said Ode.

Briar glanced down at her hands. "It was Jet, not me. She fought the wolf off you when it attacked."

A loud whistle made them both jump. Shouts echoed across the mountainside, and Jet growled.

"The shepherds are looking for you," said Briar. "We must go."

"Wait!"

Ode grabbed hold of her small, delicate hand. She gasped in surprise and he could not believe that he was being so bold.

"Come back tomorrow night," he said.

Briar shook her head.

"I need to . . ." Ode tried to think of a convincing reason. "I need to speak with you about your companion."

They both heard heavy footsteps as the shepherds approached. Briar tried to pull her hand away, but Ode held on to it desperately.

"Please!" he said.

She shook her head and this time, he did not try to stop her.

Jet was already leaping between the rocks, ready to vanish through the mountain pass. Ode watched Briar scramble over the rocks, her cloak trailing behind her.

"Ode!" the shepherds were calling, drawing nearer. "Ode, shout to us!"

Briar paused at the mouth of the mountain pass, and suddenly, she turned around to look at him.

"Tomorrow I will be here," she called in a whisper, and then she disappeared.

Ode was hailed a hero. He was even summoned to see the High-Kin and the High-Kiness, who personally thanked him for his bravery. Word spread quickly that Ode and Arrow had killed two mountain wolves, and for the rest of that day, he was overwhelmed with congratulations from everyone who crossed his path. The temple did not lose a single sheep. There had been another attack down the mountainside that night, but the shepherds had rallied together and fought the wolves away.

Ode knew he should feel guilty for receiving such undue praise, but he could think of nothing but Briar. The day seemed to creep by too slowly and he found himself glancing at the sun every few minutes, longing for it to scurry across the sky. In the eating hall, he searched for her with tired, bleary eyes, but again, he was sure she was not there. When evening finally came, he bounded up to Leai, the head of the shepherds, offering his services for the night shift.

Leai tried to dissuade him, arguing that he needed to rest, but he persisted until she finally agreed. As the sun sank below the mountains and the stars appeared in the sky, Ode found himself striding toward the flock with a grin.

When he was finally alone beside the mountain pass, Ode felt like he could not sit still. He paced up and down, counting the sheep he could see over and over again to keep himself occupied. He ran his fingers through his hair so that it would not appear so messy and practiced standing casually with his chest pushed out. Above him, peering down from a rock, Arrow watched with bemused detachment.

After a while, Ode began to wonder if Briar would ever appear. He looked at the sliver of a moon, like a slice of cream cut into the night's sky, and judged that he had already been waiting some hours. He started to feel foolish and wondered if this was all a joke. Perhaps she was lying in her bed in the temple right now, laughing at him.

Ode fiddled with his cotton shirt, chosen especially because it was the cleanest clothing he had. The ties around his neck were undone because he had wanted to show off the new muscles in his neck, but now he just felt stupid and cold. He hastily tied them up and wondered why he had ever thought Briar would be interested in him.

Ode had so thoroughly convinced himself she was not coming that when she suddenly appeared at the mouth of the mountain pass, his mouth dropped open in surprise. He jumped up from his slouched position against a scrubby bush and tripped over one of the roots, landing face first on the dusty ground.

"Oh!" gasped Briar, hurrying down the mountainside. "You be all right?"

Ode quickly climbed to his feet, his cheeks red. "I'm fine," he said. "How are you?"

Briar stopped awkwardly in front of him, burying her hands in her skirts.

"I be well, yes."

"Why are you talking like that again?"

Briar's brow creased. "Like what?" she asked.

"Like the other Kins and Kinesses. You weren't speaking like that last night."

"I . . . I be having to speak like this. Otherwise, they be suspicious."

"But they're not here. You can speak normally to me."

Briar sighed. "That is just it," she muttered. "I do not speak normally. I sound different."

A shadow slipped through the mountain pass behind her, its long tail flicking from side to side. Jet crept over the rocks, keeping her eyes on Briar.

"Why do you speak with a different accent?" asked Ode, wanting to fill the silence. "When did you come to the Castle Temple?"

Briar looked as if she might not answer him, and then finally she mumbled, "I came here when I was a baby. I do not know why I sound different."

"I think your accent is nice," said Ode truthfully; he could have listened to her soft, sweet voice all night.

"I thought you wanted to ask me about my companion," said Briar, shuffling her feet. "That is why I came."

"Yes! Let's . . . um . . . sit." Ode gestured to some rocks and they both sat, avoiding looking at each other. Briar tucked her feet beneath her and pulled her cloak into her lap.

"I have never met anyone who has a companion before," Ode began. "I just wanted to ask you about it. Where did you find Jet?"

The snow leopard slid gracefully from the shadows and butted her head against Briar's shoulder. Briar giggled and tickled the chin of her large cat until Jet purred.

"I found her when she was a baby. A wolf was chasing her, and I threw stones at it until it ran away. She has been mine ever since, and I visit her whenever I can."

"That's just like me!" said Ode. "I found Arrow when he was a cub."

Briar smiled at him.

"So, do you think Jet was drawn to you?" he asked.

Briar's smile fell away. "You mean like Magic?" she whispered, her voice faltering.

"No . . . I didn't mean . . ."

"It is *nothing* like that."

"Of course not!" agreed Ode in a squeak. "No, no, it's nothing like that," he added, lowering his voice to a deep grumble. "That would be . . . terrible."

Briar nodded, and Jet glared at Ode with sharp blue eyes.

Ode tugged at the ties of his shirt, wondering desperately what to say next.

"Is that all that you wanted to ask me?" Briar said after a long pause.

"Yes," said Ode, because he could think of nothing else to say. He knew he was ruining this moment and would regret it later.

"May I ask *you* some questions?"

"Yes!" Ode tried to mask his initial excitement with a casual shrug.

"What does it feel like when you are away from your wolf?"

Ode glanced at Arrow, who was still laying on the rocks above them, watching with a sulky expression and pretending he did not care about their nighttime visitors.

"I'm never away from him," Ode replied.

"I wish it were the same for me. I cannot be seen with Jet in daylight, because I do not know what the others would think if they saw us together." As she spoke, Briar buried her hands in the silky fur around Jet's neck. "It hurts when we are away from each other. It is like . . . like part of me is missing."

Ode nodded. "I can imagine," he said.

"What is your name?" Briar asked, suddenly. "I realized that I do not know it."

Ode had repeated her name so often, muttering it in his sleep and reciting it in his mind: *Briar, Briar, Briar, Beautiful Briar.* He had not even considered that he was nothing but a nameless shepherd to her.

"My name is Ode," he said quietly.

"Ode," she echoed, and he loved the way it sounded with her accent. He wished that she would say it again.

He glanced sideways at her, noticing the pretty curves of her legs, tucked beneath her, and her straight nose, silhouetted in the moonlight. He caught the hostile gaze of Jet and quickly looked away.

"I think your wolf does not like me," she said. "He has not moved off that rock."

"He's just jealous," said Ode without thinking, and then blushed furiously, the tips of his ears burning pink.

"I have heard Kins and Kinesses at the temple say that they come from all over the realm," he babbled quickly. "Which country did you come from? I haven't seen someone who looks quite like you before."

It was Briar's turn to blush, and she fiddled with the edge of her headdress, which folded over her ears.

"I do not know where I came from," she said. "The High-Kiness brought me back from her travels when I was a baby and she forgets where she visited. I suppose she has been to a lot of places."

"Your eyes are so blue. . . ."

"Yes, I know that I look strange."

"No, you're—" Ode stopped himself before he said something embarrassing. "You don't look strange," he corrected himself.

She bowed her head and smiled. "I have never seen anyone who looked quite like you before either," she said. "And I live with Kins and Kinesses from all over the realm."

Her eyes wandered across his face and Ode's heart thumped in his chest.

"Your skin is golden brown—and your hair is so dark. Where did you come from?"

"The Wild Lands."

"Oh, you are the Wildlander they brought back?"

"Yes."

Both Kiness and shepherd stared at the dark valley below them, sleeping and still. They could hear the faint rush of the wind through the rocks and the contented bleating of the sheep.

"I must go now," said Briar.

Ode jolted with surprise. It could not even be midnight yet; he had not expected her to go so soon.

"But . . . but . . . what about the wolves? What if they come back?"

"You will be able to hold them off," said Briar, looking away. "I have stayed too long as it is, and I must go."

Ode watched her gather up her skirts and turn to leave, dying to think of something that would stall her.

"You will not tell anyone about me, will you?" she asked.

He shook his head.

"I be seeing you," she said in the accent of the temple.

"I be seeing you," he mumbled in response.

Jet galloped ahead—a silvery shadow flitting through the mountain pass—and Ode watched with fingers clenched as Briar followed the leopard. Then she stopped, and just like last time, she turned back to look at him over her shoulder.

"If you are here the night after tomorrow then I will meet you," she said, as if she could not help it.

Ode struggled to keep a delighted grin from breaking across his face.

"Yes . . . yes! I'll be here."

Once she disappeared, he punched the air with delight.

Two nights later, the pair met again. They sat side by side on the same rocks, staring down at the valley and stealing glances at each other, blushing furiously. Ode did not dare to think that Briar liked him the way he liked her. He knew that, as a Kiness, she had taken vows against such things, but he simply could not help but find her enchanting.

Every time he looked at her, he noticed something he had not seen before, like the pretty, pronounced cupid's bow of her lips or the elegant contours of her cheeks.

As they chatted at their second meeting, it slowly dawned on Ode that Briar was lonely. He discovered that he had never seen her in the eating hall before, because she dined in a separate room, and he would not have come across her around the temple, because she kept to the classrooms and the dormitories, only venturing out for the daily ceremonies.

"Why do you have to live like that?" he asked.

"The High-Kiness says that I am in training. She thinks that I could be the next High-Kiness one day."

"But the High-Kiness walks all around the temple and—"

"That is just what she says," Briar interrupted, and Ode did not want to push the matter.

The two spoke instead of the temple and the few Kins and Kinesses they both knew, their chatter drifting into the night sky. Ode managed to make her laugh and he considered it a great triumph. To hear her giggle was, he felt, the biggest achievement of his life thus far.

"I must go," Briar said abruptly, just as Ode was beginning to relax.

He felt the same disappointment and the same frustration as before. Briar did not mention meeting him again until the very last moment, as she stood at the top of the mountain pass and looked over her shoulder. She told him the night after next she would be here again, should he wish to meet her.

Ode practically collapsed onto the ground in relief as she faded into the darkness.

They met for the third time, and so it went on. Sometimes Briar did not appear and Ode knew it was because she could not creep out of the temple. She had explained that it was difficult to leave her dormitory unnoticed if the High-Kiness was prowling around, and on the nights she did not arrive, Ode sat sulking in the chilly darkness. He knew that his feelings for her were dangerous because they could not be returned, but he could not help it.

Sitting next to one another on the rocks at each meeting, both Ode and Briar felt they had finally found someone at the temple who understood them. They did not think each other's companions odd and Ode was no more afraid of Jet than Briar was of Arrow.

"I think I have almost won him over," Briar said with a grin one night, when the wolf wagged his tail as she appeared.

Jet, too, was gradually becoming used to Ode, and she would sometimes flick her tail around his neck and rub her shoulder against his back if she was in a friendly mood.

"That means she likes you," Briar laughed the first time it happened.

Neither shepherd nor Kiness wanted to overthink their meetings. For the moment they were happy living night by night, meeting by meeting. They looked forward to seeing each other with fluttering thrills in their chests, and then, afterwards, a low sorrow when they were forced to part. If they thought too much about what they were doing, they knew they would realize the danger of it, so they tried not to think of it at all.

They established quickly that they were friends. It was Briar who said it first when they met one summer's night and shared a wedge of goat's cheese. Ode offered her the last piece and she asked, "Is this because I am your only friend?"

Ode blushed. "No, it's because you're my best friend," he said.

Briar grinned. "I suppose apart from Jet, you are my best friend, too."

"Of course," said Ode, trying to hide his joy.

"Of course," she echoed, impersonating him.

They both laughed. Friendship it certainly was. Yet, they did not realize that they were actually falling in love.

CHAPTER TWENTY-FOUR

The Changing

I t seemed Ode's life now revolved solely around Briar. He thought of her when he woke in the morning, and he thought about her all day as he dug vegetables in the valley and carried produce up the stone steps to the temple. He could not believe that she ventured out every other night to see him and a secret part of his heart dared to believe she might begin to share his deeper feelings. He knew that she was lonely and in need of a friend, but he hoped their meetings meant more to her than just friendship. The only problem in their bright, delicious summer full of love was Magic.

Ode was beginning to feel the old itching of his transformations. It was like a tickle between his shoulder blades that he could not scratch. At first, he thought it was merely due to the hot summer days, but when he began to dream again, he knew it was more than that. Now, when he went to sleep each night, it was not images of Briar and her beautiful face that danced through his thoughts, but visions of Cala. He saw her walking through sandy desert lands and searching sprawling cities. His past bitterness toward her had slowly trickled away with time and he was relieved to see her safe, but he wished that he knew what she was looking for. We wished he knew what his dreams meant.

As the summer cooled into autumn, Ode's Magic grew worse. He began to fall asleep with a sinking heart, fearful of what would happen. Several times he had woken in the shepherd's hut at night, on the edge of a transformation and only able to stop himself at the last moment. Tumbling onto the floor, he lay shaking with his teeth clenched and the white feather around his neck burning a hole into his chest. Luckily, no one else had noticed except Arrow, who whined in his ear and licked his cheek until he was calm once again. Ode did not want to turn into the white bird. He had thought that his Magic had left him and he had not been sorry to see it go. He hated to think what Briar would say if she knew about his gift and the thought made him despise himself.

"Is something the matter?" Briar asked one night, and she put her delicate hand on his arm.

Ode jumped at her touch and realized he had been staring silently at the valley below them.

"I don't feel well lately," he said.

"Oh, is there an ointment you can use? Have you asked the Kins and Kinesses at the temple? Your friend Molash is good at such things."

"Nothing would be able to help this."

Briar took her hand off his arm and pulled her cloak around her shoulders. She was silent for a moment before she asked, "Will you tell me what is wrong? Maybe I can help."

Ode winced, wishing he could. They spoke with each other easily now, laughing, joking, and teasing. Sometimes they still blushed and found looking into each other's eyes difficult, but the awkwardness of their first meetings had long disappeared. Ode wanted to tell her everything about him: his homeland, his past and his gift, but he felt she would not like it. Sometimes he hoped that if he told her, she might be able to see that he was still the same person. He had Magic, but he was still Ode. In the Room of the Gods, every evening he prayed that

Briar would one day understand, but he knew the time for that was not now.

"I . . . I am not sure I can even describe it," he said, picking at a piece of scrubby grass on the ground beside him.

Briar was quiet for a while and they both listened to the far-off bleating of the sheep and the purring of Jet, who lay stretched out nearby.

"I have not felt right recently either," she said.

Ode glanced at her in surprise. Briar was normally quiet and secretive, preferring to hear about his life in the valley with the other herders and his daily chores rather than talk about herself. If Ode wanted to hear her thoughts and feelings, he usually had to prod her for answers.

"I am worried about a friend," she continued. "I feel like she is in danger, but I do not know how to help."

"Another Kiness?" asked Ode.

Briar nodded. "It is Kayra. I think I have told you about her before? She is a good friend of mine, but for a while she has been . . . seeing one of the yak herders."

Both of them flushed and bit their lips. They knew that at the Castle Temple this was scandalous—and that it was exactly what *they* were also doing, too.

"This man was once a Kin, but he lost his way," Briar continued. "He and Kayra were friends, and she always hoped that he would return to the temple. She spent time talking to him about the gods and I–I–I think she became . . . attached to him."

Ode swallowed hard and began tearing the scrubby grass in his hands into little pieces. "That's terrible," he said.

"Yes, but there is more. Kayra has been changing lately, and I think there might be something wrong."

"How is she changing?"

"She is getting bigger, but she is not eating more food."

Briar mimed puffing out her cheeks.

"Oh," said Ode.

"Oh?"

"Perhaps she is with child?"

Briar gasped and her pale skin turned a violent red. She stared at Ode and had she not looked so horrified, Ode would have laughed.

"That is . . . that is *abominable!*" she stuttered.

Jet lifted her head and flicked her tail in concern, and from his perch on the rocks above, Arrow also looked down in surprise.

"It is impossible!" Briar cried.

With the training of a birther, Ode did not think it so strange, but he decided to keep that to himself. "Yes," he said, nodding in agreement.

"I think you have that wrong," Briar added.

"Yes, perhaps."

"No *perhaps* about it!" Briar suddenly stood and brushed down her plain skirt.

"It is time for me to go now," she said and marched primly through the mountain pass without even looking over her shoulder.

The following day, Ode worried he had offended her. He hoped that she would still appear at their next meeting, and though she took her time, she did eventually emerge through the darkness that evening. They did not speak of such things after that.

———◦∞◦———

As the fields and trees in the valley became brown and bare, Ode's Magic grew worse. It was a buzzing headache that he could never shake off and an ache in his arms and legs that would not subside no matter how much he stretched. Ode felt worn and exhausted, and it was beginning to show. After one dinner in the eating hall, Erek held him back.

"You be looking ill," said the Kin, his dark brow knotted with worry. "How many night shifts you be doing? You be needing a rest."

"I'm fine . . . it's just an early winter illness."

Erek studied his friend's bloodshot eyes and hunched shoulders. "There be something wrong," he said.

Ode glanced up and down the hallway where they stood. Occasionally, a Kin or Kiness would pass by, but otherwise they were alone. He was tempted to tell Erek everything. He did not think he could stand it much longer. The confession was on his lips, but he stopped himself at the last moment, knowing that he could not risk being cast out of the temple. Then he would never see his friends or Briar again.

"I don't like winter," he said at last, and it was partly true. "I remember how I almost died, and I remember how you saved me."

Erek nodded, and Ode prayed that his friend believed him.

"I be understanding how hard that might be for you," said the Kin. "Such fears do nay leave us easily. I be seeing what I can do."

"Do?"

"I be asking the High-Kin what we can be doing for you to make it better."

"You don't need to—"

Erek put his hand on Ode's shoulder and shook it gently. "I did nay bring you back to this realm from death to see you suffer," he chided, his brown eyes warm. "That be the end of the matter."

"Thank you," said Ode, his chest tingling with guilt. "Thank you. You're a true friend to me."

The Kin smiled and walked away. His kindness brought Ode some relief, but just a few days later, Ode's Magic felt stronger and more persistent than ever. His whole body throbbed with its fizzing pressure so that every breath was agony. Arrow glued himself to Ode's side, whining with worry and nudging his master's legs. Struggling through the day, Ode made it to the evening in a haze of pain. He felt too ill to attend dinner at the eating hall and instead sat by himself in the shepherd's hut, trying to ignore the stinging that rippled through his limbs.

He knew that he must shift or it would happen of its own accord. He had tried to fight it for too long, hoping that it would disappear again, but he could not go on like this. With his whole body aching, Ode decided that tonight he would shift just once before Briar appeared—to get it over with. Since his infamous battle with the wolves, there had been no new attacks on the flock and the shepherds had lapsed into their old routine. Throughout the summer, Ode had often been on the night watch alone, which had suited his meetings with Briar perfectly; but now that winter was approaching, the shepherds were all tightening their standards. There were frequently two or more shepherds on the night shift now, and Ode knew that he would have to try hard tonight to shake off the others. They often liked to gather to chat before spreading across the mountainside, and since Briar did not appear until later, Ode usually did not mind, but tonight it was imperative that he left quickly.

As it was, he did not find it difficult to break away from the others. The shepherds were full from a large dinner and were happy to settle down for a night of intermittent watching and dozing as soon as possible. With his whole body trembling with pain, Ode strode up the mountainside and threw down his things beside his perch. Some sheep were grazing nearby and scattered in clouds of brown dust.

Looking around to make sure he was alone, Ode began pulling off his clothes. The sky was dark above him and the moon was a pale crescent that hung low in the sky. As the cool air hit Ode's bare skin, it began to burn. He touched the white feather around his neck and felt its delicate bristles bite the skin of his hand. These past moon cycles, he had almost forgotten it was there, as if it were a familiar scar on his body that he no longer noticed. Now, it felt heavy and powerful and Ode stood with his feet apart, waiting for the shift to take hold. He knew that it would not be an easy transformation.

Ode had vague recollections of what his first shifts had been like, but just then, it felt as if they were happening all over again. His limbs contorted and snapped, morphing into the form of another. He opened his mouth to scream in pain, but the sound disappeared into the gasp of another animal. Parts of him shrank and parts of him stretched. It was all over in a moment, but it felt long and agonized, and his transformed body was sore and stiff. He had not been the white bird in so long that it took him a while to remember how to move.

He waddled forward under Arrow's watchful gaze and stretched out his long neck. In his bird form, he longed to fly, but he knew it would be foolish. The shepherds would surely see him, and if not them, someone awake in the valley would spot him. He forced himself to hop over the rocks instead, occasionally unfolding his huge white wings to flex and stretch them. The pressure that had slowly built over the days instantly vanished, and he felt giddy with relief. He was so pleased that he did not notice the silver shadow at the mouth of the mountain pass before it was almost too late.

Arrow growled a warning and a squawk of alarm escaped Ode's beak. He tumbled over the rocks to his pile of clothes, his webbed feet slipping in the dust. For a second, he feared that he would not be able to shift back. He could not remember how to do it and dread churned in his stomach. He looked over his shoulder at the silver shadow that was watching him from the mountain pass with perplexed, blue eyes. It would not be long before Briar followed Jet, and Ode imagined that he could hear her now, climbing up the rocks on the other side. Just when he thought he would be discovered, his bones began to shudder. With a cry of surprise and a stab of pain, he became a man again. With tingling fingers, he grabbed hold of his clothing and hurriedly pulled them on.

"What are you doing?" a soft, beautiful voice called.

Ode was wearing just his breeches and boots. He quickly grabbed his shirt and pulled it over his head before throwing his furs over his shoulders. With scarlet cheeks, he turned to see Briar standing nearby, her face flushed.

"There . . . there was something caught in my shirt," he said.

She stared at him.

"You're early," Ode added, because he could think of nothing else to say.

Briar's blue eyes suddenly became earnest. "Yes—yes, I hurried here," she stuttered. "I need your help."

"What's wrong?"

"My friend, Kayra, is ill. I think—I think you were right."

"She is with child?"

Briar bit her lip and nodded.

"What's ailing her?" It had been a long time since Ode had practiced being a birther and he tried hard to remember all of Cala's teachings.

"Well, I . . . I think she is having a baby."

"*Now?*"

"Yes, I think so."

"Where is she?"

"In my room."

"In a dormitory?"

"No . . . I sleep in different quarters from everyone else."

Ode was too preoccupied with thoughts of the pregnant Kiness to think how odd that was.

"Have you told the High-Kiness?" he asked.

"No, Kayra made me promise not to. She is not herself, and I can tell that she is hurting—I do not know what to do!"

Briar's last words were muffled by sobs and her face crumpled into tears. Before he could stop himself, Ode rushed to her side and wrapped his arms around her. She leaned against him, pressing her head into his chest, and he breathed in her sweet, heady scent. The warmth of her body against his made his skin tingle and he longed to hold her like that forever, keeping her safe. Suddenly, she pulled away, wiping her face with the edge of her red cloak.

"Sorry—thank you—sorry," she gasped.

Dizzy from her touch, Ode could not reply at first. But finally he said, "Tell me what is wrong with your friend, and I will try to help. I've some knowledge of such things from my homeland."

"She has pains all across her stomach and she says they are getting stronger all the time."

"She must be in labor!"

"Is that bad?"

"It means the baby is coming now," said Ode, pacing up and down.

Briar gasped and whispered a quick prayer.

"If you won't tell the High-Kiness then you need to bring me to her."

Briar hesitated.

"I know men are not allowed in the Kinesses' chambers," added Ode. "But if your friend does not receive help—then she could die."

"If that is so, I must take you. We can leave Arrow and Jet here to watch the sheep. No one need know that you are gone."

Briar took her snow leopard's great face in her small hands and began whispering to her, petting her whiskers. Ode looked at Arrow doubtfully.

"We are not used to being parted," he said.

"He cannot come into the temple. He will surely be seen."

Ode knew she was right. He put his hand on his wolf's flat, gray head and said, "Stay," as convincingly as he could manage.

But when they turned to leave, Ode looked over his shoulder to see his wolf climbing the rocks after him.

"No," he said gently. "Stay."

Arrow whined and tilted his head, and when Ode began walking again, the wolf followed.

"It's no use," he said to Briar. "He won't stay."

"Fine, but he cannot give us away," she said with a frown.

"He won't."

They climbed through the mountain pass and hurried across the rocks on the other side, stumbling through the darkness. Ode had often wondered how Briar managed to sneak out of the temple unseen, and as he followed her through snaking, dark crevices, and up a sheer cliff face, he realized that it was not easy. Panting for breath, they stopped and crouched behind a high, stony wall. Briar motioned for him to be quiet, and she carefully picked at one of the rocks until it came away.

She peered through the gap before nodding and indicating that they should climb over.

Ode watched with stunned admiration as she hitched her skirt into the belt around her waist and began climbing. He tried unsuccessfully not to look at her long slender legs and when she caught him, she frowned.

On the other side of the wall a wide temple courtyard lay before them. Multicolored prayer flags zigzagged from one end to the other and a gold statue glinted in the moonlight at the center. Ode did not recognize this place, and he realized that they must be in the Kinesses' chambers. Arrow scrambled over the wall behind them, landing with a soft thump on the flagstones.

Checking left and right, Briar waved them on. They wound through the shadows and slipped into the cool, dark temple. Smoky incense clogged the air, and Ode could hear the faint, hushed snores of sleeping Kinesses nearby. He followed Briar through hallways and around corners until they reached a heavy, red curtain that she pulled aside. Ode ducked beneath her arm and found himself in a small, glowing room. The walls were blue and there were two beds, one of which was occupied by a scared, gasping Kiness. She looked at him with round, brown eyes.

"It is all right, Kayra," said Briar, pulling the curtain back into place. "This is my friend."

Kayra regarded Ode suspiciously, but then her face contorted with pain and she clutched at her inflated belly.

"There now, there now," said Ode in his gentle birther-voice, plumping up the pillows behind Kayra's shoulders and taking her hand.

He could scarcely believe that he was being so bold, but all of his training came flooding back to him and he acted instinctively. Just the other day he would not have dared to touch a Kiness, let alone hold her hand. Such a thing was forbidden to one who was not a temple member. Yet, when he looked at Kayra now, he did not see a Kiness but rather a frightened young mother.

"We will need cloths and warm water," he said to Briar, who stood silently in the corner, watching him.

She nodded and disappeared.

"You need to stay calm and breathe," he instructed, turning back to Kayra. "You do realize what is happening to you, don't you?"

Kayra's fingers tightened around his hand as she panted. Her headdress was damp with sweat and her cheeks were slick and glistening in the candlelight.

"It be a baby," she wheezed. "I be thinking that might be it."

"Yes, it is a baby . . . and you won't be able to keep it a secret when it comes out. You'll have to tell the High-Kiness."

Kayra grimaced with fear, but another contraction shook her body and she held her hands over her mouth to muffle her scream.

"This be too much," she wailed. "I be dying!"

"Hush, it's all right. I'm here."

Kayra looked at him and nodded. "I be trusting you," she gasped.

Ode noticed Briar had returned and she stood, lingering in the doorway. He beckoned her over.

"I'll need your help as well," he said.

"I will do what I can," she replied stiffly.

Briar's face was caught in the shadow of the candlelight and Ode could not read what she was thinking. He felt that she was suddenly distant when not long ago they had been so close—so close that he had actually held her. As she placed a jug of water and a pile of old linen beside the bed, Ode hoped she would not think differently of him after this night.

A cry of pain from Kayra stole both of their attentions and they each took one of her hands, whispering words of comfort. Briar watched her friend writhe in pain and her blue eyes filled with tears.

"Just tell me what to do," she said to Ode, her voice breaking.

He smiled and nodded.

All night they stood by Kayra's side and nursed her through to morning. Although humped, the Kiness's belly was not large enough and Ode guessed the baby must be premature. He predicted that the birth would be difficult and he was not wrong. Kayra, exhausted and sick, could barely push her child out of her by the time it was finally ready to come.

His shirt soaked through with perspiration, Ode encouraged her endlessly, all the while praying that she would make it until the morning. She was inexperienced and terrified. Even if she managed to have the baby, Ode worried that she would not bond with it. He feared for Briar, also, who looked just as astonished and petrified by the whole ordeal as her friend. If he was not comforting Kayra, then he was reassuring Briar with cheerful comments he did not wholly believe himself.

"It's almost there, I can see its head!" he whispered as light began to seep through the shuttered windows.

Kayra looked both alarmed and relieved at once. "It be a boy or a girl?" she asked.

"I can't see yet. It's still inside you."

"Push!" Briar urged her. "Keep pushing, and do not give up."

Kayra followed her friend's orders, her face set in grim lines, and Ode waited with the linen for the baby to fully emerge.

"Push!" Briar cried.

"You're almost there," said Ode. "Just a little more."

Kayra screamed as she pushed with all her might, and then she collapsed against the pillows, murmuring softly to herself.

Ode held the tiny creature in his hands and rubbed it gently.

"Should it be making a sound?" asked Briar, watching his face.

Ode kept rubbing the baby's tiny limbs and tried not to look as concerned as he felt.

"My baby . . ." Kayra moaned. "I be wanting my baby . . ."

The air was split with a piercing squeak and Ode almost fainted in relief.

"A little baby boy," he announced, holding it up for Kayra to see. Briar cooed, and Kayra smiled in delight.

"Let me be holding him," she said. "Be coming to me, little one."

Ode handed over the mewing baby and just then, he forgot he was in the temple with two young Kinesses. For a short while he was transported back to the Wild Lands and he expected a ceremony to commence that evening with colored feathers and beating drums.

"What be the meaning of *this*?" boomed a voice.

Ode jumped and Arrow, who had been sleeping in the corner, barked.

In the doorway stood the High-Kiness, her mouth open in horror.

CHAPTER TWENTY-FIVE

The Man Birther

It was not without difficulty that Ode explained how he had managed to get into the Kinesses' temple unnoticed. Standing before the High-Kiness and the High-Kin that morning, their robes rumpled from their haste in dressing, Ode tried his best to avoid any connection that could be made between himself and Briar. Instead, he fabricated a tale in which he had heard the anguished cries of a Kiness while wandering around the hallways unable to sleep, and he had followed them to Kayra. That other girl, he said, had happened to be in the room and she had helped deliver the baby.

The High-Kin and the High-Kiness received this information with blank, stunned faces. The High-Kiness could not believe that such a thing had happened to one of her students, and she struggled to accept that the newborn was actually real, though she had seen it with her own eyes. She fiddled with the folds of her headdress and the lines around her eyes were deep with concern.

"How you be knowing what to do?" the High-Kin asked Ode, smoothing down his beard, which was tangled from his night of sleep.

"In the Wild Lands I was trained for such things," Ode said, resting his hand behind one of Arrow's silky ears for courage. "I delivered the babies of my tribe and helped the mothers."

The High-Kin and the High-Kiness's eyebrows shot up in unison.

"Oh . . ." they both whispered faintly.

Then there was silence.

"I nay be knowing how this all happened," muttered the High-Kiness.

"I think I must say this," said Ode, and they looked at him in surprise. Even he could not believe that he was about to be so bold. "You must teach the Kins and Kinesses about birthing and such things. Perhaps if Kayra had known about it then she wouldn't have found herself in this situation. If I hadn't been there, then she would have died—she was weak and scared. Is there no one in this temple that knows about birthing?"

"There be nay reason for anyone to know," said the High-Kin. "Well, that is what we be thinking before. . . ."

"I know a little from my travels," said the High-Kiness. "But it is nay something we be having to consider before."

"I think you should consider it now," said Ode. "The mountain people who live around the temple must be in need of help with such matters, and you are always saying that you want ways to reach out to them."

The High-Kin and High-Kiness both stared at him in amazement.

"You be a strange man," said the High-Kin with the shadow of a smile.

After more questioning that Ode did his best to evade, he was sent to the eating hall for a late breakfast. The room was almost empty, except for the Kins who were clearing up the dirty bowls, and Ode sat alone. He was exhausted and sore from the night's activities and he could barely remain upright; his body frequently slumped into sleep. He was just nodding off when a flittering shadow caught his eyes. He looked up to see Briar beckoning him from the doorway.

His tiredness forgotten, he jumped up and lurched over to her. They were alone in the hallway, but Ode could hear the distant footfalls of Kins and Kinesses going about their daily routines in the temple. He knew it would not be long before someone appeared.

"I never had the chance to say thank you," Briar whispered.

They were standing so close that Ode could smell the sweet, flowery scent of her, and he could feel her breath like little gusts against his skin.

"If you had not helped Kayra, she would have died," she added.

"How is she? And how is the baby?" Ode managed to say, trying to stop himself from throwing his arms around her again.

"They are well, and she has decided to give up her vows. The father of the child has come forward, and he and Kayra are to be married."

"Is she happy?"

"Very," said Briar, and then she paused. "But I will lose my friend," she added, twisting her fingers together.

"I'm your friend, remember?" said Ode, gently pulling her hands apart and holding them in his own.

Briar looked up at him, and they both smiled. Ode's heart thumped in his chest like the frantic beat of wings, and he felt himself leaning toward her.

"Briar!"

They sprang apart, and Ode saw the High-Kiness marching toward them, her face taut with anger.

"You be not in your room," she growled at the Kiness.

"I—I just wanted to thank him," Briar muttered.

"Well, now you be thanking him and now you be leaving."

Briar nodded meekly and walked away, disappearing down the hallway with her brown skirt swishing around her ankles.

Once she was gone, the High-Kiness stood staring at Ode for a long moment, scrutinizing his face.

"You be staying away from that Kiness," she said. "You be hearing me?"

"I only met her last night."

"That be good. You be nay meeting her again."

Ode wanted to ask why. He wanted to know why Briar did not eat with the other temple members. Why she slept in a room separate from the girls' dormitories and why he had never seen her walking around the temple with the other Kinesses.

"The High-Kin be wanting to speak to you," said the High-Kiness, casting a disdainful glance over him and his wolf. "I be taking you there now."

Ode followed her through the temple, back to the room he had stood in that morning, attempting to explain himself. The High-Kin was pacing from one side to the other, still dressed in his wrinkled robe. He smiled when Ode entered and embraced him, as was the custom.

"This matter be almost put to rest," he said. "And that be good, for it has wearied us all."

He glanced at the High-Kiness but she was standing apart, still giving Ode an intense glare.

"We be thinking what you say this morning be right," the High-Kin continued. "We be thinking that those in the temple do need to be knowing about birthing and such things."

Ode remembered his daring words and flushed.

"We be thinking you move to the temple and teach them."

It took Ode a moment to realize what the High-Kin had said.

"Me?"

"There nay be anyone else who could do it," said the High-Kin with a chuckle.

Ode opened and closed his mouth, unable to reply. He had wanted to live in the temple for so long that he could hardly believe it.

"You be right that this be a good way to reach out to the mountain people," the High-Kin added. "And it be apparent you have skills in this."

"But I haven't reached a decision about my vows," said Ode. "I've been praying, but I can't see an answer."

"Perhaps the gods be having different plans for you," said the High-Kin quietly, and the High-Kiness flinched.

"If you nay want to that is fine," she added quickly.

"No!" Ode cried before he could stop himself. "I mean, I'm honored by the offer. Honored and shocked."

"You be not having to take vows for this," said the High-Kin. "As long as you be praying and waiting for a sign then that be all we can ask. But I be urging you to think this over. We be in need of your help and your skills be wasted herding sheep now that we be seeing what you can do."

There was a pause, and Ode heard the distant chanting of a prayer from the Room of the Gods, which drifted through the open window shutters.

"Yes," he said.

"Should you be wanting to consider it first?" asked the High-Kiness, but the High-Kin beamed with delight and her question was ignored.

"I'm so thankful for this chance—" began Ode.

"You be helping us," the High-Kin interrupted. "I knew the gods be bringing you here for a reason."

The High-Kiness frowned, but Ode did not notice. He felt elated. He grinned for the rest of that day, foolishly thinking that now, since he would be living in the temple, he would see Briar more than ever.

―⸻⸻⸻―

As it was, Ode barely saw Briar at all. He moved into the temple the day of the High-Kin's offer and, though he waited at their meeting spot that evening to tell Briar the good news, she did not appear.

In a sudden rush, autumn became winter and snow fell thickly across the mountains, glazing each peak in a slather of white. Lacy frost fringed the prayer flags that hung around the courtyards, and the prayer wheels grew stiff with ice. The temple fires blazed continuously, but still Ode would awaken some mornings in his dormitory with frost in his hair. The weather did not encourage freezing midnight wanderings, and whenever Ode ventured out to the mountain pass where he had once kept watch, hopeful that *this* time Briar might be there, he found it deserted. There were no prints in the snow that might have been a leopard—no silver shadows sliding over the rocks. Briar, it seemed, had vanished.

When he was not looking for his Kiness, Ode was busy teaching the students and learning new skills himself. Erek remembered that he had once promised to teach Ode to read and they began daily lessons, working through scripture with slow precision. Ode discovered that he was both a good teacher and a good student, which gained him a favorable reputation among his peers at the temple. He still helped in the valley when he was not taking lessons, and he could feel himself growing wise as well as strong.

Ode knew that he should be happy. His teaching at the temple was interesting and his visits to nearby mountain people were also proving a success. A reserved race, they were distrustful at first, but in time they came to accept him and some even welcomed his birthing help. With such blessings as these, Ode wanted to be thankful and he often was, but he thought of Briar constantly. He did not know where she had gone or why. He thought about their last meeting over and over, considering if he had said or done something wrong. In dark moments he even wondered if she was hiding from him.

He never saw her around the temple, though he always looked. Even when teaching, if someone walked across the courtyard outside, Ode would glance through the window with hope. He was not permitted in the Kinesses' chambers, but on his days of rest he would linger nearby. His female students passed him with quizzical glances, but he would stay put until the High-Kiness appeared. Only then did he slip away. Sometimes he was not quick enough and she caught sight of him. Her eyes would narrow and her top lip would curl. Ode became convinced that she had something to do with Briar's disappearance.

Whether he was nursing new mothers in the huts of the mountain people or explaining the cycle of babyhood to a class of young Kins sitting at their desks, Briar was always present in Ode's mind. He thought that if he could catch just a glimpse of her, all would be well. However, when he finally did see her, one dark, cold evening, he almost wished he had not.

The whole temple gathered together for the Midwinter Feast and Ode piled into the eating hall with everyone, trying his best to look jolly. He had spent the morning at Kayra's hut in the next valley, where she now lived with her new husband. It was not the first time that Ode had visited, since Kayra worried often about her baby boy's well-being. As always, Ode had assured her that the child was perfectly fine, and then, as always, he had asked her if she had news from Briar. Knowing what he would say, Kayra lowered her eyes and started shaking her head before he had even finished speaking. Whenever he asked, she always gave him the same response, but Ode could tell that she was lying.

He brooded over it now, sitting at a table in the eating hall. Around him, his friends were joking and laughing with one another, but he could not join in. He did not know why he turned his head to look across the room, but when he did, he saw two blue eyes watching him. Ode was so shocked that he almost shouted her name. It was only Erek, seated beside him and oblivious to all else, who prevented him with a hearty pat on the back.

"Happy Midwinter to you!" Erek cried.

Ode did not reply. He was staring through the raucous crowd to the blue eyes on the other side of the room. She was far away, but he could see she looked sickly and thin. She stood at the edge of a group of Kinesses, who were all yelling and singing joyfully, but she was not joining in.

Ode scrambled to his feet, ready to weave through the red cloaks to her side. He did not care that those around could see. He had been longing for her too much and had barely thought of anything else. Even in his dreams he had seen her beautiful face—pale and wan and wishing for him, too. He began trying to push his way through the throng, but suddenly, she turned away from him. Dodging through the masses, she fled. Ode could not believe it. He sat back down heavily and ignored Erek's questions.

"You be looking ill," the Kin said at last. "You be better to go to sleep."

Ode nodded glumly and left the hall, Arrow trailing behind him with his tail drooping low against the ground.

The hallways of the temple were empty and Ode passed the red, peeling walls with his head bowed. All classes were dismissed for the Midwinter Feast and Ode made his way to the schooling rooms. He did not feel much like sleeping. There was an itch between his shoulders that needed to be dealt with, as if wings were trying to tear apart the muscles of his back. Since moving into the temple, he had been shifting regularly. He knew it was dangerous, but he figured that to not shift would be worse. He needed to keep his Magic under control or else it would show itself in other ways. Life in the temple was so close and communal that, should he give even the slightest sign of his gift, someone would notice. He shared a dormitory with six other men, and students and friends accompanied him from morning until night. To shift, he had to slip away at opportune moments such as these.

The schooling rooms were deserted, but Ode crept from one classroom to the next, checking. Arrow galloped about, sniffing, but he gave no sign that he had detected anyone.

With a mixture of sorrow and frustration, Ode began pulling off his furs in one of the empty classrooms. It was cold and he began to shiver as he emerged from each layer, but his dark mood left him numb to the pain of the chill. He grasped the white feather around his neck and transformed. He was almost as good at it now as he had been in the Wild Lands. The knack had come back to him quickly and he could sense his control over his Magic strengthening.

Just then, feeling as hurt and rejected as he did, he wished that he could transform and never turn back. A life without Briar did not seem worth living.

As a bird, Ode waddled about the classroom, stretching and flexing his wings. He did not often allow himself to fly unless he was far from the temple and completely convinced that he would not be seen, but today he felt reckless. He was sad and desperate. He could not forget the way Briar had run from him. He had spent moon-cycles searching for her, yet all that time, it seemed, she had been avoiding him. Had he done something wrong? He could not bear to think of it. He wanted to fly away and never look back.

Ode ran out of the classroom and began beating his wings, followed by Arrow, who growled in surprise. In the courtyard, Ode soared above the flagstones to the temple roof, circling the mountaintop. He could see the snow-covered valley filled with whiteness like a goblet sloshed in milk, and he could see the mountains that spread in all directions like an icy sea. The danger of what he was doing eclipsed some of his sadness, and he tried to focus on the thrill of it.

He stayed in his bird form far longer than he would normally have dared. The pale, wintry sun plunged behind the nearby mountains and the sky became cold and dark. Finally, Ode descended from the slate temple roof and disappeared into the classroom once more. He transformed into his human form and pulled his clothes on before he grew too cold. The flight had raised his spirits a little, but when he remembered Briar's blue eyes and her sweet, gushing laugh, he felt gloomy again. He was tired and decided he would go to the dormitory and try to lose himself in sleep.

He was about to leave when he noticed that Arrow was not beside him. Glancing around the room he did not see his wolf's familiar gray body anywhere. He frowned and the first stirrings of unease crept into his chest. He strode to the door and pulled aside the red curtain.

There, lying in the middle of the courtyard in a patch of moonlight, was Arrow. Beside him sat Briar. She tickled the wolf's soft belly and giggled when he wagged his tail in pleasure.

Ode swallowed hard and wondered if this was a vision.

Seeing him, Briar stopped and her face became solemn. She staggered to her feet, and Ode could see that she was weak. Her plain clothes were dirty and despite all the furs thrown over her, she looked tiny and fragile.

"Will you run away this time?" he found himself saying, and he was surprised to hear his voice sound so bitter.

"Will you stay human?" she asked back, jutting out her chin.

Ode felt the blood drain from his face, and he gritted his teeth together.

"I saw you just now," she added, folding her arms. "I know what you are . . . a Magic."

"Shush!" Ode cried, looking around.

They were both silent, but Ode knew that he could not stay angry. "Briar, please."

When he said her name, she immediately softened and her arms fell by her sides again.

"Why did you never tell me?" she asked.

"I was afraid. I didn't tell anyone and I thought—I thought that you would hate me."

A pearly tear trickled down Briar's cheek. "I do not hate you," she whispered.

Ode slowly moved closer to her, as if she might suddenly run away. He could see that her eyes were red-rimmed and her cheeks were ashen and hollow.

"Where have you been?" he asked.

"In the temple."

"But I've never seen you. Why have you been hiding?"

"I would not hide from you."

"Then what's happened? You look sick. What's wrong? Please tell me."

He was so close to her now that they were almost touching. He took hold of her hand, and she jumped. Her palm was icy and her delicate fingers looked cracked and sore.

"I . . . I . . ." she gasped, more tears coursing down her cheeks. "I just cannot see you. You need to understand—"

"But I love you."

The words were out of Ode's mouth before he could stop them, and Briar gasped. She snatched her hand away and shook her head, sobs shaking her body.

"No!" she said. "No, you cannot!"

"Why?" Hurt slashed across Ode's chest and he felt his hands begin to tremble.

"We are *friends*," said Briar.

"Yes, but . . . you are more than a friend to me."

"No!"

Ode knew it was forbidden, but he had longed for it. He had not expected Briar to react like this. A small part of him had hoped she felt the same way.

"I can't help it," he said. "Since the moment I saw you—"

"No!" Briar cried again, wiping her tears away roughly with the sleeve of her dress. "You cannot, and I will not let you."

She turned and began to run, her feet pattering softly against the flagstones. Ode thought about chasing after her, but his legs suddenly felt heavy and awkward. Beneath his shirt, he could feel his white feather burning, as if it were throbbing with pain. At his feet, Arrow threw back his head and howled at the midwinter moon.

CHAPTER TWENTY-SIX

The Command

Ode did not know how he survived after Briar's rejection. He felt empty. Dead.

He walked to his lessons each morning and answered the students' questions about birthing and motherhood. In the afternoons, he completed his own studies, reading with Erek or practicing to write in the language of the temple. And in the evening he volunteered to tend to the fields in the valley with his old friends. To those around him, Ode seemed normal, but inside, he ached. Whenever he could, he crept off with Arrow and hiked through the nearby mountains. There he would shift into his bird form and soar through the white-capped peaks. It was the only thing that gave him a release.

Gradually, the snow began to soften and melt. In the Room of the Gods, everyone prayed for spring, and in the courtyards of the temple, a persistent *drip-drip* sounded as the ice on the roof trickled away. Winter ended, and the voices in Ode's head began.

He was walking between classrooms one morning when he heard a shout. He stopped and looked around, causing a group of young Kinesses to knock into him. They exploded into giggles and scurried off, snickering to one another. Ode ignored them and looked up and down the hallway. He was sure that he had heard something, but there was no one else around. He shivered, although he was not cold, and went on his way.

Later that day, a voice spoke to him. In one of the temple's reading rooms, where the older Kins and Kinesses retreated to study, a low muttering began to vibrate in his ear. Around him, Kins and Kinesses sat cross-legged at low tables, scriptures spread before them and chests of scrolls at their sides. They were all silent and Ode realized they could not hear the voice. The scripture he had been reading swam before his eyes, and he clutched his head, breathing deeply. For a moment, he panicked, fearing he was about to shift as the voice continued to chatter away. Trying not to attract attention, he slid his hand beneath his shirt and touched the white feather. Its bristles were burning and the voice in his ear grew louder, though he still could not make out what it said.

A furry muzzle nudged his elbow, and Ode jumped. The voice disappeared and he looked down to see Arrow staring back at him. Ode briskly wiped his hand across his damp forehead and began gathering up his things. He had meant to stay in the reading room all afternoon, but he felt nervous and sick.

Once in the hallway, he wondered if he should go for a walk to shift alone, but there was a strong wind blowing and his legs were trembling. He blinked rapidly and showers of color burst across his vision. He had not felt like this since his illness in the Wild Lands.

Battling dizziness, Ode shuffled through the temple to his dormitory. It was a clean, bare room in a hallway of identical rooms with rows of beds and scuffed, green walls. At this time of day, it was empty, and he crawled into his bed, barely managing to pull off his furs and boots before climbing beneath the blankets. As soon as his head hit the pillow, he fell unconscious and almost immediately, a dream began.

In his dream there was a man he had not seen before. The man was tall and strong with brown hair and dark, haunted eyes. He looked as if he had once been handsome, but now his face was twisted and angry.

It was only as he crossed a dimly lit room to a table strewn with scrolls that Ode realized the man's right leg was wooden from the knee down. It tapped against the grimy floorboards.

There was a knock at the door and the man grimaced. By the small, round window in the corner, Ode guessed they must be on a boat.

"Yes?" the man barked.

A slight, blond boy entered. "Captain, a gull has brought a message," he said.

"What does it say?"

"The Scarlet Isles have agreed to the terms of the Magical Cleansing."

"We knew that was going to happen," growled the man. "They have never been Magic sympathetic."

"And the Hillands are rallying. They have formed an army larger than expected from exiles in the Wild Lands."

The man paused and rubbed his eyes. "My cousin always *was* full of surprises," he said, with a slow smile.

The vision vanished, and Ode awoke suddenly to the sound of hushed voices and running feet. The ship cabin and the man with the wooden leg were gone, and he was in his bed at the temple once more. His blankets were soaked with sweat and his head buzzed with the dregs of the vision. He sat up to see a huddle of Kins near the door, arguing in low voices. The shutters at the windows were closed and the room was dark.

"What's going on?" he mumbled.

The Kins rarely said an angry word to one another and Ode did not think he had ever heard a group arguing before. A few turned at his voice, but no one replied. They looked tense.

Ode swung his legs to the floor and shuffled across the room, his mind still reeling from the vision. He lifted his hand to his forehead and felt his burning, feverish skin. He knew his vision meant something important, but he could not understand what it was.

"There be state officials in the temple," one of the younger Kins whispered when Ode was close enough. "They be coming into the mountains to tell us the news. They be arriving just this afternoon without any warning."

"Officials?"

"Soldiers from the main island."

"What do they want?" asked Ode. "What's the news that they bring?"

"*War,*" said the young Kin, and he looked excited and terrified at once.

A crowd of red cloaks marched past the doorway and Ode caught sight of a familiar face.

"Erek!" he called.

His friend paused, but he did not wear his usual cheerful smile.

"Come back!" a young Kin squeaked as Ode slid into the bustling hallway. "We be told to stay in our rooms!"

"I need to be going," said Erek, standing aside to let a crowd of mature Kins pass. "I can nay stop to talk."

"I've been lying sick with a fever," said Ode. "I've only just woken, and I don't know what's going on. Why is everyone so afraid?"

"There be nothing to fear," the Kin replied firmly.

"People are speaking of war. . . ."

It was a nasty word that conjured memories of the Wild Lands. For a second, Ode saw the broken, limp body of his father in the dust.

"If the peoples be warring then it is nay to do with the temple. We be for the gods and nothing else. It nay be our decision what the Scarlet Isles be choosing to do. I say it again, there nay be anything to worry over."

"Is this to do with the Magical Cleansing?" asked Ode, remembering what Asha and the professor had said to him long ago.

Erek's face drew taut, and he glanced at Arrow.

"I be needing to go," he said. "I think it be best if you stay in here and out of the officials' sight."

Ode watched as his friend turned and disappeared down the hall.

No one in the temple slept that night. Everyone huddled in groups around flickering candles, whispering and waiting. It was shocking to all that the state officials had come so far into the mountains without sending messenger eagles ahead. To have gone to such an effort must mean the news was of deadly importance.

By morning everyone knew: the Magical Cleansing had come to the Scarlet Isles. As the sun rose over the mountains, it was carried in mutters through the temple rooms. When the Kins, Kinesses, and workers in the valley were called into the eating hall for a meeting before breakfast, the audience already knew the announcement. For the first time since The Red Wars, the Scarlet Isles were to join forces with their neighboring countries in the Western Realm. They were going to fight the Magics.

Standing on wooden crates at the head of the eating hall, the High-Kin and High-Kiness attempted to explain the news. Worried, tired faces stared back at them and officials were stationed in a corner, watching. There were ten of them, all dressed in uniforms of gray, which looked a little worse for wear after the journey through the mountains. It was difficult not to notice the sabers dangling from their waists and the rifles slung across their shoulders. They were young and they had the pale skin and fair hair of the Scarletions.

"We be separate from the affairs of the kingdom," said the High-Kin. "We all be knowing that, but . . . we be the Castle Temple, too, the royal temple and still akin to the Scarlet Isles. We must be living by their authority."

Ode saw those around him shift uncomfortably from foot to foot. The only authority the temple was supposed to bow to was the gods'.

"The royal family be granting us this island for our temples, for they be great followers of the gods," said the High-Kiness in a thin voice. "So it be right that we give back to them if we can."

Her words produced more fidgeting among the crowd.

"From now on, I be wanting us all to keep the Western Realm in our prayers," said the High-Kin. "Of course, we always be praying for the health of our king and kingdom, but we be praying now for strength and success in the fight, too."

There was a click as one of the officials played with the hilt of his saber.

"The king be knowing how devout we be, and he be sending these officials here to . . . watch over us," the High-Kin carried on. "They be stationed here for a while to keep us safe and be living with us."

There was an audible intake of breath from the crowd. The officials looked around with blank, expressionless faces. Ode almost thought it would have been better if they had smirked or grinned menacingly. As it was, they did not seem human.

"Because of the war, we be taking a view against Magic," the High-Kiness said. "The Castle Temple be always following the king, and we be never supporting Magics before, but now . . ." Her voice betrayed her and trembled before she finished in a rush, "Now, we be praying for their defeat and their deaths."

The hairs on the back of Ode's neck rose and he saw those around him flinch. No one at the temple ever spoke of Magic, and he wondered how the other Kins and Kinesses felt hearing such news.

"There be nothing for us to fear," the High-Kin continued. "We be making sure we are a support to our kingdom in its time of need. . . ."

A hand touched Ode's arm, and he jumped.

"I be leading you out of here," muttered Erek under his breath. "Be following me and do nay draw attention to yourself."

Ode was about to argue that the meeting had not finished, but the Kin had already moved away. Ode weaved through the crowd after him, Arrow sliding and twisting between sets of legs like Ode's shadow. Out of the eating hall, the trio walked down hallways and across courtyards to the Kins' chambers. They slipped inside a dormitory and Erek pulled the curtain across the doorway. The beds in the room were unmade and there were guttering candles dribbling wax onto the floor from a night of whispers and excitement.

"When I be bringing you to these mountains, I be thinking I brought you to a better place," said the Kin.

"You did," replied Ode. "If it weren't for you, I would have died."

The Kin shook his head. "Nay, you be in danger now."

"Why?" said Ode, struggling to keep his voice light.

"I nay be meeting a man before that had a wolf as a pet. There be something strange about that."

There was a beat of silence.

"Does everyone in the temple suspect me?" Ode finally asked.

"Before they be thinking you a Wildlander and that seemed to make sense. But now things be changing. The temple will become a different place."

"What should I do?"

"Just now you must be laying low, away from the officials. The wolf must be kept outside so it be nay bringing attention to you."

Ode glanced down at Arrow, who was watching their conversation with his green eyes as if he could understand what they were saying.

"I'm not sure that's possible," he said.

"It be the only way," replied the Kin firmly. "These officials be nay lying when they say they want Magics dead. It be The Red Wars all over again—Pervorocco, Daric, and the Scarlet Isles joining together to wipe out Magic."

"But they lost that war, didn't they?" Ode had picked up some vague understanding of history from his afternoon readings with Erek. He knew The Red Wars had ravaged the Western Realm many, many seasons ago, and that those involved had vowed such a thing would never happen again.

"They lost, yes, but there be many dead," said Erek. "And I be nay wanting you to die."

"Why?" asked Ode suddenly.

Erek had always been a comforter and a friend. Ode knew he could rely on the Kin for anything, but there was something determined about his face now that struck Ode as unusual.

"Why?" he persisted when he received no reply.

"You came to me like a gift from the gods," said Erek at last. "And they be telling me ever since to watch over you."

Ode wanted to tell the Kin that he was wrong. He was a lowly birther—a poor boy from the Wild Lands. He had been praying to the gods and they had never answered him. He was of no consequence.

"I believe you be chosen by the gods," said Erek. "I believe you be having a destiny."

CHAPTER TWENTY-SEVEN

The High-Kiness's Secret

Overnight, it seemed, the Castle Temple transformed. No longer was it a comfort to its occupants—a refuge and a place of peace. Officials prowled the hallways day and night. They claimed a suite of rooms for themselves and carried out frequent searches whenever they pleased. At the ceremonies in the Room of the Gods each evening, they stood watch, their arms folded and their rifles winking in the light of the candles. The Kins and Kinesses did their best to act normal, but none could pretend they were not afraid.

Winter became spring, but the arrival of sunny days and bright breezes did not bring the usual smile to Ode's face. Like everyone at the Castle Temple, he felt tense and drawn. Mealtimes were quiet and strained affairs in which Kins and Kinesses tried to finish their food as quickly as possible under the supervision of gray uniforms. Lessons were conducted in hushed voices with fervent glances at the door, in case a search was suddenly announced. It seemed as if everyone was waiting for something terrible to happen.

The rising pressure at the temple scared Ode, but his separation from Arrow worried him most of all. He felt lost and alone without his companion by his side. Ode knew that it was safer this way, but it did not make waking each morning without Arrow's familiar shaggy body sprawled at his feet any easier. He crept away often to visit his wolf, who had to be shut away in a hut in the valley, where it was hoped the officials would not think to go snooping. Each time Ode arrived, Arrow would almost knock him over with excitement, and every time he left, the wolf would howl with anguish. No matter how long they were apart, Ode found that it did not get easier.

His classes had been suspended under Erek's insistence, so his days were long, endless expanses of nothing. He lurked around the temple, trying to stay out of the officials' way. He snuck off to see Arrow as often as he could, but still he was bored and aimless. The High-Kin and High-Kiness were under constant supervision, so Ode could not go to them for guidance. Instead, Erek acted as a mediator, carrying messages back and forth between them when he attended meetings with the temple elders.

"The elders be saying they think you should be leaving," he muttered one spring day.

Ode and Erek stood outside the front of the temple, the valley dropping away before them, then soaring again in jagged waves on the other side. The prayer wheels were tinkling as a yak herder descended the stone steps, spinning the barrels as he went, and their chimes rang across the rocks. At the entrance to the temple were two officials, watching everything with flat, dark eyes.

"But you said before that wouldn't work," Ode whispered back. "You said there would be no way to escape without attracting their attention."

"We be thinking you be attracting their attention more if you stay. They becoming interested in everyone."

Ode tugged at his red cloak. Erek had given it to him the day after the officials arrived so he might blend in with everyone at the temple.

He had always wanted a red cloak, but under these circumstances, he found it did not hold the same value it once had.

"If I did go . . . *where* would I go?" he asked. "I don't know these mountains."

Erek sighed and pretended to point at something in the valley. The two of them were supposed to be discussing crops. That is what they had told the officials before they stepped outside.

"You be just having to go somewhere," he said. "Let me speak with the elders and we be seeing what we can do. But be ready to leave at any time."

Ode could not believe this was happening again. He had escaped one country threatened by the Magical Cleansing, and now he was about to be forced from another. If the gods had brought him here for a reason, as Erek believed, then what was it? These days he had too much time on his hands, and he brooded over his past often. If he was not thinking of such things, he was worrying about Briar. Though she had rejected him, and though he had not seen her since that fateful meeting, he could not help himself. He hoped that, wherever she was, the officials had not found her. He prayed she was safe.

At night he continued to dream. His visions were incoherent, jumbled images that flashed through his mind. He saw blood and death and red flowers. He wondered what it all meant, and he worried that he would not find out until it was too late.

But it was not only Ode who suffered from the presence of the officials. The Kins and Kinesses, who had always been gentle and kind to one another, were now snappy and irritable. They were afraid, and their fear made them harsh. Ode saw one of the officials push over an old Kin who was carrying plates across a courtyard. Whether he did it on purpose or by accident, it was difficult to tell, but the old Kin fell and the plates clattered against the flagstones, some smashing. No one came to help. The old Kin lay for a long time on the flagstones, groaning softly and clutching his ankle. Ode wanted to go to him, but the official stood watch, almost daring anyone to come near. Instead, the other Kins simply walked by and the old Kin was left to get up on his own.

The officials knocked people over often and it soon became apparent that these were not accidents. Ode witnessed a Kiness tripped in a hallway and he saw a little Kin shoved aside in the eating hall. These small acts of violence stunned the people of the temple into silence. They hated what they saw, but they felt powerless. So their anger turned to each other. Bickering broke out often at ceremonies and in dormitories. Everyone began looking for reasons to argue, and Ode knew it would not be long before they turned on him. He could feel the Kins in his dormitory watching his comings and goings. They knew that there was something odd about him, and they could see that his wolf had disappeared. They did not ask him questions, but Ode felt them quietly seething behind his back. They needed someone to blame for what was happening at the temple, and he was an easy target.

Ode realized that Erek was right: he must leave before something happened. When he next saw his friend, Ode almost ran up to him. The Kin sat in the eating hall with a space open to his right. Ode hurried over, carrying his bowl, and waited for one of the officials stalking around the room to move away.

"Have you heard any—" he began whispering.

"You be told to go to the Room of the Gods," Erek interrupted with a hiss, and then he stood up and walked away, though he had not finished his meal.

Ode was left sitting alone, his mouth open. The Kiness nearest him shot him a nervous glance, and he quickly ducked his head, eating his broth in silence. The ceremony in the Room of the Gods was not due to start until sundown, and he would need to enter without attracting attention. Once he had finished his food, he piled his bowl with the others and tried to hurry from the room as carefully as possible. When he passed an official at the door, he felt eyes on him, but he did not raise his head.

Flitting through hallways, Ode kept his head bowed. He took a shortcut through an empty classroom, and then crossed a courtyard scattered with cherry blossoms. An official marched up and down the flagstones, a rifle resting over his shoulder, and Ode shrank into the shadows, trying his best to disappear. He heard a gasp and looked up to see that the official had caught his rifle in one of the zigzagging lines of prayer flags. With a yell of annoyance, the official yanked it off and the fabric shredded, sending the whole line flopping to the ground. He bared his teeth in a grimace of annoyance and pulled the trigger of his rifle. There was an almighty bang and one of the Kinesses screamed. A puff of smoke drifted into the sunshine and those in the courtyard cowered. The shot had been directed into the air, but it was the first time many of the Kins and Kinesses had ever heard or seen a weapon fired.

Taking advantage of the confusion, Ode turned and hurried down a hallway. He passed a group of officials who were running toward the sound of the commotion, and undetected, Ode climbed the steps to the Room of the Gods. He glanced once over his shoulder to make sure no one had seen him, and then he ducked inside.

The room looked strange without all the bodies of the temple gathered into it. The great golden statue of one of the goddesses on the other side of the room glowed in the dim light and the ceiling swirled with smoke from lit incense. It was quiet and peaceful. Ode did not know what he had been sent here for, but as his eyes adjusted to the light, he saw a figure sitting on one of the benches.

"I must be speaking to you quickly," said the High-Kiness. "We be nay having long. They will be wondering where I am."

Ode frowned. He had expected to meet Erek here or the High-Kin.

As if reading his mind, the High-Kiness said, "I be unsure about you from the start, but . . . I be running out of options." She climbed shakily to her feet.

"What do you mean?"

"You be needing to leave, and I be needing you to take someone with you."

Ode felt his chest flutter. "Who?" he asked.

"I be showing you in one moment, but first I be telling you something important. You must be leaving tonight, both of you. We never be thinking that the Castle Temple ever get this way, but we never be foreseeing this war. . . ." The High-Kiness paused to rub her forehead. "I be so worried for my charge. She be not safe here, and you be needing to take her into the mountains to hide."

"Who?" Ode repeated, daring to let himself hope.

"We be writing to the king," the High-Kiness continued, ignoring his question. "And we be asking that these officials be removed. It be not safe right now, and you both need to be gone. Do nay go to another temple for there are officials everywhere. You go and stay away until we be bringing you back, yes?"

"All right. Yes."

"Tonight it be announced that there be a meeting after the ceremony. You be hearing everyone leave and that be when you must escape. She know all this already and she be telling you more. I must be leaving now."

Ode nodded, agreeing to anything if it meant what he hoped it did.

"She be here," said the High-Kiness, and she crossed the room to one of the large, colorful tapestries hung on the wall. Pulling it aside and lifting up another wall hanging underneath, she uncovered a door. "Be quick now," she said, motioning for Ode to go inside.

He paused.

"Hurry!"

The temptation was too strong for him to resist. The door opened when he pushed it and he saw a flight of stairs ascending into the gloom. He was about to slip inside when the High-Kiness grabbed his arm.

"Above all, be keeping her away from Magic!" she hissed. "Other Magic," she added, turning her face away.

Ode nodded, and then she shut the door, letting the wall hangings swing back into place with a muffled thump. For a moment, Ode was plunged into darkness, but after a while, his eyes grew used to the shadows and he managed to feel his way up the stairs.

He emerged among the rafters. Dust floated through the air and slices of fading light filtered through the slates of the roof. The Room of the Gods had a high ceiling and Ode had never wondered if there was an attic above. Old rugs riddled with holes were flung across beams and tapestries that had almost faded to nothing were slumped into corners, sticky with grime. Among it all, curled into blankets on a makeshift bed, was a tiny Kiness, her head in her hands. Her clothes were ragged and dirty, her body angular and frail. She did not wear a headdress and her golden hair fell in breathtaking folds, curling around her waist.

"Briar?"

She stirred and two blue eyes peered out at him. Gasping, her expression turned from relief to fear to delight, and then back again.

"Have you been up here this whole time?" he asked, beginning to duck under the beams and climb over the piles of old, discarded tapestries toward her.

He was thrilled and worried all at once. He could not forget the last time they had met and the way she had been disgusted by him, but the very sight of her made him long to cradle her in his arms.

"I didn't think that you would come," she said, her voice dry and cracked. "Not after how I spoke to you."

"Briar, I meant it when I said . . ." he trailed off as they both blushed. "When I said that I was your friend," he finished lamely. "I would not abandon you because of some silly argument."

He settled onto a blanket beside her and could not stop himself from taking hold of her hands. Her skin was cold and damp.

"You are ill?"

She shrugged. "I think I have been driven almost mad up here. I managed to escape at first and to visit Jet, but since the officials have come, it is too dangerous. I miss Jet and . . . I have missed you."

Her hair fell across her face and Ode's fingers ached to brush it aside. Her curls shimmered in the slanting light and threw arcing sparks that bounced from beam to beam.

"I've missed you as well," he said.

Briar leaned against him and gently lowered her head onto his shoulder. Her crown tucked beneath his chin and the warmth of her body melted into his. Ode could not bear to ruin the moment, but neither could he stop himself from asking, "But what about my . . . gift?"

Briar sat upright and looked away. "I have told no one," she said. "The High-Kiness believes there is something Magic about you, but she does not know for sure."

"How do you feel about it?"

"I do not feel anything. I'm sorry for what I said before. You are still you, and you would not hurt me."

"Hurt you?"

Briar fiddled with her torn skirt. "I do not completely understand it myself," she said. "But the High-Kiness has always said that those with Magic will hurt me. Ever since I can remember, she has worried for my safety."

"I will *never* hurt you," said Ode.

She smiled. "I know."

They lapsed into silence—the only sound was the creaks of the building.

"After the ceremony we are to leave?" asked Ode.

For an instant, Briar looked like her old self again. The anxious tightness of her features slipped away and her face brightened with joy.

"Yes," she said. "We will live in a cave in the mountains with Jet and Arrow. It will be wonderful!" She paused and glanced around the rafters. "Where is Arrow?"

"In a hut in the valley. He has also been forced into hiding."

Briar touched his shoulder, for she knew how much it must hurt him to be parted from his companion.

"Thank you," she whispered. "Thank you for forgiving me."

And she leaned forward and kissed his cheek.

CHAPTER TWENTY-EIGHT

The Warning

Ode and Briar watched the ceremony that evening through the cracks in the ceiling of the Room of the Gods. They saw the Kins, Kinesses, and workers from the valley pile into the building followed by the officials, and they murmured along with the service, their heads bent.

Ode could barely concentrate since his whole body quaked from the touch of Briar's soft lips against his cheek. He knew he should be worrying about escaping the temple unseen by the officials or planning where they would run to when they made it out of the valley, but he could not help himself. He wondered if Briar secretly loved him, too. He knew such a thing was forbidden, but life at the temple was not what it had been before. Throughout the service, he stole glances at her, studying the perfect curve of her jaw and the overwhelming radiance of her hair. It suddenly occurred to him that once they were in the mountains, he would see her every day. He would have her complete, undivided attention. The thought made him smile dreamily.

As the High-Kiness had promised, after the service a meeting in the eating hall was announced. The members of the temple poured out of the Room of the Gods followed by the officials and headed toward the main building. Ode and Briar watched them go, nervous excitement beginning to make them tremble.

"What now?" asked Briar.

"I suppose we leave. . . ."

The whole thing seemed so surreal to Ode that he could barely believe what was happening. To be sent to spend his days alone with Briar in the mountains was something from his wildest fantasies.

"Surely we should not just walk out," said Briar.

"No, of course not," muttered Ode. He was so thrilled, he was finding it difficult to think.

"I need to get Jet," said Briar, beginning to gather up her blankets. "She used to wait for me behind the temple. I cannot leave without her."

Ode also needed to retrieve his companion and they planned to go their separate ways before meeting at the mountain pass. There was something romantic about returning to the spot where they had first met and both crept down the stairs and into the Room of the Gods with happy, flushed cheeks.

When Ode pulled aside the tapestry, he almost tripped over a sack that had been dumped on the floor. Peering inside, he saw that it was filled with clothing and provisions. He suspected that the High-Kiness had left it for them and he silently thanked her. Hoisting it onto his back, he was about to leave when he saw Briar pause.

"I have lived in The Castle Temple almost all my life," she whispered, glancing around the room. "It will be strange to leave."

Ode remembered how he had felt parting from the Wild Lands.

"You will come back," he said. "We will come back once it's safe."

Briar gently took hold of one of the colorful streamers that hung from the ceiling and let it slide through her fingers.

"I do not think I could leave . . . if it were not for you," she said, treating him to one of her blinding blue gazes.

Ode wanted to reply, but he found he could barely speak.

"I will see you on the mountain pass," she added, turning to go.

"Be careful!" Ode managed to call out softly.

"I will," she said over her shoulder with a smile.

Ode watched her hurry to the entrance, pulling her cloak over her hair. He almost could not bear for her to leave, though he knew they would be reunited soon. Once she had gone, he waited, counting under his breath until he judged it had been long enough. Then he followed. The courtyard outside was empty and the sky above lay flat and black. The moon was a skinny curve that shed little light on the mountainside, and Ode was grateful.

He hastened down hallways and snuck around corners with the sack banging against his back and his head filled with happy daydreams of his future life. He did not come across anyone as he went. It seemed that the High-Kiness had managed to summon everybody, including all the officials, to the eating hall. As he stepped out of the temple and onto the first stone step that led down the mountainside, Ode felt his shoulders begin to relax. He hoped that Briar was climbing over the wall at the back of the temple at that moment.

For once, Ode did not turn the prayer wheels as he descended into the valley. The soft patter of his feet was the only sound, mixed with the intermittent bleating of sheep and goats nearby. When he reached the valley, he hurried across the fields to the huts, which climbed up the slope on the other side. He was so busy thinking of life with Briar that he did not notice the door of Arrow's hut was slightly ajar. It stood in a row of rugged, abandoned storage shacks and in the darkness, Ode did not see the footprints that led up to it.

He whistled, waiting to hear his wolf's excited scrabbling or eager whine, but there was no sound. With a frown, Ode opened the door of the hut and gasped. A pair of dark eyes stared at him in a horrifyingly familiar face.

"Greetings, little man."

Ode stumbled back, almost tripping over himself.

"It has been a long time," said Cala. "Though I have been far away, I have been watching you."

She did not look a day older than when they had last met. She wore her hair parted into two long plaits like the Taone tribeswomen, and her leather tunic was just as Ode remembered it. He tried to swallow the panic rising in his throat. He did not know what she wanted.

"Where's my wolf?" he asked.

"I have set your companion free for the time being. You will not be able to take him with you where you are headed."

Panic flared in Ode's chest. "What do you mean? Where is he?"

"Hush, hush, little man. He is safe."

Cala looked him up and down, and then nodded. She saw his tall, broad frame and his shoulder-length dark hair.

"I always knew that you would grow to be strong," she said. "If Gray Morning was here now, he would see a warrior."

The mention of his father took Ode by surprise. It was as if she had slapped him and he struggled for breath, his chest tight with emotion. He did not let himself think about his father if he could help it. He tried not to think about the Wild Lands at all. It was too painful. And it was easy to let it sink into the past in these mountains, surrounded by a new life and new people. But Cala was before him now, with her familiar earthy scent that made him think of feathers dancing on a clawing breeze and the heavy beat of drums.

"Why are you here?" he asked, his voice trembling.

"I have come to tell you that you must leave."

"I am leaving."

"No, you must return to the Wild Lands."

The panic in Ode's chest began to burn through his body. Only moments ago he had been so sure of everything. Only moments ago he had felt so happy.

"I can't. . . . I won't," he stuttered.

"You must!" Cala hissed, stepping toward him. "The Western Realm is readying itself for a war, and you need to join your side."

"No, I need to be here. There is someone I must look after—"

"You will only bring danger to Briar."

Ode clenched his fingers into fists, his knuckles turning white.

"How do you—how do you know about Briar?"

"I told you, I have been watching you. I know you care for her and that is why you must stay away."

"What makes you think I believe you?" he spat.

Cala's face became taut and hard. "Do you remember that I once told you about Abioy?"

"The sorcerer?" asked Ode, vaguely recalling the name.

"Yes. He is powerful, and you have attracted his attention. You must not lead him to Briar or you will put her in danger."

Ode did not know whether to believe her. He could not tell if this was a trick. He just wanted to find Arrow and go to the mountain pass.

"I will keep Briar safe," he said.

"You will not be able to, little man. Briar was . . . cursed as a child. Have you not thought that she is different? That is why she is here! In these mountains she was supposed to be safe. Abioy is looking for her."

Ode thrust his fingers through his hair.

"Stop it!" he cried. "You are wrong. You are trying to trick me."

"I am not, I promise. I have made you strong. I have—"

"Wait! You *made* me . . . ?"

Cala looked away and Ode's mouth dropped open.

"You did this to me?" he hissed. "You made me this way?"

"I was doing what was best for everyone."

"You made me a freak! My dar hated me, and I was cast out of my tribe!"

"I had to," Cala tried to argue, but Ode was hardly listening. "Abioy cannot succeed, and I had to do something—"

"You made me, and then you left me!" Ode cried, his voice echoing against the rocks. "You *left* me!"

"I have been trying to stop him. I have been trying to work out his plans."

Ode shook his head.

"I don't care about this," he said. "I don't care about your sorcerer, and I don't care about you!"

He turned and began running across the mountainside, sliding on the uneven rocks.

"Ode!" Cala called after him. "You must leave now! I have seen it!"

But Ode did not care, and he went on running. He did not want to return to the Wild Lands, and he did not want to take the fate of the realm on his shoulders. He just wanted to be in the mountains with Briar. If he could reach her, then together they would find Arrow and retreat to their cave. He did not want to let go of his dreams.

Ode could barely see in the faint moonlight and he almost slipped off a ledge as he ran. Finally, panting and damp with sweat, he reached his and Briar's old meeting place and with a surge of relief, he came to a halt. Dumping the heavy sack of provisions on the ground, he looked around, expecting to see a silver shadow lurking between the rocks.

"Briar?" he called softly. "Briar?"

He hoped she had not been waiting long. Perhaps she was on the other side of the mountain pass. Ode clambered across the rocks, but still he could not see her. He went back and doubt began to creep over him. He did not know what he would do if she had been caught leaving the temple.

"Arrow?" he called instead. "Arrow?"

Cala had said that his companion was safe, and Ode hoped that meant the wolf was nearby on the mountainside. When he found Briar, they would both go looking for Arrow.

Ode paced back and forth, trying to push all thoughts of Cala from his mind. Then he saw something that made him pause. A print in the mud. Spring rain had fallen the night before, turning the dusty ground soft, and stamped into the earth between the rocks was the indent of a snow leopard's paw.

Ode looked around again, but he could still see nothing.

"Briar?" he called louder this time. "Briar!"

He heard a click behind him and turned to see the barrel of a rifle pointed between his eyes.

"Stay where you are," growled a state official.

Part Five

A Kiness waited beside the mountain pass, crouched between the rocks. Her clothes were worn and tatty, and her hands were muddy and scratched, but she smiled into the darkness. Beside her sat a mountain lion with large, watchful blue eyes and a tail that flicked impatiently back and forth. Above them, the sky was vast and black, punctured with tiny, pale stars.

"Where is he, Jet?" whispered Briar, fighting to keep her voice light.

She had expected Ode to be here by now. What if something had gone wrong? Her own escape from the temple had been quick and easy, but maybe one of the officials had caught Ode. Maybe he was in danger.

The Kiness stood and peered into the valley, but she only saw the flickering lights of candles in the workers' huts. Her cloak slipped from her head and revealed her long, golden hair, which glowed like a summer moon. Despite her thin, weak body, her hair remained lustrous and bright. All her life it had seemed as if it almost had a Magic of its own.

"Ode?" she tried calling softly. "Ode!"

There was no reply, and she sank back to her knees, biting her lip. Her snow leopard nudged at her arm and she cradled its head, running its silky fur between her fingers. She wanted to escape with Ode so much. Too much. Now, she was worried that her desire for it was making everything go wrong. She wondered if the gods were angry with her for turning her back on her vows. She did not want to upset them, but she could not go on living locked in the attic of the Room of the Gods. She could not go on hiding forever.

She had fallen in love with Ode, and there had been nothing she could do to prevent it. She had tried to resist, but it had been pointless;

it was like trying to stop breathing. For a while, she had been afraid that he loved her in the way other men seemed to love her. They looked at her like something possessed, but Ode was different. Or she hoped that he was. When he was around she no longer felt lost and lonely. He made her feel at peace.

"Briar?"

The Kiness started at the sound of his voice and her full, red lips broke into a wide smile. She climbed from between the rocks and waved to the familiar figure standing nearby.

"I am here," she whispered. "You had me worried that you would not come. I thought something terrible had happened."

Ode looked as strong and handsome as ever and her breath caught in her chest. Maybe when all of this was over they could return to the temple and marry. Then they could live in the mountains like Kayra and her yak and have a family of their own. It seemed almost too good to be true. Right now, she was simply content with a summer spent living in a cave with Ode, talking and laughing with each other every day.

"I am sorry to have kept you," said Ode. "I was held up."

The snow leopard bounded across the rocks and sniffed at Ode's feet.

"It has been so long since she has seen you, she has almost forgotten who you are," giggled the Kiness. "Jet, it is just Ode, silly."

Ode put a hand on the snow leopard's head and the animal stilled.

"Do not fear," he said. "She knows who I am."

The Kiness smiled and scrambled across the rocks to him.

"Where is Arrow?" she asked, scanning the mountainside.

"Oh, he is waiting to join us later. There is something we must do first."

"But we must leave right away—"

"We need to go to the temple."

Briar frowned.

"The temple?" she said. "We cannot go back there now. The officials will see us! We have only just escaped unseen."

"I know a secret entrance. Come, we must go."

Ode took hold of Briar's arm and his grip pinched her skin.

"All right," she replied faintly. Below she saw shadows moving in the distance. "The officials!" she hissed.

"Do not fear," Ode replied. "They will not see me."

He pulled on her arm and led them onward. In the dim moonlight, his eyes flashed and they might have been silver or gold or violet. Or, maybe it was just the light.

CHAPTER TWENTY-NINE

The Official

Ode stood staring down the barrel of a gun. The small, black "O" gaped back at him and twitched in the official's hands.

"Where is the girl?" the official growled in broken mountain language.

Ode tried not to look relieved. This must mean they did not have Briar. He hoped that she had escaped.

"Hey!" the official yelled, thrusting the barrel into Ode's face. "Where is the girl? She was just with you."

Ode frowned. "What girl?" he asked, trying not to look at the rifle.

"Do not fool me!" said the official, his lip curling. "I saw you both running over the rocks. Why did you come back? And where is that . . ." He screwed up his face, struggling to find the right word. "Where is that animal?"

Ode stared at him.

"Well?" yelled the official, jabbing at him. "I saw you all just now. Where have they gone?"

"I—I don't know what you mean."

The official chuckled and shook his head. "Answer me or I'll shoot."

"But—"

"I saw you leave the temple and I saw you meet up here. I thought I had lost you, but you came back."

"No, you are mistaken. I haven't—"

"Tell me where she is!" the official roared. "Tell me or I will shoot!"

The rocks around Ode began to lilt and blur. Something was happening to him and he could not stop it. He threw out his arms to steady himself and the earth swirled and rolled beneath his feet. His shoulders were tingling and it almost felt as if he were about to shift.

"What are you doing?" snapped the official with a hint of worry in his voice. "Stand still!"

Ode felt his body begin to shudder and change. His bones snapped and reformed, his muscles twisted and adjusted.

"What—" began the official, but his words ended in a cry of revulsion. "A Magic!" he yelled.

Ode's clothes fell away in a heap and he stretched out his large, white wings. He had not shifted against his will in a long time and he felt frustrated and panicked. He squawked.

"A Magic!" the official yelled again in Pervoroccoian. "Men needed over here!" He turned back to Ode, his face screwed up with disgust. "I knew this place was not what it seemed," he said, switching back to mountain language. "I knew there was evil here."

Ode flapped his wings, but the official lifted his rifle.

"Don't move!" he cried. "My comrades will arrive, and we will arrest you. No more tricks or you will make it worse for yourself."

They waited in silence but no one came.

Ode wondered if he could fly off before the official had time to shoot. If he were an eagle he could launch himself into the sky, but his bird form was awkward and clumsy. He could not risk it.

The official stepped forward and prodded Ode's feathered chest with his rifle. Ode stumbled back and the man laughed.

"They tell us Magics are dangerous," he said. "But this is foolish. Am I supposed to be afraid of you?"

A shadow fell across the crescent moon and the mountainside was plunged into darkness. Even the stars seemed to disappear.

"What was that?" growled the official.

A wind began to blow and it grew stronger until it howled. The earth beneath them shuddered and shook, and a scream sounded across the valley.

"What is going on?" shouted the official. "Stop it!"

I'm not doing it! Ode wanted to cry, but it came out as a squawk.

The wind tugged and pulled at his wings, threatening to throw him off the mountainside. As his eyes adjusted to the darkness, he saw that the official was also struggling to stay on his feet.

"Where are my men?" the official yelled above the roar of the air. "Stop this Magic now or you will die!"

He fumbled with the rifle in his hands, fighting to aim it at Ode. He hooked his finger around the trigger and closed one eye.

A dark shape soared from the shadows and landed on the official with a snarl. The shot exploded in a bang that was lost in the screeching of the wind and the bullet bounced off the rocks. Ode honked in surprise and watched as Arrow sunk his teeth into the official's arm.

The official shrieked in agony and shook the wolf off, reaching for the rifle that had been knocked from his hands. He stumbled back, trying to find his footing on the rocks again, but the wind grabbed hold of him and hurled him off the mountainside. In a moment he was gone, tumbling down into the valley and vanishing into darkness without a sound.

Arrow almost fell after him, but the wolf stuck his claws into the rock and flattened himself to the ground. Ode wanted to shout out to his companion, but all human words were lost to him. He knew they could not stay on this mountain. Whatever was happening, he had no control over it and he did not want them to suffer the same fate as the official.

Arrow began crawling toward the mountain pass, keeping his body low and out of the wind. Ode tried to transform, but it was futile. He could barely manage to stay upright, let alone shift back into his human form.

I will follow from the sky, he tried to say, but no words came from his beak. Still, he thought he saw Arrow prick his ears as if he heard him.

Ode opened up his wings and let the wind launch him into the night. Immediately, he was flying and battling against the great gusts that tried to push and shove him. He beat his wings desperately, attempting to fly away from the sudden storm, but he could feel something dragging him backward.

Behind him, he thought that he could just about make out the Castle Temple shrouded in clouds and covered with black tendrils. He did not know what was happening, but he struggled away from it. He needed a moment of peace to understand it all. He could not think in this whirlwind. He flapped his wings and prayed to be free, his body shuddering with the effort.

Suddenly, he broke through it. Like a stone spat from a mouth, he lurched out of the wind and away into the surrounding mountains. Dizzy with relief, he flew as far as he could, followed by a wolf on the ground.

CHAPTER THIRTY

The Curse

Ode lay shivering, naked and lost. The night was dark and calm here; there were no strong winds or black clouds. After the storm on the mountainside, Ode had flown for as long as he could. Finally, he had plunged from the sky in exhaustion, landing with a thump against a rocky crevice. Arrow found him soon after and Ode clung to his companion, barely able to comprehend what had happened. Now he rested, curled on his side with his wolf's warm shoulder against his back. He waited to die because he wanted it all to end. Everything had been ruined, and he could not face life anymore.

Ode did not know how long he lay there. He closed his eyes and drifted in and out of consciousness, his body numb from the force of his Magic. Images of Briar and thoughts of his friends back at the temple flitted through his mind. Something had gone wrong, and he had a sinking feeling that it was his fault. He sensed that Briar was lost to him and he felt the temple was in danger. He could not bear the thought of either.

Erek said that the gods had chosen Ode for great things, but Ode knew his friend was wrong. The gods had rejected him. He had worked at the temple for seasons, waiting for them to call him to vows, but it had never happened. It had never happened because he was nothing but a worthless, strange birther boy. His Magic was useless and ineffective. The official had laughed at him and he had been right to laugh. What good was a white bird? It would not help anyone. It would have been better for everybody if Ode had wandered the Wild Lands forever and had never come to the Scarlet Isles. It would have been better for Briar if she had never met him and for that reason, he wanted to die.

Tucked into the jagged face of the deserted mountain, Ode lay in darkness. He considered throwing himself off the edge and imagined his body squashed on the rocks in the valley below. He thought that he would probably do it, if he could convince Arrow not to follow. Before he had a chance to think further, a fur cloak landed with a thump by his side.

Arrow yapped and wagged his tail. Ode opened his eyes and looked up at the familiar figure in the faint starlight.

"Come on, little man," said Cala. "You were difficult to find, but I am glad to finally see you. I was worried you had been caught in the enchantment. Now we must hurry and be on our way."

Ode clenched his teeth. If he did not feel so weak and wretched he would have attacked his auntie, for she surely had something to do with all of this.

"Get away from me, you evil thing!" he hissed.

Cala's face remained still, but her eyes betrayed her sadness. "I am not evil. I am here to help you. Come with me, and I will explain."

"You have explained enough!" Ode kicked away her fur cloak and coiled back into himself.

"I did not raise a man who would give up like this," said Cala. "I did not give you some of my powers for nothing!"

"What you gave me is useless," Ode growled.

"That is where you are wrong. Your gift is important, Ode, and you must not underestimate it. There will come a time when you will need it dearly—there will come a time when only *you* will be able to save us all."

"You're lying!"

"No!" shouted Cala. "I am speaking the truth!"

Arrow whined, and the air seemed to tremble at the timbre of Cala's voice.

"I know where your Briar is, little man. She is in great danger. If you will not get up for me, then get up for her."

There was a pause.

"I can barely trust you," said Ode.

"The way I see it, you do not have much of a choice. You are helping no one hiding here."

Ode shivered. "All right," he said. "Turn away and I will get up."

Cala rolled her eyes, but she faced away from him.

"I changed your swaddling when you were a baby, little man," she muttered to herself. "I have seen it all before."

Ode slung the fur around his shoulders and for the first time, he noticed how icy his skin had become in the chilly night air. His teeth started to chatter and his hands began to shake.

"We must get you to a fire," said Cala. "Follow me."

Ode stumbled after her across the rocks. His bare feet tripped on the uneven, stony ground, and he had to lean on Arrow often to stop himself from falling. They walked for some time through valleys and up cliff faces until they came to a small cave. Cala led him inside where the embers of a fire were burning and a bed had been laid in the corner.

Ode settled before the fire while Cala muttered to the growing flames in her own language, just like she used to when Ode was a boy. If he closed his eyes, Ode could imagine himself back in their tent in the Wild Lands again. Outside their home, the rest of the Taone would be relaxing after the evening meal, while Gray Morning practiced fighting drills with Blue Moon beside the settlement. It was all so distant now that it felt like another life.

"How did you escape the enchantment?" Cala asked.

They had been sitting in silence, both gazing into the flickering fire.

"What do you mean?" Ode asked.

"An enchantment was conjured back there, did you not see it?"

"I saw the dark clouds, but I didn't know it was an enchantment," said Ode, stroking his wolf's silky ears. "An official tried to shoot me, and I would have been killed if it weren't for Arrow. After that I felt something trying to pull me back, but I broke through it."

Cala nodded and stared at the shadowed walls of the cave.

"Was it your sorcerer?" asked Ode after a pause.

"Yes, it was Abioy. And he is not my sorcerer—not anymore."

"Who is he? How do you know him?"

"He is a powerful man and very greedy," said Cala, standing up. She walked over to the bed in the corner and began rummaging through a bag there.

"But how do you know him?" Ode persisted.

When she did not answer he sighed. It was all mysteries and lies again. This is what he had hated and he would stand for it no longer. He was about to tell her so when she threw a leather bundle into his lap.

"My old tunic!" said Ode, holding it up. "The one you made me when I was a boy. It was always too big but you said I would grow to fill it one day."

"Perhaps it will fit now."

Ode pulled it over his head and grinned. He was sure that it smelled of the dry rushes of the plain lands and the smoky fires at Midsummer.

"Why do you have this?" he asked.

"I have carried it with me all this time," said Cala, looking down at her hands. "Ode, I am not your mam, but I have no child of my own, and I care for you as if you were my son. I hated it when I left you, but it had to be done."

Ode swallowed and fiddled with the edge of his tunic. He remembered all the times she had dried his tears when he was a boy and the nights she had hugged and rocked him when he was afraid.

"I believe you, Auntie," he said.

Cala smiled and her eyes were glassy. "I went searching for Abioy because I thought that I could stop him, but he could not be found. I knew him when he was a boy, you see, but he believes that I am dead. Long ago he wanted to be king of the Scarlet Isles, but he was laughed out of the royal court. Now he seeks revenge."

"But why is he here? What does this have to do with Briar?"

"Ode, Briar is no ordinary girl."

Ode knew that. She was the most beautiful thing he had ever seen. "What do you mean—" he began.

"She is the heir to the Scarlet Isles and a princess," said Cala. "She was cursed as a child and brought here for safety."

Ode blinked. "A princess?" he spluttered.

"Yes. The king and queen hid her in the mountains when she was a baby. They thought that Abioy would not find her here, but they were wrong. It took him many seasons, but he has got her now."

Ode looked around the cave. "We were going to escape together. . . ." he said faintly.

"I can see that you love her and that is why you must listen to me, for she is in great danger."

Ode's breath caught in his chest, and he felt the ground beneath him tremble. His eyes wandered past Cala's head to the mouth of the cave. Outside, dawn was pouring across the mountains and warming the sky. Somewhere out there, Briar was in danger. She was a princess—not simply the Kiness he had thought—but she was still *his* Briar.

"What's happened to her? Where is she?" he asked.

"She is caught in the enchantment."

"What are we doing sitting here, then? We need to go now!" Ode tried to stand but his legs were too weak, and he stumbled.

"You must be strong first, little man," said Cala.

Ode winced. "But what can I do to help her?" he asked.

"I thought that you needed to go to the Wild Lands and join the army forming there, but I was wrong," said Cala. "The Magics are on the battlefield already, fighting from the Hillands in Pervorocco."

Ode thought of Blue Moon and Sunset By Forest. He had always imagined them in the camp with the New People.

"Are Blue Moon and my mam safe?" he asked.

"I do not know yet. I cannot always see what is going on."

Ode rubbed his tired eyes. "You must tell me what is going on," he said.

Cala walked back to the fire and sat down. "Many seasons ago, Abioy won The Red Wars and brought peace between Magics and humans, but after a while, it was not enough. Like all greedy men he wanted more. The Magical Cleansing is a cruel distraction he's created. He wants the Scarlet Isles first, and then he will try to take the whole of the Western Realm. I am sure of it."

Ode thought of Briar, trapped somewhere alone and scared. His fingers curled into fists.

"What must we do?" he asked.

"Together, we must stop him."

Ode looked at the mountains, silhouetted by light on the horizon. He hoped that wherever Briar was, she knew that he was coming for her.

About the Author

Rose Mannering is an international bestselling author and lifelong booklover. By day she works in publishing and by night she dreams up dragons, unicorns, curses that last hundreds of years, and boys who turn into swans. When she's not deep in fantastical realms, Rose is uploading videos to her book-based YouTube Channel (Rose Mannering), tweeting about what she's reading (@rose_mannering), or snapping pretty instagram photos of paperbacks (@rosemannering). Learn more at www.rosemannering.com.

Acknowledgements

I would like to send a huge THANK YOU to everyone working at Sky Pony Press and especially my editor, Julie Matysik, who let me carry on writing about this world of magic, spells and enchantments that lives in my head. I would like to send bucket-loads of thanks to my agent, Isabel Atherton, who is always such an awesome lady, and to fabulous writing-lady Kate Ormand, who is wonderfully supportive. Tons of thanks to anyone and everyone that watches my writing journey on my book-themed YouTube channel; you guys are crazy wonderful, particularly the amazing booktubers who have made videos about The Tales Trilogy: ChapterStackss, WordsofaReader, Katie Ruby, Charr Frears and Erika Chung.

Lastly, I would like to thank my family and friends, you lovely enablers you. Thank you to my mum for reading this, thank you to my dad for promising to read this, thank you to James for pretending to listen while I moan about word counts and thank you to Lyds for being my biggest fan. You're all great.

THE FIRST BOOK IN THE TALES TRILOGY

Available wherever books are sold!